D1202235

Gran at Coalgate

Winifred Cawley
Gran at Coalgate
illustrated by Fermin Rocker

Holt, Rinehart and Winston · *New York*

First published in England by Oxford University Press
Copyright © 1974 by Winifred Cawley
Printed in the United States of America

Library of Congress Cataloging in Publication Data

Cawley, Winifred.
Gran at Coalgate.

  SUMMARY: Jinnie, straight-laced English school-
girl of the 20s, learns about life when she goes
to stay with her grandmother in the north.
    [1. England—Fiction. 2. Grandparent—Fiction]
I. Title.
PZ7.C294Gr   [Fic]   75-6944
ISBN 0-03-014771-9

Gran at Coalgate

One

It was only Tuesday but Jinnie was very clean, Saturday night clean, especially her scalp which still tingled from a good going over with the fine-tooth comb. Not that Mam'd expected to find anything. There hadn't been a dick in Jinnie's hair for two weeks now: not since Jinnie'd stopped sitting next to that Gladys Wilson at school. And she'd had a bath only half an hour ago. Dad'd said it was madness to go out after a bath, she'd catch her death of cold. And she'd had a bath on Saturday night anyroad, hadn't she? Besides, there was nothing wrong with the lass but sheer hunger: it was a waste of a good three and sixpence taking her to the Doctor.

Mam'd said you couldn't tell her that the bairn was all right, constantly being sick like that. She wasn't putting off taking her a day longer. And you had to have a bath when you went to the Doctor's, hadn't you? So Dad could just look after the shop, and Robbie, and she'd be back as soon as she could. Dad had looked nearly as surprised as Jinnie felt: Mam didn't often speak up like that to Dad. Dad didn't hold with women arguing.

But here they were, Mam and Jinnie, on their way to Doctor Castle's, Jinnie with her Sunday frock on and everything clean underneath. Mam was dressed up as well, in her good navy serge coat and the hat with the new bunch of forget-me-nots that she never wore during the week, not even to the Women's Bright Hour at Chapel on Mondays. The large wicker shopping-basket looked a bit out of place with Mam's best clothes but she'd had to bring it to carry the big clay bowl and the clean red-and-white striped towel: Jinnie might be sick again. 'Mind you tell uz if you feel like it,' Mam had said: 'in good time. You don't want to go making a mess all over the Doctor's surgery, there's a good lass.'

Jinnie wasn't feeling sick at the moment, just interesting: and a bit disappointed that nobody was out in the street to see her. All her friends would be inside; it was half past five, tea-time for shipyard folk.

Mrs. Park was there, of course: hanging out of the window

1

of her upstairs flat, as usual. Pity she had nothing better to do, Dad said: and he couldn't imagine what sort of a state her house must be in. Winter and summer there she sat at her open window. Except on Saturday evenings when she and Old Park went off to the Penny Wet and got drunk together. If Jinnie'd been with Dad, they'd have walked on the other side of The Street where there weren't any houses, just the Corporation sheds. Mrs. Park wouldn't have dared speak to Dad, anyroad. As it was, Mrs. Park called down, 'Hello, Mrs. Friend. Hello, Jinnie.' Jinnie wouldn't put it past Mrs. Park to ask where they were going. Downright impittent she was, Dad said. Even Mam said Mrs. Park was too fond of putting her shovel in.

'She still looks a bit pasty, Mrs. Friend,' said Mrs. Park. 'Is she still feeling bad then?' but she didn't wait for an answer. 'The men've got their notices the day, Mrs. Friend.' As if everybody didn't know that.

'Ay, I heard,' said Mam. 'Dear knows how it'll all end. What does your man say?' Mr. Park was a pitman. 'Does he think the' really will strike? You couldn't blame them . . .' That old Strike: folks'd been going on about that Strike for weeks. ' . . . but there'll be a bonnie lot hungered if the' do . . . the bairns . . .'

'There'll be a bonnie lot hungered if the' don't, Mrs. Friend,' said Mrs. Park. Which didn't make sense.

'Ay,' said Mam, and she sighed as if she actually sympathized with the pitmen.

Dad didn't. If the pitmen and their wives didn't spend so much on pubs and horses . . . He had no patience with them. Ruin the country, they would. Him as well. If they did go on strike, Mrs. Park and the other pit wives would expect him to go on giving them groceries on tick — pay when the Strike was over, if ever — which was more than their Co-op had promised to do, he said.

That Strike could finish Jinnie's chances of going to the Secondary School, and of being a teacher. If Dad went broke, he'd never let her go; not even if she passed The Scholarship. Tunics and blouses and blazers and badges and felt hats cost money, Dad said. Jinnie had enough worry over The Scholarship exam, without the pitman and their . . . blooming . . . old Strike.

'Ah well,' said Mam, 'mebbe it'll not come to that, Mrs. Park. Mebbe the Government'll renew The Subsidy, after all.'

Jinnie didn't exactly know what The Subsidy was, although she'd heard it talked about often enough lately. She did

2

know Dad was against it, though. Yet here was Mam sounding as if The Subsidy was a good thing. And wasting time with Mrs. Park. Making them late for the Doctor's. Jinnie pulled at her mother's coat sleeve.

'All right, all right, our Jin,' said Mam. 'Well, we'd best be on our way, Mrs. Park. Bairns can't abide being still a minute, can they?'

Mrs. Park agreed, but in an absent kind of way, and she didn't try to find out where they were going. Which was disappointing, after all.

Their section of Tyne Street wasn't very long and Mam had scarcely finished her smile at Mrs. Park when they came to the green railings of the Buffs which was at the end of it. It was too early for voices, beer smells, or men playing quoits, but not very far off opening time, because you could see a light inside the Club. No light in the little window at the Dead House opposite, thank goodness. Somebody inside being cut up would have been bad luck. Jinnie could do without any of that at the moment.

'Which way'd you like to go, Jin?' asked Mam. 'On along our street, or by the High Street?'

Jinnie considered. Straight on she might just see the lucky white horse at the Co-op milk depot. On the other hand, in the High Street she was certain to pass not one, but two barbers' poles.

'Come on, wor lass. Make your mind up,' said Mam affectionately.

'By the High Street,' said Jinnie; 'and back by our Street.' The Queen's Pictures farther along Tyne Street would be open by then and Mam might, just might, let her stop and look at the photographs outside. At least she wouldn't hurry her past, as Dad would've.

At any time, the first thing that took your eye when you turned into the High Street, hanging high above the pavement, was the big clock belonging to The Clock pub below. Now, already lit up for the night, it was even more conspicuous, its firm hands black in front of the ghostly grey works that you didn't see by day. Quarter to six.

'Oh dear,' said Mam: 'later than I thought. I hope we get a good turn, so your Dad can go to the Guild. He'll not like it if he has to miss it.'

He would not. Jinnie felt guilty at the mere possibility of making Dad miss the Wesley Guild. But it wasn't her fault that she'd been feeling so queer lately; being sick and her heart thumping all over the place, and everything.

3

'And Mrs. Walker-from-High-Farm might be coming. She told your Dad on Sat'day she'd be over for sand-shoes and summer things for the bairns. And your Dad's no good with the draperies. Still, she'll wait or come back another night. She's a cannie soul: she'll not mind, when your Dad tells her why I'm not in.'

Mrs. Walker was a good customer. She was always in when Dad called for her weekly payment — not like some, such as Mrs. Baker who managed to be out every other week, just about. Dad wasn't going to let Mrs. Baker have any more tick until she'd got her present bill down a bit. If Mam wasn't in, Mrs. Walker might go elsewhere for the sand-shoes: get a ticket somewhere, at Parrish's maybe. That would mean the end of Mrs. Walker as a customer. Jinnie began to feel more worried than ever.

And what if there was nothing wrong with her after all? Mam might be vexed with Jinnie, wasting her time like this, and maybe losing customers for her into the bargain. Wasting Dad's good money, as well. There'd just better be something wrong. But it was no use. She felt all right now: perfectly all right, not the least bit sick, even if Mrs. Park had said she looked pasty.

What if the Doctor was vexed as well? Dr. Castle had a name for being sharp with folk that wasted his time. But Mam would be paying. Three and sixpence. Maybe it was only panel patients he got vexed with. And perhaps if she really tried she could be sick in the surgery.

A few shops past Smith's barber's pole Jinnie couldn't bear the worry any longer.

'Mam,' she said, and slowed her steps, 'I'm all right, now. Really I am. We don't need to go to the Doctor's. I'm better. Honest I am.'

'Mebbe you are, our lass, but we're going just the same. Come on, pick your feet up.'

'No: honest: I'm better. Let's go home.'

'The man won't eat you, lass. Anyroad, now we've got this far . . .' Suddenly Mam broke off. 'Well I never . . . Now who could that've been?' Mam had lost interest in Jinnie and was staring at the *Evening Chronicle* boards outside Hardy's the newsagent's.

Leeds bans the Charleston.
'It's war,' says Cook.

Nothing new there. Then through the wire diamonds of

4

the third placard frame out leapt a black crayon word, so conspicuous Jinnie couldn't understand why she hadn't seen it immediately. COALGATE. No wonder Mam was curious; she'd been brought up at Coalgate and all her folks lived there still.

'Saturday's March: Coalgate Wife speaks out. Picture.'

Mam put her hand in her basket to take out her purse; then changed her mind.

'No,' she said, 'we'll wait till we get home,' although she sounded excited at the idea of Coalgate being in the *Chronicle*.

'Who d'you think it could be?' asked Jinnie.

'Nay, how would I know?' said Mam. 'I don't know everybody at Coalgate.'

But she did, pretty nearly. That's what it seemed like to Jinnie when she and Robbie went there with her. Coalgate was a lovely place. She wished they went there more than just a day once or twice a year: but The Shop was very tying, she knew.

It wasn't much farther to Park Road and the big corner house that was the Doctor's. 'Mind you go to the front door and ring the bell,' Dad had said. 'You're entitled to a quick turn, we're not on his panel, you know.' But Mam went straight round to the side, to the little built-on waiting-room. The door was ajar and a notice, hanging on the knob, told them to go in.

The waiting-room was quiet. Jinnie was relieved to see that there were only two customers ahead of them: a young woman who must be first because she was nearest to the glass door that led into the main part of the house and The Surgery, and a youngish, yellow-faced man clutching a large, empty, medicine bottle. They didn't seem to be together, for they weren't talking to each other. Besides, the young woman was far too pretty and well-dressed to be with the yellow-faced man. It was her hat that took Jinnie's eye: a black Valentino, with a red rose under the brim: real silk it looked like. And her hair, black too, which showed a fringe, and a black kiss-curl plastered firmly on her cheek. Jinnie sighed with admiration and envy. If only *she* could have her hair bobbed, and with kiss-curls.

'Sit down, our Jin,' whispered Mam fiercely, 'and stop staring.' She pulled Jinnie down onto the bench beside her. The young woman smelt nice, too, even from three seats

5

away. And some day Jinnie was going to have shiny black patent leather court shoes, just like hers.

Mam planted her shopping-basket firmly on her knees, and took out Jinnie's *School Friend*. Actually, it belonged to Jinnie's best friend Edie Cole who had swopped it temporarily for Jinnie's last week's *School-girl's Own*. Mam handed it to Jinnie with a You-Be-Quiet look. Jinnie had waited a whole week to learn how Barbara Redfern and her friends would manage to escape from the cave where they'd been lured by the new gym mistress and left, gagged, and bound hands and feet, with the tide rising rapidly. She opened the paper. She shut it again: now she was so near the solution, she wanted to savour the suspense a bit longer. She'd have a Think instead -- she sometimes enjoyed a Think — not so much lately though. She'd ask Mam to get her one of those unfamiliar comics on the table over there and keep her Think for later.

The door from the house opened. A woman wearing a stiff white coat came into the waiting-room.

'Good evening,' she said.

'Good evening,' said Mam and everyone including the woman in the white coat looked surprised. The woman put a clean new *Evening Chronicle* on the table, then went into the little cubby-hole place where you got your medicine after you'd seen the Doctor. She switched on a light and started shifting bottles around.

Mam waited a minute, then she smiled apologetically at the young woman, the yellow-faced man and the little woman with a large baby who had just come in. 'Does anybody mind if I take a look at this?' she asked, picking up the newspaper.

Nobody did apparently. Jinnie admired Mam's courage. That was one good thing at least about being Grown-Up, not minding speaking to strangers. Mam turned straight to the picture page.

'Well I never . . .' Mam's voice was a mixture of disapproval and admiration but not surprise. She realized the waiting-room was listening. 'Just look at this,' she said to Jinnie in a whisper.

'What is it?' said Jinnie. Then she remembered the placard outside Hardy's. 'Who was she? Let's have a look.'

'Your Aunt Polly, of course. Who else?' Mam's voice was mostly disapproving now. She moved the big, clumsy sheets of newspaper nearer Jinnie.

But there was a whole page of pictures to choose from;

6

and Jinnie wasn't sure she'd recognize Aunt Polly anyway. It seemed a long time since she'd seen her. She was often out when they went to Coalgate.

'That one . . . in the top row . . . in the middle.' Mam put her finger on the place.

Jinnie was a bit disappointed. She'd expected Aunt Polly to be a whole picture, but she was just part of a procession, all women. Still, you could see she was somebody Special. She was right in the front of the picture, one arm linked with a woman who from her clothes must be a Cullercoats fishwife, the other arm waving straight at you as you looked. Somehow the more you looked the more Aunt Polly stood out from the rest, with her big dark eyes, her black hair, her bold laughing look. Yes, that was Aunt Polly, right enough. How had Jinnie ever thought she'd forgotten Aunt Polly?

Jinnie read the print underneath the picture. Something about the 'Women's Guild of Empire . . . and . . . Mrs. Polly Dunham, the miner's wife from Coalgate, who later addressed the meeting . . . in the Albert Hall . . .'

Her picture and her name . . . Edie Cole'd never had an aunt in the newspaper . . .

'My,' said Mam, 'I'm not sure the Coalgate folk'll like this.'

Whyever not? Jinnie wanted to ask: but she didn't. Grown-Ups sometimes said more when they forgot it was only You listening. But Mam just sighed. 'Ee, dear; poor Davie.' She put the paper back on the table.

Suddenly the bell above the door into the house buzzed. The young woman in the Valentino hat got up. My, but she must be well off; silk stockings: on a week-day. She must be a Teacher. With that skirt above her knees? And that hat? Anyway, a Teacher'd go to the front door, not wait in the queue.

It seemed a long time before she came back. She looked different now, although it would be hard to say how.

'Miss . . .' The young woman didn't hear the voice from the cubby-hole. 'Miss . . . have you got a prescription?'

The young woman still didn't hear. She only just avoided colliding with a man who was coming in, steering a great, grubby, bandaged hand in front of him.

'You want to watch where you're gannin, bonnie lass,' the man said.

The girl took no notice of him either, and was gone. She *must* be upset. Some *awful* disease. Incurable. She hadn't waited for medicine, though. And she had looked all right at first. Poorly folk were always a bad colour, pasty. The girl had looked pretty.

7

T.B.... Of course ... you looked nice when you had T.B. And they didn't give you a bottle, they sent you to Woolley, to the Sannie. Like Nora Donnelly in The Street. She was there now. And Tommy Brown: he'd died there. And Margery Wilson at school. Jinnie knew all about T.B.

What if she had T.B?

'What's the matter?' whispered Mam. 'Here, are you feeling sick again, our Jin?'

Jinnie shook her head. She didn't feel sick, just cold. Mam got the basin out of the basket all the same. Everybody was looking at them and the waiting-room was nearly full by now. A fat woman opposite clicked her tongue sympathetically. The interest and the sympathy restored Jinnie a bit. She was glad, all the same, when the bell rang for their turn. The Doctor would tell her she hadn't T.B. Mind you, if she had, she wouldn't have to sit that exam ... but she wanted to go to The Sec., didn't she? Oh dear.

On the other side of the plain glass door was, not the Surgery — there was yet another door to that — but a sort of room with broad stairs on the left and on the right the front door of the house. Absolutely beautiful it was, all white wood and coloured glass, with the outside light coming through and showing glass pictures of purple hills, blue lakes and white swans. The floor was even more beautiful: not flat and dull cement, nor shiny and cold oilcloth, nor seamed and pale scrubbed wood, but a kaleidoscope flash of tiles, blue and white and fawn and brown and red and green, that as you looked began to form lines and circles, squares and diamonds, dots and stars and stiff little flowers.

'Come away in,' said a voice through the half open door marked SURGERY.

'Come on, our Jin,' said Mam.

8

Two

It wasn't Dr. Castle, which was a relief. Jinnie knew what Dr. Castle looked like: he'd come to the house when she was so bad with the measles. This must be the new Doctor, Dr. Fife. He was young — even Jinnie recognized that — and somehow not as frightening as Dr. Castle. He asked Mam's name, then went to a set of green tin drawers. Instantly Jinnie resolved to have a set just like it one day. He pulled a drawer open. It was full of sheets of thin white cardboard. He worked through them, took one out and returned with it to his desk.

'Oh, I'm sorry, Mrs. Friend ... Sit yourself down, will you?'

There was no chair for Jinnie. She didn't mind. It was better standing, somehow. She really did feel queer now. Somewhere, inside her head, inside her stomach, she was trembling. What if she did have T.B.? Or nothing at all and the Doctor was vexed? And she'd have a desk like the Doctor's some day: it was better than the Headmistress's at

9

school. She'd have a brass stand as well with pens and ink-wells: just like the one on the desk.

Mam was telling the Doctor about Jinnie. She'd gone back to school after the measles, only last Wednesday. Then on Thursday they'd sent her home: sick. Same on Friday. 'And now again today, Doctor. Sick as a dog she'd been, the teacher's note said.'

'Come over here, will you, Jinnie?' Dr. Fife was holding out his hand, so Jinnie had to go round the desk and stand right beside him. 'Open your coat, lassie.'

He listened to her heart. It was galloping, twice as fast as usual and leaping fit to jump right through her ribs.

'Sound as a bell.'

Jinnie didn't know whether to be indignant or relieved.

Her tongue was nice and clean, and her tonsils. That was the neatest little torch she'd ever seen: like a fountain-pen. She'd have one some day, and a fountain-pen as well.

Dr. Fife examined her finger-nails. He pulled down her lower eyelids and examined them. He told her to go to the eye-testing card. The letters were a bit like the mouse's tail in last year's *Alice in Wonderland*. She was beginning to enjoy herself. She raced down them in fine style and skidded breathlessly to a halt.

'All right, all right. Stop,' said Dr. Fife, holding his hand up like a policeman, then laughed. 'That's fine. Nothing to worry about there.'

Too late now, she remembered she liked the idea of glasses. Miss Sanderson at school wore glasses. They made her look Special, a real Teacher.

Now Jinnie had to sit down: in the Doctor's own chair. Dr. Fife tapped her knees with an elegant little toffee hammer. Whatever for? It seemed a bit silly. Still, Dr. Fife was taking a lot of trouble; they would be able to tell Dad that they'd had his three and sixpence's worth.

Half of the Doctor's questions were pointless, too: just the usual Grown-Up things. Which school did she go to? Which class was she in?

'My goodness,' said Dr. Fife, impressed. 'I thought Ex-Seven was the top class. For the fourteen-year-olds.'

'Ay,' said Mam with pride: 'and not all of them get into it neither.'

Did Jinnie like her teacher? Of course she did. She didn't tell him, but she got on so well with Miss Sanderson that the others called her Teacher's Pet. Which wasn't Fair, of course.

'And what're you going to be, Jinnie?' said Dr. Fife.

10

The sick feeling had been hiding round the corner all the time, just waiting to pounce when she was off her guard.

'Haven't made your mind up yet, eh?' said the young man sympathetically.

'Oh, she's made up her mind all right,' said Mam: 'made it up on her first day at school and hasn't changed it since, have you, Jin?' Mam was proud of Jinnie's ambition, which was more that you could say about Dad; he thought you should stay in the station to which God had called you, not try to get above yourself — which was a Sin. 'She wants to be a teacher. She'll have to pass The Scholarship, though.' She didn't, mention that if there was a strike even The Scholarship might not be enough. 'Unless she gets one of them *North Mail* Scholarships. That'd more than pay the fees at the Secondary for her. The papers was hard, though.'

Dr. Fife seemed to know all about the *North Mail* competition, which had lasted a solid month. 'Oh, she did that, did she? And when's the exam for the Secondary School Scholarships, Mrs. Friend?'

'A week on Saturday, the first Saturday in May.'

'Not long, eh Jinnie?' said Dr. Fife. He was silent a moment. Then he said, 'I can't find a thing wrong with the bairn, Mrs. Friend.' He didn't seem to mind, though.

Mam sighed with relief and stopped sitting so upright. On the whole Jinnie was pleased as well that she hadn't T.B.

'But I think she's been overdoing it. What with all those *North Mail* tests, and the measles and now The Scholarship. She needs to forget about school and exams: and enjoy herself. She seems a clever lass: she'll do all the better for a complete rest.'

Jinnie crossed her fingers tight: on both hands. Folks shouldn't say such things.

'... anyway, give her a few days at home. Till The Scholarship maybe.'

'Oh Doctor,' said Mam, 'she's missed that much school lately. Can you not give her a bottle, a good tonic?' Then she realized she was arguing, with a Doctor, and went very red. 'Oh dear,' she said.

'Why don't you go up to the school, Mrs. Friend, and have a word with the headmistress. She'll agree with me I'm sure.'

Dr. Fife swivelled himself away from his desk — it was a special kind of chair was that — and stood up. Mam stood up as well, and helped Jinnie to button her coat. She looked doubtful: well she might, she'd never in her life gone to talk to any headmistress, let alone Miss Middleton.

11

The Doctor escorted them all the way to the front door and actually opened it for them himself.

'Well, good-night, Mrs. Friend: and remember, no school for the lassie. Better still, if you could get her right away: for a complete change . . . a real holiday . . . How'd that be, Jinnie, eh?' Unexpectedly he gave Jinnie an unprofessional wink, jerked his head in a conspirational way as if he'd been plotting on Jinnie's behalf. 'Good-night then, Mrs. Friend,' he said again and closed the door.

But Jinnie's heart had plummeted right into her Sunday shoes. She knew all about Real Holidays. Every Race Week Dad took her and Robbie for three days' Real Holiday to his Mother's, Gran-at-Bartons's. Three miserable days.

She didn't like Gran-at-Barton: nor her dinners: nor her teas: even if thousands of poor children *would* be glad of them. Then the Barton cousins were all too young. And the Barton aunts were just as bad as Gran-at-Barton. She might have liked the Barton uncles: ex-regular-soldier Uncle Ned, with spiked moustache; thin, bandy-legged, horsy Uncle Len; large, red-faced, squint-eyed Uncle Frank; each one nicer, a lot nicer, than the corresponding aunt. But they were Sinners, every single one — never set foot in Chapel, Gran said, from one year's end to the next.

You could never get away from Sin at Barton. Jinnie was against Sin, of course, but at home she felt she had it under control, most of the time anyroad, and that if a Testing Time ever came, she would Dare to be a Daniel and Dare to do Right.

Not at Barton. At Barton she was Sinful. Gran-at-Barton made that clear. Not liking cabbage with dripping, or gritty seed-cake; not knowing where texts came in the Bible when Grandad asked her; opening her eyes during the family prayers; not singing the hymns; humming wordly tunes when she forgot where she was; answering back; not wiping her feet properly; passing remarks. There was no end to her Sins.

Worst of all, at Barton you couldn't forget that God was watching ALL the time. Thou God seest me . . . The Unseen Guest at every table . . . The Silent Listener to every conversation . . . Reminders on every wall . . . You couldn't forget God for a minute at Barton. Or the Angels Up There, writing everything in A Book: even what you were thinking inside your own head. Which wasn't FAIR. Of course this was true at home as well but somehow at Barton it was worse. At Barton the Strain was terrible. The last thing Jinnie wanted right now was a Real Holiday.

12

'Well, what'd you think, Jin? Will I go up and see Miss Middleton, see what she says?'

But they both knew that not even a Headmistress would go against a Doctor. Not even Dad would. And how could Jinnie tell Mam that she hated Gran-at-Barton? She could only say she didn't want to miss school and lapse into silence. Why didn't that Dr. Fife mind his own business?

When they got home, Dad was in the shop with his coat and hat on and his watch in his hand.

'My, you've been a bonnie long time,' he said. 'I'll have to hurry. And the shop's been that busy I haven't even opened The Evening. Only ha'porths and pennorths an' all.' Dad was aggrieved and no wonder. He usually had a shop-free hour when the evening paper came, to study it. 'Well, what'd he say? A waste of three and sixpence, I guarantee.'

'I'm not so sure about that,' said Mam. 'Jinnie, go and change out of them good clothes. And lay them nice and straight on the bed. Go on, hurry up, there's a good lass. Mrs. Walker'll be here any minute if she's coming the night.'

Jinnie knew she was being got out of the road while Mam and Dad talked, so she left the bedroom door wide open and listened. It wasn't any good though, because they stayed in the shop and shut the glass door between it and The Room. But it didn't matter really; she'd heard everything the Doctor'd said. And they wouldn't ask *her* if she wanted a Real Holiday. Her only hope was that Dad wouldn't be able to go for a holiday. The Shop was busy at this time of year. Dispiritedly she changed back into everyday serge skirt and wool jumper and long black woollen stockings.

She heard Mam and Dad came back into The Room.

'I'll write the letter this minute,' Dad said. Jinnie gave up hope. 'It'll make uz late for the Guild, of course, but never mind. If I post it on the way, it'll get to Barton in the morning. We can have an answer by Wednesday morning, tomorrow night maybe. I can take her there on Thursday and I'll be back here by tea-time and can get to the class meeting. How'll that do, our Jin?' Dad was pleased with his planning. But this was worse than Jinnie'd ever dreamed, than had ever happened before. She was going to be at Barton: all by herself. 'Well, Jin?' but he didn't really expect an answer. 'A few days of Gran's suet dumplings and home-made bread and you'll be as right as rain.' A few days alone with Gran-at-Barton . . . .

'Well, I don't know: it's not all that urgent,' said Mam. 'It'll make you late for the Guild for sure. Len Smith's

13

starting the meeting off, you don't want to miss what he has to say.'

Jinnie held her breath and hoped for a reprieve; that would be enough for the moment. She knew Dad was a bit suspicious of that Len Smith. Dad wouldn't be at all surprised if Len Smith spoke up tonight for Darwin and Huxley and the monkeys: trying to explain things away, as if the holy words of the Bible didn't mean exactly what they said. Dad was looking forward to a show-down with Len Smith. He'd been practising his speech a whole week. He hadn't much doubt who'd win the debate either.

'. . . and I'd best go and see what Miss Middleton has to say first before we do anything.'

'Just what I was thinking,' said Dad. 'I'll get straight off then.' He felt to see if his speech was safely in his jacket pocket, jingled his collection money in his trouser pocket, patted his topcoat smooth. 'Well now, if I'm not back by half-past nine . . .' he never was but always might be '. . . shut the shop up. Just the key, mind: I'll put the bolts in. And mind you're in bed and asleep, our Jinnie. And if I see our Robbie, I'll send him home. It's time he was in for the night.'

On his way to the glass door, Dad paused, pondering . . . he was going to write to Gran-at-Barton after all . . . Jinnie's muscles tightened again. 'Oh yes, I knew there was something,' he said. 'If Mickie Donnelly comes for tabs, don't give him any: unless he's got the money, of course.' Mickie wouldn't have. He'd been drunk not just on Saturday night, but Sunday as well: long before night too. Jinnie and Robbie, on their way to Sunday School with Dad, had seen him. He'd even had the impittence to say Good-day to them. 'Well, I really will get off now. Ta-ta.' Having firmly clamped down on Mickie Donnelly and his sinful self-indulgence, Dad departed at last, full of good humour.

'Keep an eye on the shop, Jin, till I slip out of these things,' said Mam, moving towards the bedroom.

'Oh Mam,' said Jinnie, suddenly feeling that once the evening had settled down to normal she'd never have the courage to speak up; 'don't send me to Gran-at-Barton's.' As she spoke she felt herself grow more and more desperate. 'Let's stay at home with you. Or go to school. I don't mind being sick, honest I don't.' She would be crying in a minute: she cried easily although she hated herself when she did. 'There's nothing to do there, you know there isn't . . . nobody to play with . . . and . . . and . . . and . . .' But even now Jinnie remem-

14

bered you mustn't Pass Remarks, not about Grown-Ups, not your own Grown-Ups especially . . . .

'Now, Jinnie,' said Mam, 'I'm surprised at you. You should be thankful at the very idea of a Real Holiday. Just leave things to your Dad and me. And you'd best be careful what you say about Barton in front of your Dad,' she added warningly.

'But I don't *want* a holiday,' Jinnie said. 'Don't make me go.' She groped desperately for reasons. 'She won't let you do *anything* . . . and . . . and . . . she makes you eat everything . . . and she won't let you have any dinner unless you've had that suet pudding and gravy first . . .' Jinnie wept in real earnest now, at the thought of those smooth, greasy slices of suet pudding covered with thick, slimy gravy. 'And horrible seed-cake for tea . . . I hate it.' Then, in a fit of despair, it came out. 'I hate *her*.'

'Now, Jinnie, that's enough. Just you hold that tongue of yours. And think yourself lucky it's me that's heard you going on, and not your Dad.'

'Oh him . . . he's perfect: he's just as bad as she is,' said Jinnie recklessly; for Dad and his refusal to agree to pay fees for Jinnie to go to The Sec. if she failed The Scholarship were at that moment tangled up with her hatred of Gran-at-Barton and the suet pudding. 'I hate him as well.'

Mam was vexed now and no mistake. No wonder; Jinnie had shocked even herself.

'Not another word out of you, our Jin: unless you want a good hiding. Your skin's fairly cracking for it.' Mam was the one who administered good hidings. When Dad was vexed he didn't speak to you for a day or two: but Mam's good hidings hurt. 'Now be a good lass. When I've got meself changed, you can go out and play for a bit. Edie will've finished her homework by now: go and call for her.' Mam's voice was softer again. All the same, Jinnie knew it was no good Pestering any more about the holiday.

'I don't want to,' she said. She wasn't just being awkward either. She hadn't much liked being with Edie lately, somehow.

'It'd do you good to get some fresh air,' said Mam. 'What's got into you lately, our Jin? Have you fallen out with Edie?'

'No, I haven't,' said Jinnie. She hadn't, either, but it was painful to be with Edie. Edie was so lucky. She was a year older than Jinnie and already at The Sec. She hadn't passed The Scholarship, either, her mother paid the fees. Nobody knew how Mrs. Cole did it. Mr. Cole was only a pitman even if

15

he did read books and play the fiddle. Mrs. Cole was going to see that Edie became a teacher. She told everybody so in that Durham voice of hers that The Street didn't like. Edie's older sister was already at College, so it wasn't just talk. The Street didn't care for Mrs. Cole but they had to grant that she was a wonderful manager.

Edie didn't even appreciate her own luck. She'd told Jinnie ('Don't tell me Mam, will you? Cross your heart?') that she was *not* going to be a teacher. Years of homework: and for what? To be an old maid. 'Not me,' said Edie, her fingers pressing her dark hair to make the waves deeper still. Edie was going to get married. 'What if nobody asks you?' Jinnie asked, shocked. 'They will,' said Edie and looked knowing. Jinnie's friendship with Edie was a precarious mixture of admiration, disapproval, envy, and incomprehension. Edie actually wanted to get married . . . to scrub floors, poss clothes, wash dishes, mend socks, clean out stinking drains, wear a pinnie all the time, instead of having a maid to look after the house while she wore nice clothes every day and went to Paris at Easter like Miss Sanderson. Besides, Jinnie really thought it would be wonderful to learn French and Latin and . . . and . . . all those other things: but *she* might never have the chance. It wasn't Fair: it just was not.

The shop bell rang. Mam, back in her everyday pinnie, went to answer it. Jinnie heard her voice, then another woman's, and children's. Mrs. Walker. Jinnie'd forgotten she was coming. She grabbed the *School Friend* out of Mam's basket and escaped into the scullery, making as little noise as she could and pulling the door shut behind her. She moved the old green cracket as near the fire as she could get and settled down, feet on the fender, to read.

A regiment of soldiers could march through the house bagpipes playing and drums beating and our Jinnie'd never notice once she'd got her nose stuck in a book, Mam said, in pride and exasperation. Ruin her eyesight she will, Dad said. But tonight Barbara Redfern failed to absorb her and Bessie Bunter and her tee-hee were suddenly downright silly. Jinnie's own thoughts kept defeating the *School Friend*.

Once upon a time Jinnie enjoyed a Good Think. Lately thinking had been anything but a pleasure; just a tangle of worries: The Scholarship, the Strike, now the Holiday and the things she'd said about Gran-at-Barton. And she'd said she hated Dad. If Mam told him . . . It was true, though. He just would not understand how important it was to Jinnie that she should go to The Sec: wouldn't even promise to let her

16

go if she did actually win a Scholarship.

What *had* got into her? Usually she was pleased to have a Dad like hers: a Cut Above everybody else's: not a pitman nor a shipyard man but a shopkeeper; a preacher, who went to Chapel at least twice on Sunday and twice through the week as well; a once-upon-a-time-before-the-war butler who knew all about The Toffs and so was nearly a Toff himself. The Street was jealous of him: Old Ikey they called him, out of spite. At the moment, Jinnie didn't blame them.

The door from The Room into the back kitchen squeaked. Dad still hadn't oiled that hinge.

'Come back. Hi, come back here, our Lily.'

'Nay,' said Mam's voice; 'leave the bairn be, Mrs. Walker. She'll be all right with our Jinnie.'

The youngest Walker appeared beside Jinnie, runny-nosed and grinning. Jinnie had no idea what to say. She smiled uneasily and pretended to read. Our Lily stuck her thumb into her mouth and began to totter exploratively round the scullery. She reached the cupboard under the sink which sheltered Mam's pans. The snib on it opened easily. Jinnie began to feel anxious.

The shop bell rang.

'Jinnie, will you see what that is? I'm busy. And then look out and see if our Robbie's about. It's nearly time for him to come in.' Jinnie was glad to abandon Our Lily and Mam's pans. She passed through The Room. Mrs. Walker was there, and three other little Walkers, two sitting soberly, legs swinging, on Mam's high old-fashioned sofa. A third was standing on the table, in a new blue print dress with orange flowers that had only come into the shop last week. Mam was pinning the hem to the right length.

'What'd you think about that, Mrs. Walker?' said Mam: then, indignantly, as Jinnie went through to the shop, 'Keep that door shut, our Jin.' Mam was enjoying herself.

'A packet of tabs.' Mickie Donnelly: just Jinnie's luck. She hadn't the courage to pass on Dad's message. She picked up a tuppenny packet of Woodbines.

'I'll have ten,' said Mickie. Meekly Jinnie handed over a second packet. She took the dog-eared tick book from under the counter, found the page headed 'Donnelly' and added, 'Tabs 4.' Dad would have something to say when he saw that: and his first job when he came in from the Guild would be to examine the tick book. Still, she'd be safely in bed by then.

There was the bell again. Teenie Wilson this time. You had to watch Teenie. She'd pinch anything she could lay her hand

17

on: if only a fistful of yeast from the dish on the counter. She'd had a good strapping from Miss Middleton only last Friday for stealing money from the Teachers' Room. It was the belief of The Street (of the respectable folk, that is) that Teenie's mam, who was no better than she should be, egged her on to steal.

'A penny for two ha'pennies for the gas.' Teenie's voice might have been making a cash purchase of the most expensive item in the shop.

Jinnie edged carefully round to the till. She opened it only as far as the coppers section, took out a penny and exchanged it for Teenie's ha'pennies.

'Ta,' said Teenie. She grinned and showed her beautiful white teeth.

In spite of her stealing, The Street, even the respectable part, liked Teenie: except Dad, of course. She wasn't made to wash herself enough and she often smelt of horsemuck because every day after school she had to take that old barrow round the whole neighbourhood collecting the stuff for her grandad's allotment. She got a good hiding whenever her Mam'd had a drop too much. Teenie's Mam and Dad had fights and half The Street stood outside their door and listened. But nothing daunted Teenie. At her dirtiest and smelliest she had a flash of . . . something . . . of gaiety . . . of . . . charm, maybe, only charm was something Jinnie'd never heard of. Tonight Teenie was all dressed up, in her mother's best hat and best coat with high fur collar: and nice enough to be a film star on a glossy picture outside The Queen's.

'Teenie . . .?' said Jinnie.

'Ay?' said Teenie.

'Where're you going?'

'To The Pictures, where'd you think?' said Teenie. 'Second house at The Queen's. "A Kiss in the Dark." Adolphe Menjou.' She winked meaningly.

Jinnie's soul shrivelled with envy.

'But you have to be eighteen to get in to that,' she said. The Pictures was a Sin and *she'd* never been allowed to go, not even to a Saturday matinée. But she knew all about them.

'But I *am* eighteen,' said Teenie. She winked again, then twirled round, one hand on hip, the other, fingers spread, against the back of the cloche hat and her right shoulder fashionably hunched up almost to her ear.

She did look a lot more than fourteen: powdered face,

18

grown-up clothes, high-heeled shoes. She'd get in to 'A Kiss in the Dark' all right. Lucky Teenie. Teenie'd never had a chance, Mam said. Poor Teenie. Teenie'd never been taught the difference between Right and Wrong. Lucky Teenie.

As Teenie went out, Robbie came home, black as your hat and streaked with tears. He'd fallen and cut himself. Serve him right: he should have come in when Dad told him. 'And where've *you* been, our Robbie?' Jinnie said virtuously. She wouldn't mind a bit if Mam was vexed with Robbie. In fact she rather hoped Mam would be.

It must be late. Since she'd come to bed, five or was it six? trains had gone by, making the electric lines flash above the backyard wall and changing the colour of the topmost wallpaper roses. For a long time now the breathing coming from Robbie's little bed had been the fast-asleep kind. Jinnie was still as wide awake as could be. It was ages since she'd called out for a drink. Mam had brought it, shushing her. Then not so long ago she'd got out of bed and gone into The Room. Mam had been a bit vexed but she'd allowed her to put her stockings and boots and coat on and go outside to the lav. Jinnie turned over again. Her blankets and sheets had got all mixed up and she didn't feel very warm: but she durstn't call out to Mam again.

It *was* late. Half past nine. That was Mam locking the shop door. No matter where you were in the flat you could hear what was going on in every other part. Especially at night, when you could even hear the voices of the Brooks upstairs as well if you wanted to. Jerry-built, the whole place, Dad said: not as bad as the stuff they'd been building Since-The-War, though. Nothing now was as good as Before-The-War. The country was going to rack and ruin, Dad said. Strikes, strikes, strikes, and bobbed hair, and the Charleston, and short skirts, and everybody Pictures-daft. Sin and The Devil everywhere.

In the dark, Jinnie realized she was becoming Sinful herself. She'd go to The Pictures like a shot, if she had half a chance. She wasn't interested in the Charleston but she would like her hair bobbed: Eton-cropped even. She was sick of a-woman's-crowning-glory-is-her-hair, with plaits through the week, rags on Saturday nights and curls on Sundays. She turned over again: and again: and again. Her thoughts kept on turning too.

Sudden noises startled her. Thumps: one, two, three. She sat up; then recognized the sounds. Mam and Dad were letting down the sideboard bed in The Room. She must have

19

fallen asleep after all because she hadn't heard Dad come home. The thumps stopped. They'd be putting the sheets and blankets on the bed. Mam and Dad were talking in low voices. The voices grew louder but not loud enough for Jinnie to make out the words. She could make out their mood, though.

Now she could hear some of the words. She could hardly believe them: she must be still asleep. Mam was saying Dad should let Jinnie go to The Sec., whatever happened: and tell the bairn now so that she would stop worrying her inside to bits. And Mam didn't like Gran-at-Barton's either: she wasn't letting Jinnie stay with that miserable lot, all by herself, poor lass. Mam was on Jinnie's side . . . against Dad. Having her say as well, and no mistake.

Dad was having his say too. Mam needn't think Jinnie was going to stay at Coalgate either . . . Jinnie's heart leapt. She'd never even thought of a holiday at Coalgate. There wasn't room. Gran-at-Coalgate's was a one-up-one-down house, and Nan, Jamesie and Uncle Bob lived there as well. And Dad was saying something about drinking and backing horses, and mysteriously, about Aunt Polly.

On they went. Jinnie began to be frightened. Mam and Dad hardly ever had an argument; and never had a fight. Neighbours never came out to stand around the Friends' door and listen to a fight, as they did at Teenie's or at the Donnellys', farther down the Street. All the same, this *was* very nearly a fight. What if it got worse . . . if Mam threw something at Dad and cut his face . . . if Dad hit Mam and broke her nose . . . ? No, they wouldn't . . . but just supposing . . . what should she do? Fetch the police, like Johnnie Donnelly, or the folk upstairs, like Teenie? The voices grew louder still. It wasn't exciting: it wasn't funny: it was Jinnie's own family.

The sick feeling came back. Jinnie got out of bed, groped for the pot. Her head swelled to twice its size. It would burst. She vomited. She could hear herself vomiting and vomiting. Robbie started to cry.

The strip of light under the door widened. Mam was kneeling beside Jinnie, holding her forehead to help her.

'There, there,' she said. 'That's my good lass. Let it come. That's it. You'll be all right.'

Jinnie sank back onto her heels: Mam did as well, and turned her head towards Dad who was standing in the doorway.

'Now mebbe you'll believe uz,' she said and her voice was

20

quiet now but different from usual.

'Pooh,' said Dad, 'rubbish. It's naught but hunger. Sheer hunger, that's all.' Which was what he always said. 'Come on to the kitchen and have a nice bit of bread and butter.'

But his voice was uneasy, as if for once he didn't quite believe what he was saying.

Three

The carriage was for Ladies Only so Dad stopped, opened the door and got in. The woman at the window looked surprised, then forbidding, then ferocious. The shiny red cherries on the woman's hat clicked and bobbed, fit to jump clean over the brim. Dad hoisted the big brown paper parcel onto the rack. 'Come on in, Jinnie,' he said, puffing a little because it was hard work, 'and let's have that one as well. Be sharp.' Dad spoke to the woman now. 'The lass's going as far as Coalgate,' he said, 'all by herself. To her Gran's for a holiday. She's been a bit off colour lately. Mebbe you'd keep an eye on her: see she doesn't fall out or anything.'

The cherries subsided. 'Well, of course. I'm only going to Birtley, though,' said the woman. 'Come and sit yourself down, lass. Face the engine like me. You can have the window seat. That's right.'

'Thank you kindly,' said Dad. He put the smaller, flatter parcel alongside the big bumpy one. 'Now remember, Jinnie,

22

there's two parcels. And don't lose the postcard, or your ticket, or your bag. I'll just go and have a word with the guard. And whatever you do, don't open the door or try to get out before the train stops.

Jinnie was mortified. She was eleven. Dad needn't fuss so much. She could look after herself without the woman with the cherries; or the guard. Still, he was letting her go to Coalgate. And if Mam could persuade him about that, she might, she just might, persuade him about The Sec. Not that Jinnie knew in words that she was now cherishing such a hope: she just didn't feel so worried. So she smiled at Dad, and tilted her face for good-bye.

Dad gave her a pat on the cheek. 'That's right then,' he said. 'We'll all be over on Sunday.' That was another thing: Dad missing Chapel on Sunday and breaking the Sabbath into the bargain. 'Mind and behave yourself, our Jin.' He climbed down to the platform. 'Watch your fingers, now.' He slammed the door shut and walked off.

Jinnie sank back against the red plush upholstery. The strain of the last two days had been awful: tiptoeing on eggs she'd been, in case Dad changed his mind. Not a wrong word from her, even to Robbie. Poor Robbie: no Real Holiday at *Coalgate* for him. She wriggled herself more comfortable still.

There was a series of taps on the window next to Jinnie. Dad was nodding at her and a guard was with him, nodding too. Then they both stepped back, out of the steam that was quietly sizzling up from underneath the train. Suddenly the sizzle became a great hiss and the wisps of steam turned into great clouds. The train wasn't ready yet, though. The clouds thinned and Jinnie could see Dad again, talking to the guard.

Dad would've tipped the guard a shilling to keep an eye on Jinnie: he'd said he was going to. A guard wouldn't get that much very often, Dad said. Dad knew about tips. If it hadn't been for the tips Dad had got when he was in service Before-The-War and if they hadn't been thrifty and saved, of course they'd have been in a bonnie mess After-the-War. Two years of in work, out of work and on the dole and on the Gap, he'd had. Then he'd used up the last of their savings to buy the shop, the good will not the property, of course. Now they managed to rub along, only just, of course: but Dad wasn't one to be mean over a tip. So he was looking pleased as he talked and the guard was looking respectful as he listened. And now they were both pursing their lips in harmonious disapproval. I bet it's about The Strike, thought Jinnie: but indulgently.

23

The guard hadn't forgotten his job, though: his watch was in one hand, his green flag in the other. The steam was thickening and hissing again. Then through the clouds there was a great flurry. Hastily putting his watch back in his pocket, the guard wrenched open Jinnie's door. In scrambled two women, laughing and panting and bringing into the carriage a smell of fish and a swirl of long skirts and petticoats in which Jinnie momentarily drowned.

'All right lasses; leave your creels to me. I'll put them in the van,' said the guard and disappeared.

Dad was looking at Jinnie now. Through the steam his mouth was shaping words she couldn't hear: it stretched and closed in a bit of a smile. She smiled back, nodding meaninglessly.

The hiss of steam rose to a frenzy. Metal ground against metal, painful as a fork on a plate. Buffers came together high and heavy. Clanking sounds jerked dot ... dot ... dot ... along the train. The empty carriages that had been standing on the opposite side of Jinnie's platform started to slide away. No ... it was Jinnie who was moving. She stood up to wave. Dad, waving too, swivelled round to keep her in view. Jinnie swivelled. The window of the carriage door was closed and Dad was out of sight almost at once.

The platform dropped away, back into the station. The train was high above the ground now. The sun was shining, glinting on a great maze of tracks: the biggest railway crossing in the world, and Smith's in the Central Station sold postcards to prove it. Unfaltering, Jinnie's train picked out its own lines. Then came a glimpse of office windows, a great canyon of them, and real men and women working behind them: then, almost near enough to touch, the soot and stones of the Black Gate and beyond it, the old castle. The train rattled onto the High Level; that meant good luck, because it was her best bridge. Way below, cranes, the river, the Swing Bridge, a church steeple, flashed past in a jiffy, and the train was echoing into Gateshead Station, squealing to a halt.

The fishwives removed their black bonnets. Until now they'd looked alike in their striped skirts, striped shawls, white aprons and black bonnets: now you could see one was quite young. She tidied her hair in front of the carriage mirror. The woman with the cherries was inspired to take off her hat too. She unskewered the fancy steel hatpin from the heavy bun of hair at the back of her head, wincing as she did so. She placed the hat carefully in the rack and the cherries clicked for the last time. Cautiously she ran her fingers

24

through her hair and round her bun, and changed the position of a couple of hairpins. She sighed with relief.

'Feels better, a'll awand,' said the older fishwife sympathetically.

That set the conversation flowing freely: boring Grown-Up stuff about the fine day and hats and such like. Jinnie gazed out at a grimy Mazawattee Tea sign, dinted and chipped: then at the five old-fashioned boys who could only be happy when eating Fry's chocolate. Or were they all the same boy? She was never sure. A face appeared between her and the happy boy. The guard. He nodded politely at Jinnie, then tapped on the window of her door and beckoned. The old fishwife pulled hard at its heavy leather strap. It came off its brass knob: the window dropped with a bang and station smell rushed in.

'Behavin' herself, is she, Bessie?' He winked in the direction of the young woman. Jinnie would never have suspected the guard of such daftness as was now in his voice. He hadn't been like this with Dad.

'Can't do owt else, Jack,' said the young fishwife: 'unless you're getting in with us.' She shrieked with laughter.

Jinnie's eyebrows lowered. Dad hadn't given the guard a shilling to carry on like this when he came along. Common, that's what it was.

'Well, I just might at that: so watch yourselves.' More gales of laughter. Jinnie sat up straight with disdain. The woman with the hat didn't look as if she wholly approved either. 'If you're not too stuck-up to talk to old friends, that is, since Bessie got her picture in the paper again. Mind you,' his voice was more sober now, 'I was a bit surprised to see you carrying a banner for the Tories, Bessie: you and that pitman's wife.'

That made Jinnie sit up in a different way now. Would you believe it, here she was in the same carriage as the very fishwife, Bessie Somebody or Other, who'd been in the procession with Aunt Polly.

'That was my Aunt Polly,' she said to her own surprise; and immediately hoped they hadn't heard. But they had. They all took a good look at Jinnie now and Bessie said, 'Was it really? Well, a bonnie good job she made of her speech in the Albert Hall. You can tell her next time you see her. I could never've done it myself; in front of all them folk. You could've heard a pin drop.' Bessie clicked her tongue in admiration. 'Told them what it was like to be a miner's wife, she did. Sick of strikes, she was. Nothing but strikes since she

25

was wed: and many a time not knowing where the next bite was coming from . . .'

But Uncle Dave was a big money man, had been for a long time, at least that's what Jinnie'd heard Mam say and he had a whole pound a week for his pocket . . . 'And they all gawped as if they'd never seen a pitman's wife before. No more they had, most like. Cheered like mad, they did, especially when she called Cook a Bolshie. Called him worse than muck, she did. Time he thought about the women, she said. It was always the women who went without; before the men did . . .' Bessie sighed noisily. 'It's true you know . . . Oh ay, it is,' she said to the guard. But he wasn't inclined to argue, not with Bessie anyroad.

She was still talking about Aunt Polly and the meeting after the train left Gateshead station.

The young fishwife, who seemed to be Bessie's daughter, wondered if Aunt Polly's man had read the big report of her speech in *The Echo*: and what he'd had to say about it all.

'Don't suppose he'd like it,' said Bessie. The notion clearly was part of her respect for Aunt Polly. 'Made a bit of a fool of him, some might think. Wouldn't surprise me if she got a bonnie good hidin'. They're a rough lot, is pitmen . . . Don't *you* go marrying a pitman, lass, like your Aunt Polly,' she added unexpectedly, drawing attention to Jinnie again. As if she would . . . Jinnie felt herself go red at the very idea. Before she could explain that she wasn't going to marry anybody, ever, the young fishwife said, surprisingly, 'A good hiding'd be no more than she deserved. Women's got to stick by their men when all's said and done. And mind their own business.'

'Mebbe it *is* their business,' said Bessie. 'I reckon that if the men just got on with their jobs and left the women to manage things, they'd get settled a sight faster; and better, most like. They could hardly make a worse mess than the men've done with their wars . . . and their strikes . . .'

The idea was so revolutionary that Jinnie tucked it away to take out and examine later.

' . . . Your Aunt Polly'd sort their woollens for them, that she would. *And* she'd manage the bosses all right,' Bessie concluded. 'Scared of nobody. And a way with her she has.' She looked knowing, Grown-Up knowing.

Aunt Polly had made a big impression on Bessie, no doubt about that. Of course, Aunt Polly was a big woman: and she had a loud laugh . . . and black hair . . . and that was about all Jinnie really remembered. When they went to Coalgate it was

26

mainly to Gran's. It wasn't much use going to Polly's, Mam said; she was usually out: Uncle Dave as well. She had come once or twice to see them at Gran's, of course, and at Wallsend too. Jinnie hoped she'd manage to see Aunt Polly this holiday. Aunt Polly was obviously Special. And now she'd concentrate on the journey: she'd missed enough of it already.

Street after street crawled from the railway fence right up to the sky. Rows of houses, flats mostly, mirror-matched each other then passed out of sight. Prim, flat, front streets alternated with back-lanes cluttered with projecting sculleries, stair-tunnels, backyards, end-of-the-week washing that flapped lazily and reached half-heartedly for grimy wall-tops.

Then the streets stopped going right to the sky. Trees and fields started to appear above the houses . . . between the houses . . . between the stations. Then the landscape was punctuated with pit heads and pit wheels. And all the time, just outside the window, the telegraph wires were rising, rising, rising until a pole came along and dragged them suddenly to earth again. Then they rose, rose, rose and soared out of sight once more, until the next pole started it all over again. It was a great mystery how they did it. And all the time the wheels chanted a metal song, wordlessly happy like Jinnie. Train journeys were rare and Special. They should be savoured, mile by mile, station by station. Ordinary trains were best. Express trains were in too much of a hurry for you to have a good look at anything. Express trains took you to Gran-at-Barton's: fast, because you didn't want to go. Ordinary trains took you to Gran-at-Coalgate's: slowly, because Gran-at-Coalgate's was too good to be rushed at.

So she enjoyed the way every station enfolded the train and gently pulled it to a halt. She liked the names the porters called out: Low Fell, Lamesley, Beamish, Pelton, and half-way, Birtley, where the woman with the hat left them, begloved, behatted and a stranger once more. She listened each time for the thud and slither as the bundle of racing papers was thrown out of the guard's van: and for the rattlings, thumpings and scrapings as crates and wicker baskets and parcels were unloaded.

Even the guard's face at the window and his silly jokes with the fishwives became part of a pattern that must not end too soon.

But it would. This time the voice on the platform was shouting, 'Annfield Plain, Annfield Plain.' The last station

27

before Coalgate. The young fishwife was smoothing her big apron, putting on her shawl, settling her bonnet. Getting off here then, to sell Friday fish.

The faithful guard opened the door.

'Taking your time, aren't you?' he said. 'Can't bear to leave uz, eh?' He winked knowingly at Jinnie, who pretended she hadn't seen. 'I've fetched your creel, Bella. Save you a walk to the van.'

'Oh, ta,' said Bella. 'See you the night then. No, me Mam, not you, impittent,' she said to the guard. She gave him a dig in the ribs. 'Ta-ra, well. And if you can't be good be careful.' She hoisted the creel on to her shoulder and was on her way. The guard watched her, shaking his head with admiration. Then he turned to the train again.

'Next stop, lass,' he said: as if Jinnie didn't know.

'Yes,' she said.

'Mind you wait till I come along,' he said, 'and I'll get your parcels down for you.'

But Jinnie wasn't going to wait, she didn't approve of him. The minute the train started again, she took both parcels down from the rack, even the heavy one with the groceries for Gran, and put them on the empty seat beside her. She began checking: big parcel, flat Sunday-clothes-change-of-underwear parcel with the Arrived Safely postcard tucked under the string; handbag — Christmas present from Aunt Nell and Uncle Reg — it had never been out of her hand; gloves, they'd never been off her hands; hat, still on her head. Jinnie'd had no intention of spoiling her holiday by losing anything on her way. Ticket, in her handbag, in the outer compartment. She checked that it was the right half, Newcastle to Coalgate, and tucked it well down inside her glove. Now she was ready to enjoy to the full the last, best part of the journey.

The track was curving so much now that she could see the engine, belching and busy, and the first characterless carriage, its windows blinded by the sun. The track straightened, the engine and carriage disappeared. Another pit head appeared: the one she'd been waiting for. Unmistakably the Eden: Jamesie's, Uncle Dave's, hers. The pulleys were running gaily round, as if they knew she'd hoped they would be. Now came the pit heap, and overhead wires and swinging coal-tubs, full and empty, coming and going along the wires, miraculously always at the same distance apart, never catching each other up. And squealing and clanking above the beat of the train.

28

All passed in a minute. The countryside was green and innocent again, scarred only by ragged gorse bushes, black and gold and early green. The pit was still there, though. She couldn't see it, but it was still there. Hundreds and hundreds and thousands and thousands of feet below, miles and miles of little passages, pitmen crawling about in the dark, burrowing, burrowing. Ponies going blind. Uncle Dave might be down there this very minute; or Uncle Dave's lads; or Jamesie. If Jamesie was, he'd be knocking with his pick on the roof of coal, now, this moment, calling up 'What cheer?' He always did when Mam and Robbie and Jinnie were visiting. He knew what time they'd be above his seam. But how did he tell the time down there? How could there *be* time where there was no night and no day?

She hadn't thought about it before. Mam and Robbie had always been with her. They always laughed at the idea of Jamesie knocking on the coal; and pretended they could hear him. Without them Jinnie didn't feel like laughing. She shivered and swallowed: hard. The dark was pressing down on her: no sun, ever; no moon, no stars, ever. The walls of the tunnel bearing down, suffocating her. Great cliffs of coal and rock pressing down, squeezing out the air. Slowly, slowly, always, they pressed down. The pit props creaked, groaned. At any moment they'd snap, like matchsticks. Slowly, slowly, yet all in a second: first a trickle, a slither, a rattle, then a great roar of coal and stones and rock and dust. And the passages vanished and the men were dead, as if they had never been.

Or the water rushed in black and cold and treacherous: and it didn't matter whether you could swim or not because all the galleries were filled and there was no air to breathe. Or gas and poison crept up behind you and pressed silent fingers on your throat. And you were dead. Before you can say Jack Robinson, said Jamesie's voice, and laughed. But Jamesie never talked about such things: nor any pitman that Jinnie'd heard. She knew about them, all the same: she didn't know how.

A little farm passed them. She was glad of its familiar, dirty, whitewashed walls and the wrong-way-round rusty S on its chimney-stack, and the lurching apple-tree. Big parcel, flat parcel, handbag, gloves, ticket: her eyes checked them again.

At last: St. Ives' Nan's church on the hill; just below it the little stone school that Mam had gone to; below that the stone playground wall; below that again, St Ives' church hall, raw and red. And St. Ives' Road: a long terrace running

29

down the hill to the station and the main part of the town, where the pit families lived. St. Ives' Road was Coalgate's posh street: low walls, little iron railings, rusty hedges, big bay windows looped with lace, or venetian-blinded against the midday sun.

The train slowed down. St. Ives' Road was blotted out by a last-minute cutting, reappeared behind a row of yellow-green railway bushes, and was level with the train at last. The platform slid round Jinnie for the last time, pulled the train to a stop.

'Coalgate, Coalgate', and the final slap and slither of the newspapers.

'Well here you are, lass. D'you want for me to open the door? It's a bit heavy for a bairn.'

The fishwife didn't wait for an answer. She made for the window, a great bundle of apron and heavy skirt and flannel petticoats.

The door didn't open. Bessie pushed it harder, with her knee. If it opened suddenly, she'd fall out. But it didn't. Bessie opened the window and tried the door again. It was still stuck.

Jinnie heard hurrying feet, and a man trotted past with a big bundle of papers. Jinnie was alarmed. The train would start again. She'd be carried on to Consett... after all the times Dad had warned her... It wasn't her fault ... that guard. Just like him not to come along the only time he was needed. A whole shilling he'd had, as well.

'Here, come on. It's a man you want on the job. Out of the road a minute.'

Thank goodness.

Bessie got out of the road with a flounce of make-on indignation that was positively embarrassing. All the guard except his legs came into the carriage.

'Is that yours?' he asked. 'Sure you've got everything?'

'Yes,' said Jinnie rather coldly. She was relieved to see him. All the same, he ought to have come faster.

'That's right then,' he said. 'Hand them to me.'

Jinnie hesitated. She knew she ought not to argue, but she would rather get the parcels out herself. She didn't trust him to carry the flat one. And he might drop the Arrived Safely postcard out on to the line and the train might run over it. Dad'd have something to say about that ... but all the time she really knew that she was just putting off the unexpectedly awkward moment when she'd have to greet Gran.

'What's the matter, lass? Is it too high? Will I lift you out?'

30

That did it. Jinnie jumped. The guard moved hurriedly back: and just missed treading on a brown and white terrier, trailing a leash and barking crazily, which arrived outside the door almost at the same moment as Jinnie. The barking changed to a brief snarl and warning snap of the teeth at the guard, then to a choking whine as the dog leapt up at Jinnie, grinning and flapping his tongue in a great frightening slaver of welcome. Vic, and not far behind him, a weekday, workday Gran that she hardly recognized for a moment.

'Well here you are then,' said Gran, smiling. Jinnie felt warm and glad and scarcely shy at all.

'Is this your Gran?' said the guard.

'It is that,' said Gran. 'Get down, Vic,' she said. She stooped, recovered the leash and gave the dog a business-like slap. 'And just you behave yourself.'

'Here she is then, missus,' said the guard. 'Safe and sound like I promised her Da.'

'Thank you kindly,' said Gran. 'And now let's be having the lass's things. Is your ticket handy, Jin?'

Jinnie showed it to Gran.

'That's right then. *Will* you get down, our Vic?' She gave Vic a still more businesslike smack across his rump. It sobered him, for the moment anyroad. 'Here, Jin; take his lead till we're out of the station, will you?'

The guard came with them as they walked along the platform to the porter who was unloading basket after murmurous basket of pigeons.

The porter nodded to Gran, took Jinnie's ticket, said, 'She's come then, Mrs. Dunham,' and swooped his arms back into the van for the next basket, all in one breath. 'You'll tell Jamesie I'll be seeing him the night, Mrs. Dunham then?'

'Ay, Jimmie, I will. Come on, Jin. You'll be ready for a bite to eat, a'll awand. You can run on ahead, if you like. Stretch your legs. And you can cross by the line.'

'Watch out, mind. Look both ways, lass,' the guard called after her. Busybody . . . And how old did he think she was?

She did look both ways, though. But not because the guard had told her to; because Gran hadn't.

Safely on the platform on the down side of the track, Jinnie stopped to try the chocolate machine as she and Robbie always did. She pulled hard at the drawer. The thin gold and red bars inside the machine jiggled a little, but the drawer refused to come out. Still it had been worth a try: Coalgate was the sort of place where Special things might happen.

31

Vic, used to her already, inspected the machine also. He sniffed critically around the pedestal: then cocked his leg. Nasty dirty brutes, dogs, Dad said. Jinnie pretended she hadn't noticed and dragged Vic away. She still liked him though.

Just inside the little brown gate at the top of the long ramp that led down to Watling Street she waited, and watched Gran come towards her. Today's Gran was different from the Gran Jinnie had been holding in her mind. It would take a minute or two longer to get used to her.

It was her clothes. Jinnie'd never seen them before. Everyday, not Company, they must be. The long black skirt and black boots were as Jinnie had expected, but Gran's blouse was grey and white striped flannel instead of black silk and black lace. And she was wearing a big crochet shawl, home-made, not her good black coat. And a man's cap.

It was all right for Gran to look old-fashioned but she shouldn't look so ... so ... poor ... so ...

common ... so Pit Folk. Jinnie'd never though of Gran as Pit Folk before but it was out at last, the thought Jinnie hadn't known she'd been dodging ever since she'd got off the train. Gran-at-Coalgate was Pit Folk. Gran-at-Barton wouldn't even own a shawl like that: as for a cap ... a man's ....

And Gran-at-Barton would never carry Jinnie's parcels,

32

either; or let her cross the track by herself; or come to the station to meet her; or anybody for that matter. If she did, she'd be wearing a proper coat, right enough; and a real hat. Always. Yes, and underneath the hat, her hair would be scraped back, nearly to the top of her head, in a tight bun. It would be smooth and hard and steely grey: and every single hair would stay exactly where it had been told.

Jinnie looked towards her best Gran. Gran-at-Coalgate also pulled her hair into a tight bun: but no bun in the world could ever be tight enough to straighten out all the waves or hold in check all the soft little white wisps and curls. And Gran-at-Coalgate's face was . . . well, Jinnie was never scared of Gran-at-Coalgate. A wave of warm, defensive, shaming love swept over Jinnie. She met Gran's brown eyes and, not knowing it, smiled; and walked back destroying the distance between them.

'Want to race him down to the street, Jin?' asked Gran. 'Not this time? All right then.' She unclipped the lead from Vic's collar. 'Off home with you, lad.'

Tongue flapping, teeth grinning, Vic looked expectantly, doubtfully, at Jinnie, then raced down the ramp. At the bottom he braked himself to a stop that sent his back legs past his front legs, then shot off round the corner. He wasn't even in sight when Gran and Jinnie turned along Watling Street to go under the railway bridge which was dark and smelt of old trains. From the track above, water slid down, slow and fat and hardly like water at all, over black-grey moss, the sort that belonged only to railway bridges. Jinnie sighed with happiness. She was here, at last: at Coalgate: for a Real Holiday.

Surprised, she heard the guard's whistle. Already it was strange to remember the train. She had done with it: it had no right to be there still. Shuddering and clanking and setting the ripples faster down the wall, the train started across the bridge above, gathered a little speed and moved off into the past.

33

Four

They emerged from the under-the-bridge railway smell into the smell of fish and chips, distant, but a reminder that this not-like-any-other day was in fact Friday. In a minute Jinnie would see McElwain's Corner, which wasn't a corner at all but a cross-roads where Watling Street, St. Ives' Road, Iveson Road, and Grove Street, which was Gran's Street, came together. It was the main place in Coalgate, with space enough for a market, if Coalgate had had a market. As it was, four of the pubs and half the shops of Coalgate somehow contrived to present front, back, or side to the cross-roads. But you never heard it called anything except McElwain's Corner, or just Tommy's Corner.

Tommy's establishment combined a billiard saloon, Coalgate's only one, with an ice-cream, sweet, cigarette and pop shop. It had to itself all the corner made by Iveson Road and Grove Street. More important still, the pavement here was by some chance so wide you could hardly call it a pavement at all. So Tommy's Corner was Coalgate's meeting-place: for men — pitmen. Pitmen were a wild lot, Dad said: pretty Sinful, too: all that gambling and swearing and drinking and going on strike. Outside Tommy's they always seemed peaceful enough: harmless: standing, or leaning against the long, green-painted, blanked-out saloon window, or, mostly, sitting comfortably on their hunkers. It was only the hunkers that told you they were pitmen; because the men didn't go to Tommy's in their pit dirt. Here they were off duty, clean, enjoying themselves: talking, sitting silent, chewing a blade of grass, turning over a quid of tobacco and spitting out a long squirt of tobacco juice, studying *The Sporting Man,* watching Coalgate go by. But you never knew, of course; all those pitmen. Anything might happen. It never had; but You Never Knew.

The minute Watling Street curved into the cross-roads, Jinnie saw that today Something *was* happening. The men outside Tommy's looked different, for a start. Not a single man was on his hunkers, or leaning on the window, or watching the cross-roads. They were all on their feet, and

34

looking towards Tommy's door, at a giant of a man standing there and talking, making a speech more like. And they were angry: anger was in their backs, and elbows, and arms, and heads; above all, in their voices.

Jinnie moved closer to Gran.

'Is it a fight, Gran?' she asked. It didn't look quite like a fight, and it was a queer time of day for one. But pitmen's times and days were queer, anyroad.

'Nay lass, it isn't,' said Gran. 'Leastways not the sort you mean. Ah well, we'll be hearing soon enough.'

She didn't say any more and Jinnie didn't like to ask. Curiosity killed the cat and just asking a Grown-Up a simple question could be Pestering. All the same, it usually took a lot to stop Jinnie asking when she really wanted to know. However, today she was still a bit of a stranger, a visitor, to Coalgate. Besides, Gran sounded upset: not angry, more like sad. Except that Grown-Ups didn't get sad: angry, irritable, vexed, but not sad. Unless somebody died, of course. Maybe that was it: somebody had died. At Coalgate men were always getting themselves killed down the pit.

The voices at Tommy's Corner weren't sad, though. Jinnie was sure of that. Now she was near enough to glimpse some of the faces, they weren't sad either, but angry. Jamesie's as well. She'd never seen him angry before. And he didn't even glance her way. And he hadn't been down the pit when she'd been thinking about him. Like the rest of them Jamesie was seeing nothing but the big man in Tommy's doorway: a giant of a man, even allowing for the doorstep. He was the angriest of them all, fairly spitting out names, words . . . Baldwin . . . Ramsay MacDonald . . . and subsidy and owners and districts and executive and minimum. The Strike again. Jinnie ought to've guessed straight away.

Maybe The Strike was beginning now, not on May Day. Bolshie Day, Dad called it . . . Blood in the Streets . . . they'll not be happy till there's blood in the streets . . . like in Russia . . . Calling for a General Strike. Dad had closed his eyes and sucked in his lips at the thought . . . Never been such a thing in this country . . . Coalgate wasn't a safe place for a bairn, Dad had said, just now. 'Don't talk so daft,' Mam had said. Jinnie had forgotten, till now, this part of the night Mam and Dad had argued about Jinnie and the Holiday. The Strike hadn't worried Jinnie much since she'd started to think that maybe Mam really wanted her to go to The Sec. and might persuade Dad in the end. Now The Strike was real again. Yet different from the way it was when Dad talked

35

about it. The Strike words sounded different as the big man was shouting them.

There were new words too. Especially two and tenpence. How could two and tenpence be so terrible? Yet all the men were in a rage about that two and tenpence.

Gran didn't slow down at Tommy's: in fact she quickened her steps. Jinnie found herself almost trotting to keep up with her, with no chance to look back and listen. Quickly the pavement rounded a bend and they came into Grove Street. Vic reappeared through Gran's archway and raced towards them. He skittered round the pair of them, then raced up the street. He stopped at Gran's front door and waited, not knowing whether to watch them or the closed door.

The newer brick houses on one side of the street were in shadow but the sun was shining on the little stone houses on Gran's side. It even poked into Gran's archway, not as far as the big backyard, of course. It separated the cobble-stones on the street with light and shadow.

Without knowing it, Jinnie sighed with wordless relief. She forgot the noise at McElwain's and the big man and his anger. Here it was warm and peaceful and the street hadn't changed. Next door to Gran's, Lizzie Dobson's door was open as usual. Opposite, Mattie Mathieson was still sitting in his wheelchair that took up most of the narrow pavement. The shiny black cover was still trying to hide what everybody knew, that Mattie had lost both legs in The War. It was rude to stare. Jinnie tried to keep her eyes away from that shiny black cloth. It was hard, though: the shiny black cloth was like a magnet. What *did* anybody look like without legs?

'Well, Mattie, the owners've posted the new rates,' Gran called across to him. 'Two and tenpence a shift off.'

Mattie didn't reply. He often didn't. Folk going by mostly stopped and talked to him just the same.

Then, 'The Strike'll be on, then,' he said. The Strike roused even Mattie out of his silence.

'Ay,' said Gran. 'The General Strike and all, most like. Might as well make a job of it when they're at it.' Gran . . . in favour of a General Strike. Jinnie didn't believe it: she wasn't hearing properly. What would Dad've said?

'Nay,' said Mattie, 'they promised once before, and backed down when it came to the push.'

'Not this time they won't,' said Gran. 'There'll be no more Black Fridays.'

'That's to be seen,' said Mattie: 'but there'll be no more Red uns. No more Subsidies. That I *am* sure on,' he added

36

gloomily: then his face returned to its usual flat indifference.

Blacks and Reds; it was so confusing that Jinnie gave up trying to understand. She looked into Lizzie Dobson's. Lizzie believed in fresh air. You nearly got blown through her back door when you sat at Lizzie's fireside, Mam said. As well as the street door the inside door into the downstairs room was open. A little wooden gate was in position across the lower part of the opening. Lizzie's baby must be old enough for crawling now, or walking, maybe. In the depths of the room Jinnie could see a bright fire, flames leaping among spurts of white smoke. Lizzie was such a fanatic for cleanliness even the smoke was clean, Mam said. Mam liked Lizzie. Everybody did.

Lizzie herself was in full view, standing beside the table in front of the window. She was spooning food, neatly and efficiently, into an eager baby, bobbing like a bird in a great nest of bib and towel that hid most of him and nearly all his high-chair. She saw them.

'Hello, Jinnie,' she called out, tidying the baby's chin with a swoop of the spoon. 'How're you keeping now, lass? Any better?' Jinnie was surprised for a moment. She'd forgotten the reason for her Holiday. 'And how's your Mam? And Robbie? Come on in, the pair of you.'

Jinnie hesitated. Would she be cheeky if she answered or rude if she didn't? You never knew where you were with this kind of Grown-Up question.

Gran settled the matter.

'She's a bit pasty, Lizzie, but a few days with her Gran'll put her right. No, we'll not come in, thanks; it's getting on to dinner-time. Kate's champion, they're all champion. They're coming through Sunday, to see if she's behavin' herself. I'll be wantin' a ribbon-cake, Lizzie, if you'll can manage.'

You could tell from Gran's voice that she knew Jinnie *would* behave herself, and from the ribbon-cake that she also knew that it was Special, extra-Special, for Mam and Dad and Robbie to be breaking the Sabbath and missing Chapel to come to Coalgate.

'I'll manage it, Mrs. Dunham, without fail,' said Lizzie. The baby gave a bellow of impatience. 'All right, you greedy little gissie-pig,' she said lovingly, and spooned another mouthful into him. 'I'll bake the cake Sunday, after dinner, Mrs. Dunham. Nice and fresh it'll be then.'

'Nay, you bake it when it suits you, Lizzie lass,' said Gran. 'A few hours is neither here nor there.' The baby was ready for more and bellowed again. 'Nay, Lizzie, I don't know

37

which is in a bigger hurry, babies or dogs,' she added, for Vic had come to add to the noise, whining pitifully and looking up at her appealingly. 'Go and let him in, will you, Jin?'

Before the door was a quarter open, Vic shot past Jinnie into the tiny, oilclothed space at the bottom of the stairs. The big brass button that lifted the sneck of the inner door was awkward to get hold of but Jinnie managed it.

Warmth and half-darkness greeted her: and the smell of something good in the oven. Rabbit: and jacket potatoes. It couldn't be: Friday was fish. It wasn't cod that was cooking here, though. She sniffed thoughtfully. She still thought it was rabbit. Not that she cared. She didn't care if it was greasy cabbage and slimy dumplings. But it wasn't: it wouldn't be: not at Gran-at-Coalgate's.

The smells receded. Things emerged: the big table in front of the window with Gran's funny-shaped black-handled knives and forks already laid out on the worn oilcloth; the tops of an aspidistra and scented geraniums showing just above the window edge of the table. Jinnie's eyes moved. A great shock of yellow smoke combed upwards on the far wall. Then round it the kitchen range asserted itself, black and shiny. Friday: black-leading day. The mantelpiece was valanced, as always, with dark red cloth and gold wool bobbles. On the brass rail Jamesie's pit clothes were warming: shirt, breeches and thick purple stockings. Everything was just as usual. The steel fender still gleamed. The big steel coal bucket on one side of the black and white checkerboard tin hearth still balanced the heavy pit boots on the other. Nothing had changed. Already stretched on the rag mat in front of the hearth as if he'd been there all morning, Vic opened an eye at her, then closed it again. The basket chair by the fire suddenly creaked for her attention. There it was, the same as ever, crochet cushion seat, crochet shawl back. The big wooden armchair, with its patchwork cushion, still faced it. The busy cottage-loaf clock ticked somewhere up on the mantlepiece out of sight.

Shapes began to appear everywhere. Baskets dangled from the beams, and a bamboo carpet beater. Gran's sewing-machine loomed mysterious near the back door. Above it still hung the picture and inside its wide wooden frame dim figures still lived, remote and rich and like no one Jinnie had ever seen: a lady with strange, puffed-up hair, tiny waist and enormous sleeves, at her feet a boy-girl clutching a queer-shaped railway engine; a man in a strange uniform, spiked helmet and one arm in a sling, who was separated from the

38

lady by a low garden fence.

Slowly she looked round the rest of the room. The washing-up table showed itself. More wooden chairs. The dark space under the stairs relented, to reveal, but only dimly, the big bed that belonged there.

'Come on, wor lass,' said Gran's voice behind her. 'Let's in.'

The things receded, retreated into the background and began immediately the process of becoming unremarkable, unnoticeable, as things like tables and chairs usually were.

Five

It *was* rabbit for dinner. There wasn't anything Jinnie liked better, especially if she'd been poorly. It had strips of bacon in it, just like Mam's, and without even asking, Gran gave her her favourite bits, a plump pink leg and the tiny heart and kidney. But first 'A does of Phosferine for you, lass,' she said. 'I've got a bottle for you. Strengthen your nerves.' Nasty bitter stuff it was, but Jinnie swallowed it without a grumble.

Jamesie came home just as Gran was breaking open Jinnie's big jacket potato for her.

'My, my, look who's here. If it isn't wor Jinnie. And how's wor bonnie lass the day?' You'd never guess from his voice he was a pitman and had been in that noisy crowd at McElwain's Corner. But he wasn't a pitman, he was Jamesie, Mam's youngest brother who never seemed like an uncle. He took off his cap and with an exaggerated gesture tossed it at the hook on the back door. 'There you are: every time a winner.' He threw his muffler also. 'Well, nearly every time.' He went and picked up the muffler and hung it with his cap. Jamesie would never grow up, Dad said. Ay, Mam always agreed. He's just a great daft lad still. But her voice didn't mean it in Dad's way at all.

'Well, if it isn't rabbit stew,' said Jamesie. 'You want to come a bit more often, Jin. We get a bit fed-up with kipper dip.'

'Just you come and sit yourself down, and let your meat stop your mouth,' said Gran, unmoved. She took a warm plate from the hearth and began to spoon out Jamesie's stew.

Jamesie sat down next to Jinnie, pulled her plait and pretended elaborately that he hadn't.

'Did you go for me pay, Ma?' he said.

'Ay,' said Gran: 'before I went to the station.'

'Well, don't go spending it all at once,' he said. Then his voice changed. 'You heard about the owners posting the pay cuts at the pit head? Two and tenpence a shift cut for the Durham pits.'

'Ay,' said Gran: 'I heard.' Her voice was serious too. 'Ah well, we never died a winter yet.' There was a little pause.

40

'You'll mebbe be glad of a slice of kipper dip before you're done; so get on with your rabbit,' she said.

Jinnie wasn't sure what kipper dip was but she understood you'd have to be hungry to want to eat it. A bonnie good hungering is all their strike'll get them, Dad said. Why can't the clowns see it? But it seemed they could see it: so why . . . Jinnie dursn't ask: if she listened, maybe . . . .

But Jamesie was starting on his dinner.

'What're you trying to do, our Ma? Burn me mouth out? These taties is hot as hell,' he said indignantly.

'They've come from a hot place,' said Gran calmly; 'and just you mind your manners. Jinnie's not used to that kind of language, Jamesie Dunham.'

They ate their meal in companionable silence. After they'd finished, and rabbit bones and potato skins were hissing cheerfully in the fire that was now roaring away, a real pitman's fire, Gran made the tea and Jamesie moved to the basket chair.

'Now, our Jin,' he said, 'have you heard the one about the Englishman, the Irishman and the Scotchman?' And away he went, firing at Jinnie a regular volley of stories and riddles.

Jinnie had heard them all, with Robbie, the last time they came to Coalgate; and the time before that, and the time before that. Which was one reason why she loved them. She always remembered the beginning of a story and always forgot the end. Except for the riddles. She couldn't bear not knowing the answer to a riddle and having to admit it.

One particular riddle Jamesie always saved till last. 'Geordie and Bill and some of their marras were in a field. You know the one, Jin: just behind St. Ives' school. Playing pitch and toss. Now here's where the trouble was. Listen now, Jin. There was four coppers in that field, one at each side . . .' Jamesie paused ominously, as usual: and, as usual, Jinnie wondered fleetingly what Dad would have had to say at this moment . . . pitch and toss was not only against the law, it was Gambling: a Sin as well . . . 'Now, Jin lass, how d'you reckon Bill and Geordie and their marras got out of the field without the coppers picking them up?'

Jamesie was leaning forward in his chair, legs apart, forearms resting on his thighs, hands dangling between his knees, head tilted to get a good look at Jinnie's face.

'Well, come on, slowcoach.'

This time Jinnie pretended not to know the answer although she couldn't have explained why. She looked questioningly at Gran, who was now pouring tea from the big

41

brown teapot, filling Jamesie's pint pot. Gran stopped pouring and pretended to mouth the solution. Jamesie sat up and shook his fist.

'Don't you go letting on the answer, our Ma,' he said threateningly.

'Don't know,' said Jinnie at last. 'Give in. How?' She watched Jamesie's head set for the final moment of laughter.

'It was Bill and Geordie that picked the *coppers* up.'

He waited a second to make sure that Jinnie understood, then abandoned himself to his glee so whole-heartedly that Jinnie, Gran and even Vic had to laugh with him.

'And you know, Jin,' he said at last, fishing in his pocket, as he always did at this point, 'you'll never believe it, them same four coppers is here in this room this very minute. Here they are. Come on, let's have your hand. C'mon, c'mon.' Awkward and shy again, Jinnie held out her hand. 'One. Now the other hand . . . Two . . . That's *your* pay fettled for this week.' He stretched across to the table. 'Three. Four . . . that's for our Nan when she comes in.' He put another two pennies on the table.

'Well,' said Gran, 'I'm glad to see you're not spent up from last week yet. And while you're on, you might as well be having your own pay for this week.' She took Jamesie's pay-packet from the caddy on the mantelpiece where she had put it when she and Jinnie came in from the station.

Carefully, with a sharp knife from the table drawer, Gran slit it open and drew out first a piece of paper, then one . . . two . . . pound notes: and shook out some coins into her hand. Half-crowns, shillings, pennies. My goodness, that was a lot of money. No wonder Dad said there was naught wrong with The Miner's Pay-Packet and that there was an awful lot of rubbish talked about it.

Gran studied the piece of paper, the tip of her tongue pressed the corner of her mouth as she calculated.

'Well,' she said, 'the deductions is up from last week, but it seems right. A good week. You *have* been in a good seam lately.' She picked up some of the coins. Jinnie didn't like to look to see exactly how much money they made. 'Well, here's your spending-money. I'll put a bit extra aside for Dottie's Savings again this week.' Dottie was Jamesie's girl and they were getting wed this summer, as Jinnie knew.

'Nay,' said Jamesie. 'Mebbe you'd best keep more for yourself this week. Only one more Pay Day and then I'll not be bringin' aught in for a week or two, mebbe.'

'Just mebbe?: said Gran. 'Nay, it's a moral certainty you'll

42

not. And not for a month or two, never mind a week or two.'

'Nay, our Ma,' said Jamesie, 'there's hope yet of The Subsidy . . . or summat . . .'

'That's just what there's not,' said Gran. 'The last Subsidy bought all the time the Government wanted: the'll not be buying any more. You've waited too long, lad: the lot of you. You might've won a strike last year or in nineteen nineteen, just after the War: that was when you really had them on the run.'

'Hold on,' said Jamesie. 'I was only fourteen. What could I have done in nineteen nineteen?'

Gran ignored that. 'The pitmen could've had anything then, if they'd stuck out . . . Nationalization even.'

Gran thought Nationalization was All Right. Gran wanted Nationalization. What if she talked like that on Sunday? The very idea upset Jinnie. Dad might . . . would . . . take Jinnie straight home and never let her come back to Coalgate again. Nationalization was Bolshie, Dad said.

' . . . Nay, I'm not blamin' the Miners' Executive for not seein' it then; we're all troubled with after-wit. But, best face up to it, all you'll get now will be what the Owners want — longer hours for less pay.'

'So we should just lie down for them to walk over uz. Is that it?' said Jamesie.

'Nay, I've never said that neither, our Jamesie. You should strike all right. You'll lose: but you should strike.' Which was another bonnie queer thing for Gran to say.

'You're wrong, our Ma. The' can't do without coal. We've got to stay out long enough, that's all. Till wor bellies is flat ag'in wor backbones, if need be.' Jamesie was starting to look like Jamesie at McElwain's Corner.

'Nay,' said Gran, 'I'm sorry I started this: we've been over it all before. We'll had wor whisht now. Anyroad, Jinnie's here for a bit of holiday, a rest and a change. She doesn't want to hear uz going on about The Strike. D'you, Jin? Get enough of that at home, a'll awand, eh?'

Gran went to the fire-place. She lifted the lid of the teapot still warming on the hob.

'There's plenty left,' she said. 'Want a fill up, Jamesie?'

'No, thanks,' said Jamesie. 'I'll wait till Tot comes. He'll be here any minute. Save a drop for him. As long as it *is* tea, and not water bewitched and tea begrudged by that time.'

'It'll be wet and warm,' said Gran: as if Tot was ordinary, maybe, even, as if she wasn't all that fond of Tot. But she must be. Jinnie's imagination was running away with her. It's

43

something you'll have to watch, our Jin, Mam said. Jinnie knew about Tot, although she'd never seen him. Tot had saved Jamesie's life, when Jamesie was just a bit of a lad, first down the pit. Tot was a Hero. Tot was Special. Even if he was a Catholic, an Irish Catholic at that, the worst sort. Real bigots, Dad said. Coalgate was full of Catholics. Irish ones.

'Here Jin, give's a hand with the dishes, will you? Then I can get on with the clippie mat and you can have a nice read. Nan's got a whole stack of new papers. Dottie's missus passed them on. And you, our Jamesie, I fetched them laces you asked uz for. You can get them put in your boots while you're waitin'. You can wash if you like, Jin, and I'll dry.' Trust Gran to know that washing was nicer than drying and to let Jinnie do it. She'd get the pots extra clean, to show she could.

'You've done fine,' said Gran, as she picked the last of the pots, Jamesie's pint pot, from the puddle on the draining-tray. 'You can sign off now. I'll empty the bowl. Dry your hands properly mind. The towel's on the oven door.'

Warm toasted towel; warm, water-soft hands; roaring fire; Dottie's missus's books — real books maybe; Gran's praise;

44

rabbit stew; Jamesie's coppers: Jinnie really belonged at Gran's now. She relaxed comfortably into herself. She pushed back the skin at the base of her finger-nails. You should have nice half-moons, Miss Sanderson said, and no nail biting. You should take a proper pride in things like that, girls: never mind plastering yourself with paint and powder, ruining your skin, and making yourself Common and Cheap, Miss Sanderson said.

Jinnie surveyed her nails with satisfaction: then looked up. Jamesie was watching her with a smile. One eyebrow went up and his forehead wrinkled. He looked comic and knowing, pleasant and friendly, but Jinnie felt she'd been caught out and blushed. Our Jin can't bear funning, silly lass, Mam said. Hastily she clenched her hands to hide her nails. She was glad when a moment later the street door opened with a bang against the wall.

'This'll be Tot,' said Jamesie, and Vic leapt joyously at the great fair giant of a man who'd been at McElwain's. Of course: she should've guessed. There couldn't be two men as big as Tot.

'What cheer, Mrs. Dunham? What fettle the day?' he said. 'And who's this? Who's this? Nay, you'll know uz next time you see uz, lass,' but he said it good-humouredly.

Hastily Jinnie looked away. She'd been Staring again. But she couldn't help it. She'd heard often enough about Tot, and he was so big: great shoulders, great chest, thick strong neck, massive arms. The legend about him was true: for the first time she believed it wholly. He brought the story into the room with him: the warning creak of pit props, the groan of straining rocks, the shout: Jamesie paralysed by terror: Tot's blow stunning him and knocking him to the ground: the giant kneeling over him, his great back an arch that held up the straining timber, while one man died, another crawled away for help and the rest worked like madmen to shore up the props until that help came. Jinnie believed every word of it all right and Dad, for once, was wrong, pooh-poohing it and saying it was against all reason. She Stared again.

'Well, if you're staying, you might as well sit down,' said Gran, but not as if she was pleased to see him: but she must be, mustn't she? She didn't offer him any tea after all, although the pot was still on the hob plain to see. And this was TOT. It didn't make sense.

Tot didn't seem to notice, though. He just kept on talking. His voice was as big as the rest of him.

'This'll be Kate's lass, then? Jamesie said about her coming.

45

Been poor-like, he said. Doesn't look as if there's owt much wrong with you now, lass. Coalgate's done you good already, eh?' He gave a great roaring laugh that nobody joined in. You'd've thought somebody would, for politeness' sake, never mind Tot's. Jamesie put his cap on.

'Well, I'm ready, Tot,' he said.

But Tot was in no hurry.

'Not much like her Mam, though, is she?' he said. It had begun. From now on everybody would be telling her she wasn't like her Mam: must take after her Dad; and Gran would say, ay, Jinnie was a Friend all right. Jinnie didn't mind taking after Dad, but she didn't want to be a Friend. The folks-at-Barton were Friends. Jinnie'd rather be a Dunham, especially at Coalgate.

'Ay: she's a Friend; takes after her dad.' It was Jamesie that said it, not Gran. 'It's Robbie that's the Dunham. Spitten image of Nan, Robbie is.' That was something else folk always said. Sometimes it made Jinnie want to be nasty to Robbie. 'Well, come on, Tot. Ta-ra our Mam.' Jamesie was in a terrible hurry to be away, to his pigeons or wherever it was he and Tot were going.

Still Tot made no move to go: still Gran said nothing. Something was going on. But it couldn't be: she was imagining things again.

'Will her and Nan be going to the Dance on Monday, Mrs. Dunham? Tell Nan our Kevin was asking if she can do the Charleston.' He winked knowingly at Jinnie.

A Dance. The Charleston. Jinnie didn't even see the wink. The Charleston was a Sin: worse than The Pictures. It might even be the Sin against the Holy Ghost, the way they went on about it at Chapel. Now was the time for Jinnie to Speak Out: to dare to be a Daniel. But in a single terrifying flash, she, Jinnie Friend, a good Methodist, wanted to go. To a Dance. To see the Charleston. Coalgate was her only chance. There'd never be another. She crossed her fingers on both hands and waited. Tot's question had been directed straight at Gran. She had to speak to him now.

'I don't know,' she said reluctantly. 'Mebbe. I'll have to see.' Jinnie's spirits soared, almost out of sight. This was nearly a promise. 'Aren't you ready yet, our Jamesie?' Gran went on, unfairly. She was nearly rude. You'd think she wanted to get shot of Tot.

'No hurry yet,' said Tot and somehow he seemed to be defying Gran.

'He needs his sleep, before the night-shift,' said Gran.

46

'Don't stay out long, our Jamesie.'

Jamesie was looking uncomfortable and Gran's voice was sharp.

'She's in a bonnie big hurry to get shot of the pair of uz — or is it only me?' Tot said it as if it was a joke, but there was a challenge in his voice, somehow.

He laughed. Again, nobody else did. Jinnie simply could not understand what was going on. Or *was* it her imagination running away with her once more?

'Ah well,' said Tot and laughed yet again. 'Come on, Jamesie lad. So long, then: and I'll see he gets back for his beauty sleep.' But Gran didn't seem to hear, perhaps because just at that moment she was picking up the washing-up bowl to take it outside to empty it. Tot turned to Jinnie. 'So long, Jin-An,' he said familiarly, winked solemnly and departed. Triumphantly, without a backward look.

Now how did he know Jinnie was Jane Ann? Jamesie must've told him ... and that Jinnie didn't like to be reminded of the name. He had no business winking at her, either: he didn't know her. Winking was Common, anyroad. If Gran had turned against Tot, Jinnie didn't blame her. She was on Gran's side, any day: against anybody.

Six

'Just time for an hour or two's peace at the mat,' said Gran, when she'd emptied the teapot and everything was cleared away into the pantry. 'What're you going to do, Jin? Read?'

Jinnie had already decided Dottie's books could wait; would be better for waiting even. And she was itching to find out about that Dance. She'd wait till the right moment came to ask, of course. Now she asked Gran if she could watch her making the mat and together they set up the frames, which had been hiding where Jinnie couldn't see them, in the corner on the far side of the kitchen range.

'Who's it for, Gran?' But Jinnie guessed that the mat was for Jamesie and Dottie. 'It's lovely,' she said.

And it was, even half-finished. Enough had been filled in of the navy-blue border, mixed grey and blue background, and centrepiece of red flowers and green leaves for you to see it was no ordinary mat. The clippings for this mat had been carefully matched, some of them dyed especially most like.

'For Jamesie,' said Gran, 'and Dottie. There's a house coming empty on Front Street: Nin Bell's going to the Aged Miners' at Medomsley. It's a hewer's house. Jamesie's spoke to the manager for it. And . . .' she hesitated ' . . . and Tot's asking for him at the Eden Lodge. He's a big man there, a delegate you know. So one way and another, Jamesie's got a good chance for it.'

Houses were hard to get. Jinnie crossed her fingers for Jamesie's sake, and wished.

'Him and Dottie's gettin' wed this year, anyroad,' said Gran.

She sighed: which was a bit strange. But getting wed was a queer business altogether. Sometimes Grown-Ups were pleased about it. Sometimes they went on as if it was a disgrace. Gran sounded sad. Maybe she didn't like Jamesie's lass. It was warm and peaceful and Gran usually gave you a straight answer: Jinnie summoned up the courage it needed to ask one Grown-Up about another.

'D'you not like Dottie, Gran?' she said.

48

'Dear me,' said Gran, and her hands paused: 'what's put that idea into your head, Jin? Nay, there's nowt wrong with Dottie. And our Jamesie fair thinks the sun shines for the lass. It's a poor time for young folk to be gettin' wed, that's all.'

Jinnie had never heard Gran sad before. Gran liked a good laugh. When she came to Wallsend, she and Mam laughed so much sometimes that they vexed Dad who couldn't see what there was to laugh at. Not that that stopped them. Gran was the only person Jinnie knew who didn't seem to realize when Dad was vexed.

'And of course there's no knowing what'll happen about the house, once The Strike's on. It's no sort of start, without a house.'

'Would they come here and live with you, then?' said Jinnie, enjoying the Grown-Up conversation.

'Nay,' said Gran. 'We've no room. It'd have to be at Dottie's. And Jamesie's not over-fond of the old man. Nor's Dottie, come to that. Bonnie and cantankerous he is, I must admit.'

Jinnie was surprised. Weren't folk always fond of their father and mother? Then, fleetingly, she thought of Edie Cole who said awful things about *her* mother.

Suddenly Gran laughed. 'Nay, lass,' she said, like herself again: 'no need to look like that. They'll get by. We'll all get by. Everything's mixed with mercy, Jin. You'll find out.' She picked up the progger and a clipping from the navy-blue heap. 'Just you be a teacher, that's all, Jin. No short pays, no strikes, no lay-offs, no lock-outs. I'll see that our Nan gets to be one.' Gran looked positively fierce for a moment. Then she smiled. 'If it kills her. Your Mam's got the same idea for you an' Robbie. But don't let on I told you.' She smiled conspiratorally. Jinnie floated on happiness. It hadn't been a dream that Mam was on her side about The Sec.

Gran started work on the mat again. Jinnie watched her busy hands: old and shiny, ridged with veins, mottled with little patches of brown: ugly hands: hands that had done an awful lot of work for an awful lot of years. Old woman's hands. I wish she wasn't so old, thought Jinnie, unexpectedly sad, then in panic she pushed away what she was thinking.

'Show uz how to do it, Gran,' she said.

Gran's hands had made mat-making look easy, but it wasn't. The hessian backing was tough, the navy serge clippings were hard and strong and the hook Gran gave her was large for Jinnie's hand and difficult to manipulate. Gran was

49

putting in at least a dozen clippings for every one of Jinnie's. But she said Jinnie was doing champion, so Jinnie didn't mention that her fingers were aching.

It was so peaceful. No shop bell rang to interrupt them. Only twice did they stop working and talking. Once when the Co-op horse (a lucky white one it was) and cart came with Gran's weekly grocery order, extravagant with double string and thick, shiny brown paper that was a pleasure to feel. Of course Co-op prices were pretty steep, as Dad said. And a second time, when Jamesie came back, about four, to sleep in the big bed under the stairs until it was time for him to go on night-shift down the pit.

Gran and Jinnie kept their voices low until they heard Jamesie's gentle snore. After that, it didn't matter, Gran said: within reason, of course. Jinnie'd never had such a long talk before with a whole Grown-Up all to herself; Gran, at that.

For the first time, she began to get to know her Coalgate relations, those outside Gran's own house, that is, that she'd hardly thought about before. Like the O'Neils, children of long-since-dead-and-gone Aunt Nan, who'd married an Irishman. They had strange non-family names like Bernadette and Alowishus and were nearly grown-up already. 'You're not likely to see them, though, they don't often come to Grove Street,' said Gran. She seemed to know quite a bit about them, all the same.

Then there was Uncle-Dave-and-Aunt-Polly's lot. Jinnie had seen Uncle Dave and Aunt Polly of course but she couldn't remember the cousins at all. It was mostly about Joe, the eldest, that Gran talked. What a good wife that lass Eva was making him; and her only barely seventeen. Getting wed was the best thing that had ever happened to Joe: never had any real home before. 'You know what your Aunt Polly's like, Jin . . .' Jinnie did: in her mind Aunt Polly was Special, an exciting figure, who went to London and Spoke Out . . . never in her own house and the bairns just left to hing as they grow . . .' Aunt Polly became less Special at that.

Eva's baby was lovely and Joe could hardly bear to let him out of his sight. That was another Grown-Up mystery, babies: sometimes a good thing and sometimes a bad. Jinnie was beginning to be curious about Grown-Ups: she wasn't sure that she really wanted to know more about them, though. She'd be different when she did. So she didn't ask all the questions, although she felt sure Gran wouldn't tell her not to Pester. Gran wouldn't dodge questions either.

Jinnie heard about the neighbours as well. Lizzie-Next-

50

Door's husband, Anty, missed a lot of shifts these days. Gran was beginning to wonder about Anty: he had a bonnie queer look at times, and that cough of his . . . Mrs. Varley, next door on the other side, had had another bairn, her tenth, poor soul. Mrs. Fletcher, Ellen's mother — you know who I mean — had died, and two of the lads no more than bairns. Ellen had left The Tech. to stay at home and look after the family; managing better than her mother an' all, if truth was to be told.

Time passed. The border of the mat grew. Jinnie forgot to think about The Dance anywhere at all in her mind, although at first it'd been there all the time.

Then Lizzie-Next-Door's Harold tapped on the window on his way home from school. S.O.S. Mad on the Scouts was Harold, Gran said. Then you could hear shouting and games out the back, and at the front the day-shift began to clatter past.

'Time for more taties in the oven,' said Gran.

A while after that the stew was put in to warm.

At last Vic got to his feet, shook himself awake, scratched fiercely and ecstatically behind his ear with his back paw, then went to his drinking-bowl near Gran's machine. He emptied it expertly — how did he manage with only his tongue? — then came and put his head on Gran's knee, looking up at her expectantly.

'All right,' said Gran indulgently. 'Just give us a minute to put the frames away. Then you can go and meet him.'

Vic trotted to the door and waited, looking back and forward between the door and Gran. Then his tail began to thump the door, more and more impatiently, and the noises in his throat grew more and more urgent, but in a strangled sort of way, as if he knew he must not waken Jamesie.

'Open the door for that dog, will you, Jin? He'll go daft in a minute and wake Jamesie,' said Gran. 'It's about time, anyroad.'

Before Jinnie could say Jack Robinson, Vic had put himself through the two doors with a quick, buttonhook movement and was racing off up the street, barking wildly, beside himself with happiness.

'But how does he know when Uncle Bob's coming?' asked Jinnie, filled with wonder.

'Nay, he always comes home at the same time every day: you could set the clock by him,' said Gran.

Which, when Jinnie thought it over, was no explanation at all; for once more a Grown-up putting you off. No, not

51

really, and it wasn't fair to call Gran a Grown-Up.

Uncle Bob, now: he was a real Grown-Up. Not that he ever said a lot, but his silence was worse than speech and as heavy as he was. When he did speak his voice was usually loaded with disapproval. Jinnie didn't even know what right he had to be Uncle Bob. He wasn't Mam's brother. His name was Lunn: there were no other Lunns in the Family. Still, relationships were complicated. Once upon a time Jinnie'd thought (*if* she thought) that Nan was Gran's daughter: she called her Mam, after all. But Nan wasn't, she was Gran's grand-daughter. More Grown-Up things waiting to be sorted out one day. In the meantime Jinnie wished Nan was here now: facing Uncle Bob would've been a lot easier.

'Well, here we are, Annie,' said Uncle Bob. That was another thing: it didn't seem right for anybody to call Gran Annie: and only Uncle Bob did.

'So I see,' said Gran, immediately busy.

She could hardly help but see, and hear, what with Uncle Bob's bulk and Vic's sniffling, panting and jumping up and licking. You'd think there was only Uncle Bob in the whole world, the way the dog was going on. Stupid thing.

Uncle Bob pulled his bait tin and his tin water-bottle out of his big pockets and deposited them on the main table, at the door end. Then he hung his sagging jacket and his dusty work-cap on one of the pegs at the bottom of the stairs. Next he came and sat by the fire, in the Windsor chair. Slowly, deliberately, he undid the strings round his moleskins and loosened the laces of his great hob-nailed boots. He grunted comfortably and sat back; undid the button at the neck of his shirt.

'Well, you've comed.' He spoke to Jinnie at last. That was all. Ponderously he heaved himself out of the chair again. He rolled up his thick flannel sleeves. Then he washed his hands, methodically rubbing, inspecting, clasping, unclasping them in the basin of warm water Gran had placed on the washing-table. At last he was satisfied and dried them, just as methodically.

He was so slow that Jinnie was stiff with impatience by the time he sat down at the table, at the head, with his back rumpling the curtain which covered the shelves in the recess between the kitchen range and the window wall. With two fingers and a thumb he felt in his waistcoat pocket. It was hard work: his old-fashioned walrus moustache drooped even lower and his heavy chin pressed further still into the folds of his neck. At last, the fingers and thumb emerged, holding a packet.

52

'It's Friday,' he said and laid the packet on the table.

Gran set an outsize plate in front of Uncle Bob.

'Get straight on with it,' she said. 'Don't let it get cold. You know you don't like stuff cold.' So the pay-packet stayed unopened in front of his plate while slowly and solemnly Uncle Bob ate his dinner.

Uncle Bob's table manners were shocking; worse than just Common. Even eight-year-old Robbie could manage knife and fork better, Dad said: although how Dad knew was a mystery since he never came to Coalgate and Uncle Bob never left it. It was true, though. And he champed when he chewed, and he sucked the gravy through his moustache. It was so Awful, it was fascinating. Twice he belched loudly, and he didn't cover up: didn't even say Pardon.

At last it was over: the second pint-potful of tea had been drained. Uncle Bob belched for the last time, sat back and folded his arms across his stomach. His chair creaked and the curtain elastic dipped a bit lower.

'They've posted the notices,' he said. They were back at The Strike again.

'Ay,' said Gran.

'They'll all come out,' he said.

'Ay,' said Gran.

There was a pause.

'Happen we'll all come out,' said Uncle Bob, sucking his moustache thoughtfully.

'Most like,' said Gran. 'D'you want any more tea?'

'I'll have just one more fill-up,' said Uncle Bob. 'And where's our Nan? Taking her time, isn't she?'

'She said she would be late. It's Friday. Choir practice after school. I thought she'd've been here by now, though. She must've just missed a bus.'

'Bus,' said Uncle Bob disapprovingly. 'If I can walk from the brickworks what's stoppin' our Nan from walkin' from school? It's not as far. You should have more sense than to give her the fare, Annie. Makin' her soft.'

Gran was on her way to the pantry to fill up the kettle. She didn't hear Uncle Bob. But Uncle Bob didn't seem to expect a reply. He got a case from the mantelpiece and took out a pair of glasses. Jinnie knew he couldn't read. What did he want glasses for? Carefully he put them on, one ear at a time: adjusted them, ear, ear, nose. He studied the outside of the packet. Then, unexpectedly, his chin disappeared completely into his shirt neck and Uncle Bob looked over the top of his glasses at Jinnie. She was Staring again, she realized

53

guiltily. Embarrassed, she stood up.

'I'll just have a look down the street to see if Nan's coming,' she said.

'Put your coat on then,' said Uncle Bob severely. 'We don't want you going home with a bad cold. Josh'd have summat to say. Here, Annie, check this, will you?' He was opening the packet.

Jinnie didn't wait to put her coat on but went straight out into the street. Not a sign of Nan. It was too bad of her not to hurry home today. Even if it was choir practice. Suddenly Jinnie wished she hadn't come to Coalgate.

'Hi, you young monkey, come and get this on.' Gran was at the door, holding out Jinnie's coat. She gave Jinnie a sort of squeeze and between them they got her into her coat and Jinnie felt better.

'She can't be much longer,' said Gran. 'There's another bus any time now. Walk down to the terminus if you like. You know where it is. The bus could be in by the time you get there.'

It was. In fact, it had already turned round and the driver and conductor were sitting in the end seat, side by side, backs to the window, heads bobbing sociably, smoke wreathing. A group of uniforms was standing on the pavement outside the bus: neat navy-blue coats; navy, red and yellow scarves hung round necks as carelessly as if they were any old ordinary scarves; round felt hats with red and yellow hatbands; schoolbags, real leather, lying anyhow on the dirty pavement. Jinnie felt a pang of envy: and most of all she coveted the schoolbags, bulging with books about French and Latin and chemistry and goodness knew what else.

Nan was there; and two other girls. And, oh dear, two lads. Nan didn't notice Jinnie; Nan wasn't in a hurry to get home either. She was just standing there, talking and laughing in a way that Jinnie couldn't have described. A new sort of way. There was something new about Nan altogether. She had changed. She was a different shape somehow: and her face wasn't plump any more. There was something else. For a minute Jinnie couldn't think what it was. Then she realized. Her fat plaits had gone. Nan's hair was bobbed. Jinnie's hair would never be bobbed. Dad wouldn't allow it. It wasn't Fair. Nan had everything anybody could want.

Suddenly Jinnie couldn't face her. She turned away as inconspicuously as she could and started back to Gran's.

54

Seven

It had been a silly thing to do, though. Jinnie soon realized that. If she arrived back at Gran's without Nan they'd want to know why, especially that Uncle Bob. Nice and daft Jinnie'd look, saying, yes, Nan'd been on the bus but she, Jinnie, hadn't liked to go up to her. It would most likely come out as well that Nan had been standing talking to lads. Nan mightn't want that. At home, Edie Cole could get anything she liked out of her sister Mollie just by threatening to tell their mother that Mollie Stood and Talked to Cyril Tinkler. Jinnie didn't want to tell on Nan, even though Nan didn't bother about hurrying home to see Jinnie.

She didn't want to tell lies, either. Up There, Somebody would be listening all the time, even at Coalgate, and writing down every single lie you ever told: even the lies you couldn't help, the ones Grown-Ups forced you into with their questions. She needed a minute to think. Her steps had been slowing down. Now they stopped, at a paper shop. 'Collapse of Coal Conference. T.U.C. asks Baldwin.' Her half-seeing gaze moved past the placards to the window.

Then she began to look properly.

Right in front of her was just about the nicest pencil-box she'd ever seen. Four tiers, open like a fan: shiny, pale wood, lid painted with a design of red roses, and so filled with pencils it made your fingers itch. In fact, the middle section of the window was arrayed with all the things that Jinnie coveted most. Steeples of pencils; towers of exercise-books; streets of ink bottles; roadways of rubbers; rivers of pen nibs. But best of all was the pencil-box. Jinnie ached for that pencil-box ... yet it soothed her somehow. She'd have one like it some day: soon, maybe. Perhaps she'd buy it for Robbie's holiday present: Robbie'd let her play with it, she was sure. She would go and meet Nan and not run away this time.

Then it occurred to her that Nan might not be at the bus stop now. Explaining would be just awkward if Nan arrived home without Jinnie. Jinnie abandoned the pencil-box and ran.

Nan was still standing there: still swinging her school hat,

55

still talking. Still in no hurry to get home to Jinnie. This time she did see Jinnie : straight away. She said something to the others. For a moment they all looked at Jinnie, then Nan detached herself.

'Hello, our Jin,' she called. 'I didn't expect to see you here.' Her voice was warm and she sounded pleased to see Jinnie. Jinnie's resolve to be hurt dissolved. Nan was Nan again, her favourite cousin. For the thousandth time Jinnie wished she had a sister and that Nan was it.

Nan let Jinnie carry her schoolbag. Good-humouredly, she answered Jinnie's questions about school and promised to show her all her schoolbooks and teach her some French words. She seemed to have forgotten that Miss Hall, the French teacher, was wonderful but said there was a new maths master who was young and good-looking and who had been seen in Newcastle at The Oxford, dancing with Miss Robson, the gym teacher, whose dress was the shortest ever. Yes, the Charleston. It would take an hour or two of good solid talk to hear all that had been happening at The Tech., Nan's Secondary School. Jinnie savoured the prospect.

When they got home, Gran had company: which didn't surprise Jinnie. At Coalgate pit folk were never off each

56

other's doorsteps, Dad said. When Mam visited Gran, she was Kate Dunham again and old friends popped in to see her. So Jinnie knew a fair number of them, and their children. She recognized Gran's visitors now, although Betsey Smeaton had changed since Jinnie'd seen her last. Her hair wasn't just bobbed, like Nan's: Betsey had an Eton crop. Her lips were redder now, and her cheeks pinker. And she was pretty. Jinnie'd never noticed before that Betsey was so pretty. There was still something about her that Jinnie didn't like, though.

Betsey's mother hadn't changed. She was old and drained, with sunken cheeks: she still hadn't got her false teeth. She still smiled all the time, showing her gums. Her head still bobbed up and down anxiously: like the little china girl on the mantelpiece at home who nodded and trembled every time the shop door opened.

'My,' said the woman, 'hasn't she grown? I'd never've known her.' Grown-Ups had a habit of saying that. 'Not like your Kate, is she?' They always said that as well. 'She's not a Dunham, is she? Takes after her Dad, does she?'

'A bit, mebbe. Mostly takes after herself, Liza,' said Gran. Jinnie was grateful. 'Like your Betsey does,' Gran added.

Betsey was talking to Nan. Jinnie would much rather have been listening to them than to Mrs. Smeaton, but she knew her Manners. Hearing her own name, Betsey glanced sharply at the Grown-Ups, especially her mother, listened for a moment then returned, rather rudely it seemed to Jinnie, to her own affairs. Poor Mrs. Smeaton looked more nervous than ever but she didn't stop.

'Clever, you say? as well as bonnie.' She smiled ingratiatingly at Jinnie. 'Like your Nan. And is she going to College, like Nan?'

'She will, if our Kate has owt to do with it,' said Gran. She picked up some shirts which had been lying on the table, smoothed them, then went and put them on the sewing-machine. 'Well, I'll try and have the collars turned for you by Monday, Liza, then,' she said, in a good-bye tone of voice. 'I'll send one of the lasses up with them Monday tea-time, if I can. I'm not promisin', mind.'

'Thanks, Mrs. Dunham,' said Mrs. Smeaton. 'Ah well . . .' She sighed, as if she didn't know she was doing it. 'And tell your Mam I was askin' after her, Jinnie. Don't suppose I'll get to see her Sunday . . . Liza Daly, you know. Her and me was at school together.'

Jinnie knew this already. Half Coalgate seemed to have

57

been at school with Mam. She didn't know what to say to Liza. She smiled politely and said nothing.

Betsey and Nan had finished their conversation.

'Come on, our Mam,' said Betsey. 'Have you not done yet? I haven't had me tea yet, remember.'

'No more has Nan,' said Gran. She said it politely: but you could tell she didn't think much of Betsey. You could tell, also, that Betsey didn't care what Gran thought. 'And she's had nowt but a few sandwiches since half past seven this morning.' She turned to Liza. 'Kettle's boiling. A fresh pot'll not take long to mash. What about a cup, Liza?' Yet, a minute ago, Gran had seemed to be indicating it was time for Liza to go.

Liza hesitated, as if she was going to stay, glanced placatingly at Betsey, then changed her mind.

'Thank you kindly, Mrs. Dunham, but we'd best be off. The Da'll be wanting his tea an' all. Ta-ra, well.'

'See you soon then, Nan,' said Betsey. As an afterthought: 'You can bring *her* if you like,' she added ungraciously. At the inner door, she turned back. 'Ta-ra, Mrs. Dunham. Ta-ra, Mr. Lunn,' she said, and there was something a bit cheeky in her voice. Not that Uncle Bob replied. He had been asleep in his chair all this while and he didn't open an eye even now.

'And what was all that about, our Nan?' said Gran, as soon as the street door had closed behind the Smeatons.

'Just . . . I said I would go up to Betsey's after tea . . .' Nan sounded a little embarrassed '. . . to practise . . . for the dance on Monday. She's got a new record for the gramophone.'

So Nan was expecting to go to The Dance: Jinnie's heart leapt at the thought. But she was hurt as well. She'd been looking forward to a whole evening with Nan all to herself, for once not shared with Robbie.

'Well,' said Gran, 'and there's me thinking you didn't like Betsey. Nor her you, neither, for a matter of that. What's made the pair of you so kind all of a sudden?' Gran sounded really surprised: a bit vexed as well, maybe. Jinnie didn't mind if Gran was vexed with Nan. Serve her right for wanting to go to Betsey's. 'And who said you could go to the dance on Monday? Tuesday's a school day, in case you've forgot, our Nan.'

'Oh, come on, our Mam,' said Nan; 'don't be a skem. You promised.'

'I never did owt of the sort,' said Gran firmly.

'Well . . . you nearly did.' Nan was almost sulky now.

58

'You'll just have to wait and see,' said Gran.

'Oh, that's what you always say,' said Nan.

Uncle Bob opened his eyes. 'That's no way to talk to your Mam,' he said, his jowls wobbling with disapproval. 'I don't know, our Nan,' he said, 'young folks is never satisfied these days. You get to Consett every Saturday night to the pictures.' Please God let *me* go to The Pictures tomorrow night, Jinnie prayed instantly. Just this once. Then she remembered it was no good praying for something Sinful. She crossed her fingers instead. And her ankles. 'What more d'you want? D'you think we're made of money? You want to be spending as little as possible, these days: not as much.'

It was a long speech for Uncle Bob. Nan looked rebellious, half pulled a face, but was careful it was in Jinnie's direction, not Uncle Bob's. Gran shook a warning head.

Gran took the faithful brown jar out of the oven for the last time. Nan finished off the stew while Gran and Jinnie ate bread and jam and tea-cake. Then the three of them had cups of tea, strong enough for a spoon to stand up in. Nobody said a word. Nan was probably in the sulks. Jinnie was dumb with excitement, hope, and apprehension. If Nan was going to The Pictures tomorrow night, she would be going too. Jinnie was sure of that. The Pictures was a Sin: like telling lies; backing horses; swearing; asking for tabs on tick; wasting money on shop cakes or fish and chips; short skirts; Answering Back; Pestering; drinking beer; Passing Remarks; dancing, especially the Charleston; and quite a lot of other things as well. Here was another chance for Jinnie to Dare to be a Daniel, Dare to do right: and Speak Out. But here she was, again, *not* Speaking Out: against The Pictures this time. Even worse, she was sending thoughts in Gran's direction, and Uncle Bob's, not to stop Nan, and her, going to The Pictures.

Some devil had got into her lately; she was discontented with her lot: she wanted to go to The Sec. even if she didn't win a Scholarship: wanted her hair bobbed. A few hours ago she was wanting to go to a Dance, now it was The Pictures. Just once would be enough. She wouldn't even mind Dad finding out afterwards: and he would. He could be as vexed as he liked: afterwards. Her ankles and her fingers ached from all this crossing, but she wouldn't uncross them yet.

It was Uncle Bob who broke the silence. He cleared his throat, spat into the fire. 'Anyroad,' he said, as if there had been no silence since he last spoke, 'you know what that Betsey's like. What's made her come after you all of a sudden? She's wantin' summat.' He spat into the fire again.

59

'You mark my words. See if she isn't. Don't you go gettin' kind with her.'

'Oh she just wants somebody to practise with for the dance. That's all. Not much harm in that,' said Nan. Her voice sounded as if she had come out of her sulks. Nan never sulked for long: not like you, our Jinnie, Mam said.

'Oh ay, that's what she *says*. I'd've thought you knew Betsey by now. You haven't had sight nor sound of her for weeks: nay, months, more like. Then all of a sudden she comes in here with that poor mother of hers. And all she wants is to practise for the dance.' Uncle Bob's voice was animated: for him. 'And what about your homework, anyway?' he added. 'When's that going to get done, if you're off to the pictures the morrow?'

Nan flushed. Jinnie could see the dull red of her face and neck even in the dim room. 'Oh, you . . .' said Nan. Jinnie held her breath. She felt The Pictures trembling in the balance, never mind The Dance. But Nan thought better of whatever it was she had been going to say. Jinnie's breath came back.

'Well,' said Gran, 'suppose we let Jinnie choose. She's the visitor. Would *she* like to go to Betsey's. What'd'you say, Jin? Would you?'

Jinnie had wanted to stay at home and see Nan's latest schoolbooks and watch her do her homework, and maybe have some of it explained.

'Yes, all right, Gran. I don't mind going to Betsey's,' she said. She had to be on Nan's side against Uncle Bob.

Uncle Bob sniffed. Nan was pleased.

'All right then,' said Gran; 'that's settled. But mind you,' she added, 'if the pair of yuz not back in this house by eight — not a minute after — there'll be no going to Palmer's for fish and chips. The bairn needs her sleep.'

It took Jinnie a second to take it in, Gran said it so casually, as if Fish and Chips were ordinary. Fish and Chips tonight AND watching Nan practise dancing; The Pictures tomorrow; and on Monday, a real Dance, maybe. No wonder Dad hadn't wanted to let Jinnie come to Coalgate.

60

Eight

The Smeatons lived in the big house at the top of Gran's yard. They didn't have a share in the yard, they had a garden all to themselves. It ran across the whole width of the yard and cut off Gran's part of Grove Street from the next section. Although you'd never guess it from Eliza, Mr. Smeaton was a Cut Above his neighbours, an Official at the pit, a deputy or something; he must be, for them to have such a house and garden. They had a gramophone as well and Nan told Jinnie that just lately Mr. Smeaton had got one of these new wireless sets.

Nan had scarcely tapped on the scullery door when Liza appeared, smiling at them and at the same time frowning and nodding a warning in the direction of the kitchen. There at a table sat someone who would be Mr. Smeaton. The contraption in front of him must be the wireless set. His left hand was holding earphones precariously in place on his big bald head. His right hand was clenched into a tense fist except for a big little finger that was touching with enormous care a funny hammer sort of thing on the set. He frowned absently as, led by Mrs. Smeaton, the back of her head still nodding and smiling, Nan and Jinnie progressed cautiously across the room to the door on the other side. Mrs. Smeaton pulled aside the heavy velour door curtain. Brass rings rattled on the freckled bamboo rod. Mrs. Smeaton's nod congealed, but Mr. Smeaton said nothing. Mrs Smeaton's neck relaxed and she opened the door. Instantly music came straight at them. Jazz, wicked Negro stuff. The whole country's going back to the jungle, Dad said. The sound jerked and twitched round Jinnie and Nan and Liza and made for Mr. Smeaton. He bellowed:

'Now look what you've gone and made uz do, Liza, opening that bloody door. Just when I'd nearly got this thing right. If that —' he used a word Jinnie had never heard before but recognized at once as Swearing ' — row gets in here just one time more, I'll . . .'

Mr. Smeaton was too vexed to say just what he would do. But it would be something Awful. Pitmen thought nothing of half-killing their wives, Dad said. Jinnie was nearly frightened

61

and it was a Judgement on her for coming to watch Dancing. Yet at the same time she was busy making notes on the Smeatons' kitchen and despising the untidy table with its dingy oilcloth and dirty plates and mugs, its giant bottles of sauce and vinegar, the wicked jug of gleaming beer. And especially Mr. Smeaton sitting there shirtless, his wrinkled braces sagging over a grubby woollen vest with frayed, unbuttoned neck. He was scarcely decent. Outside, the house might be a Cut Above, inside it wasn't. Mr. Smeaton wasn't, either.

'Get them — bairns to hell out of here,' he went on.

Liza quivered with indecision, fluttering placatory looks and wordless apologies back and forward between Nan and Mr. Smeaton.

'Well there you are. Not before time. I thought you were never coming.'

Betsey appeared at the passage door, jigging and jerking like the music that was still going on. At this rate Betsey's ankles would soon thicken, Jinnie thought with satisfaction. One and a half inches thicker in a fortnight, the preacher had said at Chapel last week; that's what you got for Dancing.

'Well, come on then, you two; into the front room,' she said, and ignored both her mother and father. The music whined to a stop.

'I'm telling you, our Betsey . . .' but Betsey just turned her back and went into the front room, and Nan and Jinnie hurried after her. Betsey slammed the door shut, deliberately. Fond brazzen was Betsey, right enough. No wonder Gran and Uncle Bob didn't like her.

'Pooh: him and his old wireless. And his news. Who cares about Baldwin and whether the pits come out on strike or not? Come on, Nan. Jinnie can wind and you and me'll practise. That's the "Red Red Robin" that's on: and here's the other records. And the needles.'

So that was the idea! Jinnie was to do all the work while Betsey and Nan did the dancing. It would be a pleasure now to Be a Daniel, to Speak Out and tell the pair of them what she thought of their dancing and their jungle music. She opened her mouth. But the words didn't come out right.

'I can't, our Nan. I don't know how to. I might break the record. Or the gramophone.'

In fact, the gramophone was sadly the worse for wear already. The wooden part was scratched. The big tin horn, which was so like the advertisements you could hardly believe it, had not one but two nasty dints in it. Jinnie had an

62

impression that there wasn't a single thing at the Smeatons' that could be spoilt. She'd never seen furniture so chipped and scratched as the sideboard, for example. A real sideboard it was at that, not a bed in disguise like the one back home.

'No, you won't, Jin,' said Nan soothingly. 'You'll soon learn.'

'And there's plenty of books over there,' said Betsey, 'so you can read. In between.'

Jinnie decided that was just what she would do — read, and show them she wasn't interested in them and their old dancing.

As she might have known, Betsey hadn't any real books at all: not even tuppenny school stories or adventures. Just a pile of old papers that lay on the hearth near the grate where ancient ashes still crumbled. But Jinnie had made up her mind to pay Betsey out by not watching her. She started going through the heap. And would you believe it, even Betsey's papers were wicked. *News of the World* or something called *Thomson's Weekly News*, most of them. Horrified, Jinnie read one crime report after another, full of razors and blunt instruments and illegal instruments, whatever they were, and coshes and jemmies and knuckle-dusters. All kinds of things that she couldn't understand exactly. She felt sure, though, that they were far too nasty ever to be in Dad's papers.

The language of the stories was so obscure at times, and she had to stop so frequently to crank the gramophone that it wasn't long before she began to tire of Thomson and his News in spite of its nastiness. Between her and the pages, Betsey's music began to insinuate itself. She didn't want to listen, ought not to listen, but it twitched and tossed and just wouldn't be ignored. Nan and Betsey tossed and twitched with it. Jinnie listened and watched.

Betsey became aware of Jinnie's eyes. She whispered to Nan. Nan giggled and whispered back. Betsey started to sing in time with the record. 'I'm sitting... On top of ... the world ... Just singin' a song ... Just rollin' along.' That's how the song should go, Jinnie'd heard girls at school singing it: only Betsey was mispronouncing the words, and Nan was giggling still more, and Jinnie knew that the pair of them were sharing something and keeping her out of it.

What had come over Nan? She'd never been like this before. Unexpectedly Jinnie started to think about home. Friday night. No school tomorrow. Mam would've let Jinnie play outside tonight till eight. Or she might have let Edie come in to play: at Drawies, or Consequences, or Something, a lot

63

better than Dancing. As it was, Edie could be with Teenie, making up their quarrel. She might even be plotting with her, to fight with Jinnie when she came home. Edie was a bit like that. It served Jinnie right for not Speaking Out against Dancing. That wasn't much consolation, though.

Jinnie's eyes blurred. Cry-baby, cry-baby. Stick-your-finger-in-your-eye-baby. Her face and throat ached with the effort but she mustn't let the tears roll down. She wasn't going to give that Betsey something else to snigger over.

The record came to an end. She let it go on hissing softly round and round and made no move.

'Hi, switch it off,' said Betsey. Jinnie ignored her.

'What time is it, our Nan?' she said. She was relieved to find that her voice sounded all right. 'You know what Gran said. About eight o'clock.'

'Oh heck,' said Nan. 'I was forgetting. Go and see the time, Betsey, will you?'

Grudgingly Betsey went to the kitchen.

'Pooh,' she said, when she returned: 'it's early, only half past seven. Come on, Jinnie. We'll have " 'Bye, 'bye, Blackbird" now.'

But Nan was a kind-hearted girl and she was feeling a little bit guilty. Jinnie was a cousin and a visitor even if she did seem to have turned into a bit of a spoilsport. Betsey wasn't a real friend: she had a gramophone, that was all.

'No, we'd best be off,' Nan said; 'unless Jin'd like to have a turn at the dancing. I'll wind the gramophone and you can show Jin, Betsey.'

'What'd'you take me for?' said Betsey. 'She's just a kid. Don't be so mean. Oh, come on. Just one more record then.'

But Nan had started to straighten the pile of papers that Jinnie had scattered.

'Oh, don't waste time on that. Nobody'll care if you don't tidy them. Come on, Nan.'

Nan took no notice.

'There. That's it. Ready, Jin?' she said. 'See you at the dance then, Betsey; on Monday.'

'What's wrong with the morrow?' said Betsey. 'It's Saturday, isn't it? You'll be goin' to Consett, won't you? To the pictures?'

'Well, yes.' Nan was put out as well as surprised.

'That's all right then,' said Betsey. 'I'll come with you. Call for uz about half past five then. I'll be lookin' out for you.'

They left Betsey's by the front door and so avoided Mr. Smeaton in the kitchen. Nan was silent. Her pleasuring didn't

64

seem to have done her much good. But that was the way with Sin. Nan'd enjoyed the dancing: she couldn't expect to be happy when the dancing stopped. Jinnie herself knew she would go to The Pictures tomorrow night. And enjoy it, but she also knew she'd Pay For It afterwards, one way or another. That was only Fair. She was silent too.

'A minute to eight,' said Gran. That Betsey had told them a lie about the time; just like her. 'That's good lasses.' Gran looked up from the long black stocking she was knitting. She smiled over the top of the Woolworth's glasses that she wore for knitting and sewing and reading. 'Palmer's'll be just nicely opened by the time you get the papers sorted.'

Nan dragged a stack of papers from the shelf behind the curtain. Mostly *The Sporting Man*. Pitmen wasted half their money on horses, Dad said. Jinnie hadn't realized before that Jamesie was a Pitman like that. She would never tell Dad, though. She helped Nan to separate crumpled or grubby papers from the good clean ones. *The Sporting Man* looked very boring.

The next stack from the shelf was made up of *Northern Echoes*. Dad didn't take the *Northern Echo*; it looked strange, quite different from the *North Mail* or *The Daily Mail*. She turned some pages. The puzzle corner was good. How many monkeys in the tree? Twelve easy ones. She twisted the page sideways: thirteen. Then again: fourteen, fifteen.

'Hi, come on, our Jin. You're supposed to be sorting them, not reading them.' Nan's voice made Jinnie jump. And *she* hadn't grumbled about Nan's dancing.

Uncle Bob joined in, disapproving: 'You don't want to be reading in this light. You'll be ruining your eyesight.' People were always telling Jinnie she'd ruin her eyesight. 'You'll be needing glasses next,' he said, as if that were a threat.

As a matter of fact, Jinnie rather fancied glasses. Maybe they'd make her look clever: like a Secondary School girl. Like Nan. Like Nan . . . She looked at Nan. No wonder Nan looked different today: she wasn't wearing her glasses. Fancy her not noticing. And fancy Nan not saying anything. She hadn't said a word about her bobbed hair either. It was rude to Pass Remarks but Jinnie just had to, now.

'Nan,' she said, 'where's your glasses? Have you broken them?'

'Oh no,' Gran said. Nan just didn't need them any more. The doctor said her eyes were all right now. Jinnie knew Nan had worn glasses to correct a slight squint. Waste of money,

65

Dad said: sheer vanity. It'd've been different if Nan couldn't see. Gran hadn't agreed when Dad said it.

'How do you like uz without them, Jinnie?' said Nan, pretending she was hardly interested, but Jinnie knew she was. 'I look better . . .' Jinnie didn't answer immediately. 'Don't you think?' asked Nan a little less nonchantly.

Jinnie didn't think anyone looked better without glasses; any glasses: and Nan's hadn't been ordinary. Tortoiseshell, they'd been.

'Oh yes,' she said, 'you look lovely,' and then hoped she hadn't overdone things.

'Handsome is as handsome does,' said Uncle Bob with a heavy frown.

'Oh, you,' said Nan who obviously wasn't frightened of Uncle Bob at all.

Jinnie could tell that Nan was pleased. Anyway, she realized with surprise, Nan *was* lovely. There was no end to Nan's good luck. Lucky Nan. It wasn't Fair.

Nine

It was a treat being out late. Dad didn't hold with bairns running the streets at night so Jinnie and Robbie were always shouted in long before anybody else. It was one of the *dis*advantages of being a Cut Above the rest of The Street.

It was almost dark now. Coalgate was changing. The houses in Grove Street and Front Street and Watling Street that looked so alike during the day were retreating, windows coloured now and all different: cheerful pink, ghostly green, lace shadowed cream, sandy, tide-marked brown.

From the gloom outside McElwain's you could see right inside, beyond the ordinary counter, pop bottles and sweet jars, to the Saloon itself. Light, neat as a ruler, shone on shirts and heads and hands and sticks and hard green rectangles invisibly moored in space like stiff magic carpets, while everywhere else was awash with darkness full of dim shapes.

The pubs — there was one at every street corner in Coalgate, Dad said — were awake now. Pubs fascinated Jinnie. They were strongholds of the Devil, and of Strong Drink. Jinnie knew about Strong Drink, of course, and what it did to your character and your inside. But nobody at school, Sunday School, Chapel or Band of Hope had ever explained why folk went into pubs in the first place. By day, they were gloomy places, asleep behind bolted doors, bottle-green or gingery-brown tiled walls, and dead windows that you couldn't see through. At night, they weren't much better, not at Chapel time which was when Jinnie passed them: no longer silent, that was all. As for Strong Drink itself, the very idea of drinking the smell that seeped out of pubs would make you sick. Altogether, Jinnie didn't think she'd ever have much trouble Being a Daniel about Strong Drink. All the same, pubs were interesting. When she passed one she always crossed her fingers against the Devil and hoped the door would open for her to have a look inside.

She was in luck now. As she and Nan reached The Hat and Feathers, its big double doors swung open. Same old dull brown paint, globes of gaslight, high counter and men standing at it. Through the opening-closing arc of the doors, Jinnie

67

thought one of the men might be Uncle Dave. She couldn't be sure, though: all the men seemed to be wearing navy-blue suits and white mufflers and were little and pale and grey like Uncle Dave.

But there could be no doubt about the couple outside The Colliery Engine farther down Watling Street. The woman was Aunt Polly all right. She saw them, halted, and called out to them in a loud pleased-to-see-you voice that had a laugh in it as well, then went inside. Jinnie was shocked. A man who went into pubs was bad enough, but a woman . . . Aunt Polly hadn't minded being seen by The Family either. And it hadn't been Uncle Dave she was with. There was no

mistaking the giant Tot although Jinnie'd seen him today for the first time. That was another thing: women went to places only with husbands or other women, didn't they? Aunt Polly wasn't like most women, that was a certainty.

'That was Aunt Polly, wasn't it?' said Jinnie, preparing for a chat about Aunt Polly.

'Yes,' said Nan.

'That wasn't Uncle Davie she was with, was it? Wasn't it . . .'

68

'How would I know who it was?' said Nan, interrupting.

Jinnie was surprised that Nan hadn't recognized Tot, Jamesie's friend. But something in Nan's voice stopped Jinnie from telling her who Aunt Polly had been with.

All the way down Watling Street the bundle of newspapers Jinnie was carrying grew heavier and heavier but the smell of fish and chips was coming closer and closer. At last, there it was, set back from the houses on a piece of waste ground, Palmer's fish and chip shop, no ordinary establishment, but an old railway coach, on stilts instead of wheels. Jinnie sighed with pleasure, there was nothing like it in Wallsend. Trust Gran-at-Coalgate to have the best fish and chip shop ever.

Jinnie followed Nan up the steep wooden steps and through the open door where light and steam and smell came together in a thick curtain stirred and frayed by the night breeze. Today, Friday, was Pay Day and there was a sizeable cluster of customers at the counter at the far end of the coach, mostly children, unnaturally quiet, subdued by Mr. Palmer's reputation, no doubt. Palmer's fish and chips were the best in Coalgate, Nan said. They had to be, she said. Mr. Palmer was disagreeable. He never spoke a pleasant word to anybody: and Mrs. Palmer wasn't much better. At the moment Mr. Palmer's back was turned on the customers. Mrs. Palmer wasn't in sight but from behind a green curtain on the right of the range came an interesting succession of clumpings, swooshings and rattlings. In front of the curtain, at the counter, a girl was busy folding and slicing newspapers beside a big pair of black scales. This would be Millie Palmer, who was in Nan's class at The Tech. She had been one of the girls at the bus stop with Nan, so Nan had told Jinnie. Jinnie thought that fish and chips must be just about the nicest kind of shop to have but Nan said nobody ever wanted to sit next to Millie at school because she always smelt of old fish and chips: which was something Jinnie had never thought of.

Nan and Jinnie made their way towards the counter past half a dozen white-lino-topped tables — Palmer's was a real sit-down café as well as a shop — Millie looked up, saw them and smiled. Jinnie would never have recognized her out of her Tech. uniform. She weighed Nan's bundle of papers first. Brow furrowed, lips squeezed, she juggled with big black weights and little brass ones, consulted a piece of cardboard nailed to the counter then gave Nan threepence. Three whole pennies for a bundle of old newspapers. But Gran's papers brought top prices, Nan had said. The Palmers knew they came from a clean house and wouldn't need sorting.

69

Now it was Jinnie's turn. Tuppence ha'penny. Jinnie was delighted. Not because of the money: it wasn't hers anyway, it would go to Gran for next time's fish and chips, which would be after Jinnie's holiday was over, but it meant she could carry nearly as heavy a bundle as Nan, who was three and a half years older and always did things better.

Suddenly Mr. Palmer who, through the mirror above the range, had been silently despising his customers all the while, went into action. First he attacked the fires under the big pans. He clattered, raked, shovelled, slammed. Then, red-faced, he straightened up and went for the pans themselves. The lid of the main pan concertina-ed, splashed, disappeared under the mirror. Mr. Palmer seized a giant wire scoop, swirled it round in the fat, brought it out again, dripping and loaded with chips. Scornfully he pinched one, two, three chips, shook the scoop, tossed the chips into the warming compartment.

'Maggie!' he shouted and scooped out another load of chips.

The noises behind the curtain ceased. Mrs. Palmer pushed through, her shoulders dragged down by two enamel pails loaded with raw chips. She deposited the pails near Mr. Palmer.

Now Nan spoke up. 'Mine's five times, Mr. Palmer,' she said, for all the world as if Mr. Palmer was an ordinary shopkeeper.

'Five more fish, Maggie,' said Mr. Palmer contemptuously.

The customers were impressed, if Mr. Palmer wasn't, and two small boys turned round to look at Nan with respect and envy.

Mrs. Palmer disappeared again. Mr. Palmer picked up a bucket. In the big pan, the empty fat was chuckling and rippling idly. But not for long. An arc of chips swung across the mirror, slithered into the fat. It leapt and spat and sent a cloud of blue steam hissing at Mr. Palmer. He ignored it. The steam rose to the ceiling, then, defeated again, washed across the ceiling towards the door. The fat settled back into a resigned murmur.

Mrs. Palmer returned with a little criss-cross pile of fish which she handed to Mr. Palmer, and a trough of swaying white liquid, which she hooked to the side of the second, smaller pan. Mr. Palmer took a fish by the tail, slopped it in the white liquid then dropped it into the hot fat. It exploded to twice its size in a great fleece of batter, then bobbed exuberantly up and down, well aware of its own importance. When all five fish were safely in, Mr. Palmer resumed his stare

70

into the mirror. Straight at Jinnie. Guiltily Jinnie transferred her gaze to Millie, still stolidly slicing newspapers.

Mrs. Palmer cupped white paper and newspaper in her left hand. 'All right,' she said. It sounded just like Ready, Steady, Go at the Sunday School Races. Selecting a boy with her eye, 'What's yours?' she said.

There was no debate, no argument about turns. Mr. Palmer's back didn't encourage it nor did Mrs. Palmer's voice. Away she went, snatching paper, shovelling chips.

'Maggie,' said Mr. Palmer suddenly to the mirror. 'Tables.'

Mrs. Palmer put down her shovel. She swooped under the counter, produced a box of knives and forks, pushed it along to Millie. The little crowd of customers parted as obediently as the Red Sea to let Millie creep out under the counter flap. Mrs. Palmer put a match to the gas-ring at the farthest end of the counter. With a plop, blue flame ringed the big brown kettle that had been sitting there, waiting for this moment. From under the counter Mrs. Palmer brought, in rapid succession, a tray perilously covered with upside-down mugs: a white pudding basin full of sugar, a large white jug and an outsize brown teapot. She checked them sternly, with silently moving lips, then returned to her scooping. Some day, when she was a teacher and had a lot of money, thought Jinnie, *she* would have fish and chips sitting down in Palmer's, and quite forgot to remember that shop fish and chips were a Wicked Waste.

Mr. Palmer was lifting out the fish at last. Mrs. Palmer shovelled chips on to five tiny squares of white paper, added five fish and rolled the whole lot in several sheets of newspaper. Nan paid and Jinnie claimed the parcel. 'See you Monday,' said Nan to Millie, now back with her paper-cutting, and 'Good-night,' to Mrs. Palmer, who actually replied with a nod.

At the door they had to step aside to let in a new cluster of customers. Somebody hailed Nan boisterously. 'Hello, Will,' said Nan. 'It's Will,' she said to Jinnie as if that explained him. And it did, really: Aunt Polly had a son called Will. Will's voice was loud and his manner a bit queer. He'd just got off the Consett bus: been to the pictures. 'The Volga Boatman.' 'A bit of all right,' he said and winked as if he knew something Special. He'd come to have his supper before going home. His face changed.

'She'll've left uz nowt but a bite of bread and dry cheese,' he said. 'Pay Day an' all. I wonder where's she's off to the night, spendin' wor good money and makin' fools of the lot of

71

uz.' Aunt Polly's family must be still vexed about her trip to London, although that was a week ago now. Mam had said folks wouldn't like it. 'Have you seen owt of the owld bitch, Nan?' What a way to go on: swearing, and about his own mother! Smoking, as well, and Jinnie thought that might be beer that she could smell through the smoke.

'No, we haven't,' said Nan.

Jinnie opened her mouth to remind Nan that they *had* seen Aunt Polly, but Nan gave her a sharp little push with her knee.

'Come on, Jin: we don't want the stuff to get cold. Ta-ra, Will. See you at the dance. Or before, maybe,' said Nan and didn't stop for an answer.

Jinnie could hardly wait until they were down the steps. 'Was that Will Dunham?'

'It was.'

'Well then, you told a lie, our Nan. We did see Aunt Polly. Or did you not remember?'

'Of course I did,' said Nan. Her voice was queer, too, although in a different way from Will's. 'But Will was mad enough already. And he'd had a pint or two, I would think . . .' as if a pint or two didn't shock her at all. 'Didn't you see who Aunt Polly was with?' Jinnie nodded wisely. Of course she had: it was Nan who'd said she hadn't. 'Well . . . there you are . . .' Nan hesitated, then said with a rush, 'Will's wild, Mam says . . . he's just finding out about Aunt Polly . . . If you know what I mean, Jin?' Jinnie didn't. But she wasn't going to say so. Nan was always three years ahead of her. She knew so much more and could do everything so much better . . . Jinnie didn't want Nan to think she was a Baby and not worth bothering about. Besides, Nan was offering to share something Special: Jinnie wasn't going to spoil the moment with ignorance and questions. She grunted in an understanding way. 'Well, now you know then. And our Mam says Aunt Polly's in the Family and so we'll just have to put up with her; and not go putting our shovel in, and keep our big mouths shut.' My goodness, they *were* upset about Aunt Polly going to that meeting in London, against the miners. But . . . keeping their mouths shut? Aunt Polly's speech had been in the paper. Of course, there was Aunt Polly going into a pub, with Tot. In some strange way he might be part of the trouble. All the same, Jinnie didn't understand. There was no doubt though, that Aunt Polly was Special: what kind of Special Jinnie wasn't sure. Bad Special, Nan's voice seemed to be suggesting.

72

Jinnie waited for more clues to Aunt Polly, feeling the fish and chips parcel become hot in her hand and in the lamplight noticing the newspaper wrapping begin to turn black and nearly transparent, from the fat.

'Anyroad,' said Nan, 'she's good-hearted. There's something about her you can't help liking, Mam says . . . well, most of the time.'

Which was not what Jinnie had expected and only added to the mystery of Aunt Polly.

That night, after they'd gone to bed, Jinnie had Nan all to herself at last and a chance for a real talk. Talk they did, for a long time. Nan told Jinnie all about The Tech. and Jinnie could never hear too much about that. She told Nan all her worries about The Scholarship. Nan was positive Jinnie would win one: Gran thought so too, because Jinnie was clever. And even if she didn't, she would go to The Sec. Gran had discussed it with Mam and so Gran *knew*. Mam had never said anything to Jinnie because Dad wouldn't like her to. So Jinnie hadn't to let on at home about what Nan was telling her. No, Dad hadn't actually promised, but Gran was confident he would let her go. Jinnie wasn't so sure. Well, Nan said, Aunt Kate's draperies were a good part of the shop's trade now, weren't they? Jinnie supposed they were: she hadn't thought about it before. Anyroad, what had Mam's draperies to do with it? Well, said Nan, fair's fair: if Aunt Kate earned money, she was entitled to a say in spending it, wasn't she? Jinnie admitted Dad was fair-minded, she'd heard him say so. She was persuaded. There was something very soothing about Nan. She was a bit like Gran for that. Gratefully Jinnie forgot her own affairs and listened to Nan.

Nan told Jinnie about her Coalgate friends, some of them scarcely more than names to Jinnie and all of them less interesting than Nan's Tech. friends, but she listened. And she did know Betsey now. Not that Betsey was a friend. Nan suspected that the reason why Betsey had turned so kind all of a sudden was that she was interested in Will. Maybe Betsey had a pash on Will, Nan said. On *Will*? thought Jinnie, half asleep now. Or maybe she was going after him because Nora . . . remember Nora? . . . liked him an awful lot. At this point, Uncle Bob thumped up at them. A few minutes later he came to the bottom of the stairs and said in a penetrating whisper that Jamesie was still abed and they'd better be quiet. Anyroad, *he* was going to bed now and needed his rest if they didn't. 'Our Nan,' he added as an afterthought, politely putting all the blame on Nan. They went on talking

73

just the same but in whispers now, and under the bedclothes.

Nan's voice started swaying from side to side like seaweed in a rock pool.

'Did you really mean it, Jin? About liking my hair bobbed? And what you said, about me not wearing glasses any more?' Nan sounded a very long way off now.

'Yes,' said Jinnie. She heard quiet voices downstairs, and the oven door opening and shutting and a renewed smell of fish and chips came up the stairs: Jamesie up and having his supper. 'Yes,' she said, making an effort to please Nan, 'I really do. You look grand.' Nan grunted contentedly.

Suddenly Jinnie wondered what *she* looked like. What if she was homely? Beauty's only skin deep, Dad said. Ay, and ugliness goes to the bone, Mam said. Still, it didn't matter. You didn't have to be beautiful to be a teacher. She would like to be, though.

What had got into Nan? Worrying about how she looked: and making Jinnie worry about herself as well. And talking to lads. Obscurely, Jinnie felt that all kinds of things were changing for Nan. And would for her, too, one day. She felt threatened. She wanted to stay as she was now: for ever. She felt guilty too. Some Daniel she'd turned out to be. She tried to make a bargain with Them Up There. She wouldn't go to The Pictures tomorrow: or ever have fish and chips again, if she could go to The Sec.

If only she was back at home, safe from all temptations, with Robbie's soft breathing coming comfortably through the dark, and Mam and Dad in the next room. Could it really be only this morning she'd left them?

She hadn't said her prayers! She prepared to get out into the cold: prayers-in-bed didn't count. She heard the front door move: then heavy boots outside. Downstairs the gas light plopped out. It was too late for prayers, Gran was coming upstairs. She loved Gran, but it was Mam she wanted now. A tear squeezed from under her closed eyelids: another: and another. She was glad Nan was asleep now. Jinnie changed her own breathing and pretended she was asleep, too.

74

Ten

Gran let them wear their Sunday clothes to go to The Pictures. Jinnie liked hers, especially the hat which made her look like a Secondary School girl, she thought. But Nan grumbled. Her coat was old-fashioned, she said. The waist was far too high. And you could see where the hem had been let down. Her hat sat too high on her head: it was a kid's fashion, she said.

'A man on a gallopin' horse'll never notice it: nor you neither,' said Gran. 'And if you don't want to go, you can stop at home.' Shut up, Nan: please shut up, said Jinnie inside her head. 'Of course, there's your school things: you could put them on just this once, if you like.'

Nan should be happy now. Uniforms were expensive and strictly for school and you changed out of them the minute you got home. But Nan said, 'School clothes on a Saturday night? For the pictures? Betsey got a new coat and hat for Easter. I bet she'll have them on tonight. Why can't I have a new coat? Or a new summer hat, anyroad?' Nan's hat had been new last year, Jinnie knew. She couldn't really expect another one yet. But then, Gran spoilt Nan, Dad said. So you never knew. 'Of course,' Nan went on, 'Betsey's working.' She said this as if it was a threat: yet Jinnie had always thought that Nan wanted to stay at school and then go to College, as much as she herself did.

'You don't think it was Betsey bought that coat and hat, do you, our Nan? How much d'you think she earns up at the Vicarage for goodness' sake? Not a penny more than three and six a week, I'll be bound. If that. Liza Daly's up to the ears in debt for that lass,' Gran said. 'Everything bought on tickets and poor Liza frightened to death her man'll find out. Can't even get herself a pair of false teeth, can't poor Liza. And all because she can't say no to that nagging, selfish little . . .' Jinnie didn't like Betsey but she hadn't realized that Gran disliked her so much as well. 'Clothes daft. Lad daft, an' all. She'd better watch herself, that lass, else she'll end up in Trouble Street. What's more, you know I don't like you havin' owt to do with her, our Nan, neither.'

75

'Ay, just you mind what your Mam says another time: you don't want to be like Betsey Smeaton.' Jinnie had almost forgotten Uncle Bob was there in his chair by the fire. His voice quite startled her. Vic, who was stretched out on the hearth-mat, under Uncle Bob's foot, opened an eye, and stirred his tail. 'New hat,' said Uncle Bob. 'Where'd you think the money'd come from? You'll think yourself lucky to get a bite to eat afore long.'

'Oh give over, Bob,' said Gran. 'It's only natural for the lass to want nice things. She'll have to wait for them, that's all. Your turn'll come, lass, never fear.'

When she's a teacher, thought Jinnie.

When Nan and Jinnie were ready, and sitting waiting for Ellen Fletcher to call for them, Gran took her purse out of the machine drawer. She put four pennies in a neat pile on the window table.

'That's for our Nan, for the pictures,' she said. She laid down a penny, and a threepenny bit on top of it. 'That's for our Jin,' then she added a penny to Nan's money and a half-penny to Jinnie's. 'That's to come home on the bus.'

This was a bit awkward. You mustn't let your Gran pay for anything, Mam had said. The Consett Iron strike was just over, she'd said, and the National Strike was looming up, and at the best of times Gran hadn't money to spare. But how did you argue with Gran? Everybody said Jinnie was too fond of Arguing and Answering Back.

'Oh no, Gran,' she said now. 'Mam said not to. I've got my own money. She gave me half a crown for the holiday. I needn't take any of it back, I can spend it all. And I had sixpence saved up as well. Look.' She held out her handbag.

'Oh that Mam of yours. I'll have to have a word with her when she comes the morrow,' said Gran severely. 'Here, give uz your bag.'

Jinnie handed over the little bag and watched Gran put the money into it.

'Why don't you come as well, Gran?' she said. 'Why don't you? You'll be here all by yourself,' for Jamesie had already departed to Dottie's for the evening and she knew Uncle Bob was going out later.

'Nay, lass,' said Gran. 'What'd an old wife like me be doing with the pictures? Nay —' her brown eyes smiled and she gave Jinnie's hand a little squeeze — 'I'll be glad to be shot of the lot of yuz. I'll have an hour or two's peace for a change.'

Vic woke up again, completely this time. He growled.

76

Uncle Bob's foot pressed him more firmly, then Uncle Bob bent down and took a grip on the dog's collar.

'That'll be Ellen,' said Gran. 'Go and let her in, Nan.' For the door had not opened after the polite knock. 'Come away in, lass. Sit down a minute, Ellen hinnie. And how's things? Still managin' all right, a'll awand, eh?' Gran's voice was full of liking for Ellen. 'And how's Clark's cough, Ellen?'

Ellen was small and dark-haired and rosy. She smiled at Gran and her teeth were white and pretty.

'Grand, Mrs. Dunham. Everything's champion. Clark's cough's on the mend. I'm still keepin' him in, though. Richie's stayin' in the night and Madge's doin' the tea dishes and seein' the lads to bed, so I've nothin' to worry about.'

Richie was the oldest of the Fletchers. He'd been going down the pit since he was fourteen and he was grown up now. He did his best to help Ellen. So did Richie's girl, Madge. They'd even put off getting wed for a few months. Quite different from that nasty, selfish, spoilt Alan who'd been his mother's favourite. She'd fed the others on kipper dip to send Alan to College, Gran had said. He had repaid her by getting married and leaving home the minute he was teaching. Never came near them now. Gran had told Jinnie all about the Fletchers yesterday.

'Well, just enjoy yourself, Ellen lass,' said Gran. 'And

77

remember, if ever you're stuck, and want a hand . . .'

'I know, Mrs. Dunham. Thanks.'

'Hey, hurry up, you two,' said Gran. 'Can't you see the lass's waitin'? And mind, straight home after the pictures. Quarter to nine bus.'

'Oh, man mother,' said Nan. 'We were going to go round to market, just this once. It's special this week. It's got that Powsey. Don't say you've forgot. There was a bit about him in the *Echo* and you said I could go and watch him.'

'I never said nowt of the sort,' said Gran. She wouldn't have done, either. Gran never made promises, Mam said. That way you never disappointed anybody, Gran said.

'Oh go on, Mrs. Dunham. Let them,' said Ellen. 'I wouldn't mind a walk round the market myself. And a look at Powsey. We wouldn't be all that late home. His first jump's at half past eight, the paper said.' Nan hadn't mentioned any Powsey to Jinnie, although he was obviously Special. But then, Nan was used to Special Things. 'You can't hardly believe he'll do it, can you? Jumpin' into a blazin' tank. From a hundred feet up a height. And settin' hisself a-fire first.'

Jinnie's heart leapt at the thought of such a sight. Powsey must be as good as Benaiah, who killed a lion . . . in a pit . . . on a snowy day. Or a kind of Apollyon, only not sinful, of course. What a thing to tell Edie about, and Robbie. She wished hard in Gran's direction.

'That's right, Annie. It'll be summat worth rememberin'. I was thinkin' of stoppin' and havin' a look at his half past ten jump meself,' said Uncle Bob, rather surprising Jinnie, who never hoped for much from Uncle Bob.

'Well . . . I don't know . . .' Gran hesitated. 'How're you goin' to get your bath, if you're home late, our Nan? Once you're at the market you'll go forgettin' the time. No. I'm not havin' you comin' back on the pub bus, not on a Saturday night.'

That settled it. But Jinnie didn't mind, not really. She must learn not to expect too much, Mam said. The Pictures was Special enough. Anyway, she didn't want to be on a bus with drunks. A drunken man was just a wild animal, Dad said.

Nan hadn't given up yet. 'Betsey's got a watch,' she said. 'She'll have it on, most likely. We'll get the time from her.'

'I know that Betsey: she'll say owt that suits her . . .' said Gran.

'Please,' said Nan. 'Just this once.'

All in a rush, Gran gave in. 'Oh, all right. If you promise to

78

leave Consett not later than the quarter past nine bus. I'll have the bath out waitin', with just the hot to put in.'

Nan, Ellen and Jinnie walked a few doors farther up the street to Whitehead's shop, to call for Nora, Nan's other Coalgate friend. It wasn't a real shop with a proper shop window, like Jinnie's, just a one-up-one-down house exactly like Gran's, except that when you went in from the street, instead of a whole door into the downstairs room, there was only the bottom half, and it had a broad slab of wood across for a counter.

The three girls could only just squeeze into the little space at the bottom of the stairs because two customers were there already: Joe and Harold from Lizzie-Next-Door-to-Gran's. Nora, hat and coat on, was waiting patiently for Joe and Harold to make their once-a-week choice. Over their heads and past Nora, Jinnie could see Mrs. Whitehead, plump, fair, placid, on her knees beside a little Whitehead in a big zinc bath in front of a great fire and an equally large fireguard which was draped with nightgowns. Firmly and methodically she was soaping the little Whitehead. Lizzie, the oldest Whitehead, was standing in front of a looking-glass hanging above the chest of drawers in the window corner. She was combing her hair and dividing it into sections. Two in-between Whiteheads, barricaded in by a teetering wall of biscuit tins, sat over a late tea, or early supper, at the table under the window. Their jaws moved slowly and thoughtfully as if they didn't want to finish too quickly. They didn't seem worried by their audience or the tins.

There were biscuit tins everywhere, full ones on the table and on one side of the chest of drawers: a wonderful selection ranging from Tea Tyme Dayntees down through fig rolls, coconut puffs, custard creams, Nice, to plain Maries and cream crackers. There were tins all over the floor too: empty ones with their lids inside them. Mrs. Whitehead must have a good biscuit trade. A good sweet trade as well, for where you didn't see biscuit tins, you saw boxes of soda lunches, gob-stoppers, licorice all-sorts, sweet cigarettes, wine gums, mint imperials, sweet tobacco, licorice straps; and glass jars of black bullets, glacier mints, paradise fruits, pear drops. In the corner on the far side of the kitchen range, towards the back door, stacks of wooden crates of pop reached higher than the mantelpiece. Whitehead's wasn't a proper shop, but it was nice: a luxury shop, really.

Over a soapy spike of the little Whitehead's hair, Mrs. Whitehead, calm and unsmilingly pleasant, greeted them.

79

Lizzie saw them in the looking-glass. She turned round and grinned at them through her hair. She took a pair of tongs out of the fire, spat on them. They sizzled. Lizzie swung them round, blew on them, spat again. No sizzle this time. She twisted a strand of hair round the tongs, held it in place, studied it in the looking-glass.

In front of the pop crates, Mr. Whitehead, large and still in his big wooden chair, stared morosely into the fire, unmoved by the female busyness around him. There was Something Wrong with Mr. Whitehead from The War. Like Mattie. Coalgate seemed to have more than its share of casualties of either The Pit or The War.

They were a silent family, the Whiteheads, all except Lizzie, who talked and laughed enough to make up for all the rest, Gran said.

'Which one's taking you out tonight, Lizzie?' asked Nan, for Lizzie's laughter was irresistible and she had a whole string of lads after her.

'Wouldn't you like to know?' said Lizzie into the mirror, pulling the tongs slowly out and leaving a fat sausage curl. She laughed and the little bulges above her corset dimpled and quivered.

Lizzie-Next-Door's lads made their choice. Nora counted out aniseed balls. Joe and Harold gave up their ha'pennies and pushed their way out of the shop.

'Well, if there's nothin' else, our Mam,' said Nora.

'That's right: you get off,' said Mrs. Whitehead.

'I'll serve anybody else that comes in before the bairns is all bathed,' said Lizzie. 'Have a nice time, our Nora.'

Nora opened the counter door gently, with one hand keeping the scales safely in place.

'Mind you close the front door properly,' said Mrs. Whitehead. 'I don't want the bairns catchin' cold.'

The heat in the room, even at the foot of the stairs, was so solid that the most determined draught would bounce straight off it, but Nora shut the door carefully, and gave it a gentle bump with her knee to test that the sneck was securely in place. Nora was a quiet, gentle girl altogether.

The Smeatons lived five houses farther still up the street. Betsey opened the door and came out before anyone had time to knock.

Jinnie stared. Done up like a dinner, Betsey was: new coat the height of fashion, well above her knees; long shiny stockings, real art silk, flesh coloured — they couldn't have cost a penny less than one and elevenpence ha'penny; black

80

patent court shoes. She was wearing one of the latest helmet hats, with a pompom of feathers on one side. It was pulled right down on her forehead, almost to her eyes and not a hair was showing except two kiss-curls, stuck flat, one on each cheek. Her lips were very red: and her cheeks were pink. There wasn't a trace of shine on her nose. She smelt good, too. No wonder Nan had sounded envious of Betsey. Betsey made her and the others look shabby and old-fashioned.

Jinnie gazed in admiration and the beginning of envy. Then she came to her senses. Decent girls didn't get themselves up like that. A grown girl showing her knees. As for those red lips . . . a Scarlet Woman, that's what Betsey was. Jinnie knew what Chapel folk thought about Scarlet Women. If Dad'd been here he'd have had something to say about Betsey. To Betsey, most like: Dad wasn't afraid to Speak Out. Betsey was . . . Jinnie, outraged, searched for more words for Betsey. A Flapper. Fast. A Fast Flapper. Jinnie soothed herself with the words and succeeded in the end in despising Betsey's clothes as well as Betsey.

'Well, at last. About time you got here. I nearly went without you,' said Betsey, but she didn't mean it. Her pale eyes moved from one to another of them, watching, to see how they were affected by her appearance. They were speechless.

'My goodness, Betsey,' said Nan at last: 'you don't half get some clothes. You aren't half lucky.'

'Pooh,' said Betsey, gratified, 'this's nothin'. Just wait till I get a new job. I'll do better than this: you see if I don't.'

Nobody asked about any new job, so they must know about it. Jinnie wished Nan would tell her things.

There was a knocking on the window of Betsey's house. Liza had pulled back the lace curtain and was nodding and waving, her gums grinning with pleasure. They all smiled and waved back. Except Betsey, who didn't even look that way. Mrs. Smeaton's smile faltered and slipped a little, then the curtain dropped back and hid her.

The party was now complete. Consett, The Pictures and Powsey, were not much more than a mile away. Betsey wanted to take the bus.

'Might as well,' she said: 'now there is one. More convenient than the old train.'

'We've only got money for one way. If we take the bus there, we'll have to walk back,' said Nan; 'and we've promised to be back by the quarter past nine. Anyway, I'd rather do the walk before the pictures than after, in the dark.'

81

'I've got the fare for uz, from me Mam, so we can ride back as well,' said Betsey. 'And we don't want to miss the beginning of the picture or not get in.'

'We'll not do that, we've got plenty of time,' said Nan. 'So you give that money back to your Mam.'

'Give it back? What'd'you take me for?' said Betsey. 'Anyway, I couldn't. She didn't give uz it. I took sixpence out of her purse last night. She's never even missed it. She wouldn't.' Betsey laughed.

Nobody said anything.

'You didn't believe uz, did you? You lot aren't half easy to kid,' said Betsey. But she hadn't been kidding. 'I was just havin' you on.' Nan, Ellen and Nora looked at one another, but not at Betsey. 'I never took the rotten sixpence. So don't any of you lot go sayin' I did. The Vicar gave uz it: for stoppin' late last Tuesday. So there.'

'All right,' said Ellen at last. 'Let's forget about it. And there's nobody stoppin' you gettin' the bus yourself if you want, Betsey.'

But Betsey stayed with them. She grumbled, though. First they were walking too fast. Next her new shoes were hurting her. Then court shoes weren't for walking, they'd be ruined.

In spite of Betsey's grumbling, it wasn't long before the meadows and the gorse-scattered waste, called Robson's Fields, between Coalgate and Consett came to an end and bay windows, iron railings and privet began.

Suddenly Betsey looked back over her shoulder, then started a tottering run that set the low, half-belt on the back of her coat bouncing shamelessly up and down on her behind.

'You lot can do what you like,' she called, 'but I've had enough of walkin'. See you in front of the Royal.'

'Well I never,' said Ellen, 'and we're more than half-way there. What a waste of good money.'

'What on earth for did you let her tack herself on to uz, Nan?' It was quiet Nora who spoke, her pale face flushed and pink. 'You know we can't stick Betsey, for one thing. And anyway, it's much better with just the three of us. We can talk properly, then.'

Poor Jinnie almost wished herself at home with Gran, or even on the bus with Betsey. She was hurt, and surprised and a bit resentful as well. They hadn't stopped talking since they'd set out. Not to her either: not about school, or French or history or anything Jinnie was interested in. Not even

82

about The Strike — at least she knew something about that — not about The Pictures they were going to — she'd have liked that. But about shortening their skirts, whether they should, or could, or would be allowed to: and about dancing: and more boring still, about Will Dunham and some friend of his, some Kevin, that Ellen seemed to like, and other lads whose names Jinnie couldn't remember now. Worst of all, they'd been enjoying themselves, talking and giggling in a way that made Jinnie feel excluded, although she couldn't have said why and had pretended she was enjoying herself also.

'We don't mind *you*, Jinnie,' said kind Ellen.

'Of course not: she knows that,' said Nan.

Jinnie managed to smile but she now felt about six years old and it was worse not to be minded than to be objected to like Betsey.

'Well, what *did* you ask Betsey for?' persisted Nora who was more animated now than she'd been at any time during the walk.

'I didn't,' said Nan. 'She asked herself. She just said she was coming. Then this morning her Mam came to pay back half a crown she'd borrowed and Betsey came as well: and asked what time would we call for her tonight? What could I say, with her Mam there?'

It was Nan's fault, all the same, going to Betsey's last night. Just for the sake of a gramophone. If she hadn't gone, even Betsey wouldn't have had the cheek to tack herself on to them, as Jinnie very nearly pointed out.

'And why did she suddenly *want* to come?' said Nora. 'With *us*? Have her and that Elsie Nattrass fallen out all a sudden? Fast cats, they are, the both of them. I thought they got on like a house on fire.'

'Well,' said Nan, weighing her words and not looking at Nora. 'I think she might be a bit struck on our Will. She kept on asking questions about him last night: I couldn't help wondering.'

Nora turned pinker still. She pressed her lips tightly together and said nothing.

'But what about Joe Telford?' said Ellen, surprised.

'Oh, that's finished, didn't you know?' said Nan. 'Anyway, you know Betsey. If she thinks somebody else likes a lad, she'll be after him.'

'If she's after him, she'll get him,' said Nora bitterly. 'She always does. All those clothes. Look at us: what chance've we got? Gives the lads the glad eye and everything, she does, an' all. And it works.'

83

'Well, she'll not get our Will,' said Nan but her voice lacked conviction. 'He's got too much sense. And he likes you, Nora.' Then she added consolingly, 'Anyway, if she does, you know what she's like. She'll soon drop him and be after some other lad.'

'And you know yourself, Nora, she's said often enough she's going to do better for herself than a pit lad,' said Ellen. 'A traveller, or an insurance man that's what she's out for. That's why she's lookin' for a place in Jesmond. She'll get one soon most like.'

'Then why doesn't she leave pit lads alone?' said Nora. 'And one of these days there might be one she'll want to hang on to, or that she'll have to wed. It's all very well for you, Nan Dunham. You're going to College. And you're good-looking. And so're you, Ellen Fletcher.'

'There's nothing wrong with you, Nora,' said Nan, pleased by the reference to her good looks but trying not to show it. 'You've got lovely eyes. And your hair . . .'

'Oh shut up, Nan,' said Nora, and she quickened her steps.

Nan looked at Ellen, raised her eyebrows a little, turned down her lips a little, gave a tiny shrug. Nobody said any more and they all walked faster.

Jinnie had plenty to think about. All this new worry, not about really serious things like Strikes or Scholarships, but about how you looked. First, yesterday, Nan, with her bobbed hair and no glasses; today, Nora; Ellen too, most like; Betsey certainly. Not that Betsey actually worried: she was *sure* she looked better than the others. It had something to do with lads, Jinnie realized. It was because of lads that Betsey got herself up like a Scarlet Woman: and because of Will, Nora was so fierce — Nora who Nan had said was always calm and quiet. Jinnie thought about Will. He wasn't ugly, she supposed: but he was bad-tempered, and he swore, and drank beer. He was awkward and clumsy. His hands were big and rough. His clothes didn't look right. Altogether, he didn't measure up to Laurie in *Little Women*: not even to second-best Mr. Brooke. Yet quiet Nora hated Betsey Smeaton, because of Will.

Jinnie couldn't understand it. She was fascinated and a little frightened as well. *She* didn't intend to get Worked Up about any lad, ever. She wasn't going to get married and scrub floors and poss clothes all her life. She was going to be a Teacher.

84

Eleven

'Come on, kidder, let's be getting there,' said Ellen, touching Jinnie's elbow. 'Wake up, lass. You must be thinkin' of gettin' wed, starin' so long at Gillis's.' She giggled. 'Look, she's blushin'.'

'So she is,' said Nan. 'Come on, Jin, tell us who he is?' She giggled too.

Jinnie was furious. She always hated herself for blushing so easily, sometimes for nothing. And Ellen wasn't being fair, either. Jinnie'd been hoping they wouldn't be late for The Pictures, not thinking about any daft lad. It was Ellen herself that had wanted to stop and gawp at fat chairs, shiny side-boards with bulbous feet and stupid carpets that only rich folk could ever buy. Even the window next to Gillis's, Madame Irene's, all liberty bodices and stays, laced, strapped and buckled, round massive pink plaster hips and stomachs, was less uninteresting. Which was saying something. Then again, farther down Main Street, they'd walked straight past a window full of school panamas and blazers, tennis rackets, tennis balls and Special white sand-shoes, and no one had even thought Jinnie might like to look.

'Oh you, our Nan,' she said. 'You ... you're ...' She couldn't find any words. Nan just laughed and didn't understand how Jinnie felt. Nor did Jinnie herself, strangely enough. Outraged she certainly was, yet somewhere, secretly, a tiny bit of her was flattered and pleased by their funning which made her, for a moment, one of them.

They didn't stop at any more shops, thank goodness, and soon came to a place where Main Street was interrupted by a side street. And there it was, facing them across an ordinary little street, The Royal. The Pictures. It was a bit like The Boro at home: a big canopy: above the canopy blind walls, below it a wide entrance, and posters, and easels loaded with photographs. A double row of lights, pale in the not-yet-dark, was spluttering round the canopy: and lights shone on the easels. The Royal wasn't open yet: a wide metal trellis spanned the entrance, and only a handful of folk clustered round the photographs. No question of not getting in: they'd

85

have their pick of the seats. Jinnie breathed in a deep gulp of happiness. Then she remembered Somebody was watching her, and listening to her thoughts. She breathed in deeper still. It was no good: she still wanted The Pictures. She crossed her fingers defiantly, pushed such thoughts into the future and concentrated on the pleasures of now.

'Just look at that: just look. You never told me he was comin' to The Royal, Nan Dunham. You said he'd seen "Go West" already. But you told *her*.'

Now what was Nora on about? Jinnie was growing a bit sick of Nora. Then at the nearest easel, she saw a coat and hat bobbing about. They became familiar. So did the fur-trimmed sleeve giving a playful push at a stolid serge arm beside it.

'No, I didn't, Nora,' Nan protested. 'And he has, hasn't he, Jin?' Not that Jinnie had the slightest notion. 'They met on that bus, I bet. That'll be it.'

'I hate her.' Nora's voice was hard and tight. 'I hate that Betsey Smeaton.' You could tell she really did. Jinnie could only marvel and stare at Will, clumsier than ever in best navy-blue. 'One of these days . . .'

'Nay, shut up, Nora,' said Ellen. 'Don't go upsettin' yourself. And don't let them hear you. You'll only make yourself cheap.'

'Cheap!' said Nora, her voice notes higher than usual. 'Cheap! I'm about fed up of folk talkin' about not makin' yourself cheap. *She's* not scared of makin' herself cheap and she can get just about any lad she likes.' All the same, Nora paused, and when she went on, her voice was lower again. 'Oh well, if he's daft enough to fall for Betsey, she's welcome to him.' She pressed her lips together, stiffened her neck and somehow made her face expressionless again. 'Well, I'm goin' in before they see uz. You lot can do what you like.'

Fortunately for Nora, The Royal was opening now. A big man, all gold braid uniform, was unlocking the gate across the entrance hall. He gave it a push. It clicked, shuddered, rumbled, then in a rush, clashed and scissored and became tall, thin, and unobtrusive. The way in was clear now. At the same time lights came on in the entrance hall and in the pay-box. The board behind the arched opening in the pay-box window whisked away, revealing pale hands, white lace wrists, black satin sleeves and fat rolls of purple, and red and yellow tickets. Half a dozen lads had materialized from nowhere and were scuffling into a queue at the window.

'And leave Will to Betsey Smeaton?' said Nan to Nora. 'You know what a softie he is: like as not he'll pay for her,

86

the little gold-digger. No bloomin' fear. Wait a mo, Nora.' But she was speaking to Nora's back. She didn't go after it, though. Instead, she moved towards the group at the easel, Ellen and Jinnie following.

'Well, here we are, Betsey. Hello, Stan,' to the other lad standing there, then, 'Hello, Will.'

Will turned round from the photographs. 'There you are then, our Nan. Where's Nora? I thought she'd be with you.'

'Getting her ticket,' said Nan.

Will swung further round still, saw Nora, smiled, made an uncertain movement towards her. But Nora was so busy with her change that she didn't seem to see him. His smile flickered out and he stood still, but he kept on looking at Nora as she moved away from the office and disappeared through the inner entrance curtains. Betsey pulled a face at nobody in particular, shrugged, and the feather pompom on her hat bounced fashionably.

'Well, you've seen the big picture,' said Nan. 'You won't be wanting to see it again, Will.'

Will looked embarrassed and muttered something about it being worth another fourpennorth but Nan ignored that.

'Ta-ra then, Will. See you Monday at the dance,' she said. 'Come on, you lot: before there's a big queue.'

She took Betsey firmly by the arm, which was surprising: you'd have thought she'd be only too glad to be shot of Betsey. And Betsey came, as if she wanted to. Jinnie couldn't understand that either, but then Nan's friends were about as unaccountable as Grown-Ups: Nan herself too. Maybe they were Grown-Ups now but at that moment Jinnie had no time to spare for such a disagreeable thought. She got out her fourpence and followed Nan.

Anticipation is Better than Realization, Dad said: so did her writing-book at school. It was a lie. Jinnie had never anticipated anything half as wonderful as The Royal. It looked like King Solomon's Temple, Aladdin's Cave, Babylon, Chapel at Harvest Festival. Red and gold every- where: opulent velvet and rich dark wood in row after row of empty seats. It smelt like spring-cleaning and carpet beating, the doctor's surgery and the chemist's and Uncle Reg who smoked too much.

The others had left her behind. She hurried down the aisle and the rows of seats rotated round her as she went.

'What'd you want to sit so near the front for?' Betsey was saying. 'This is just about among the kids in the three- pennies.'

87

'If you want to go and sit at the back among the courtin' couples, you can,' said Nora, who was already seated. She didn't look at Betsey or any of them. 'This'll do me. I've come to see the picture.'

Nan said doubtfully that Nora *had* chosen a place a bit near the screen.

Jinnie waited for them to make their minds up. She didn't care how long they took. There was so much to see she hardly knew what to look at first.

Straight in front was the screen, an enormous gilded frame thousands of times bigger than the magic lantern screen at the Band of Hope. Right in the middle of it was a bouquet of red roses, cartwheel size and dripping greenery: Anderson's, 197-199 Main Street. At one o'clock from the bouquet, a leg of lamb, white and lacy, juggled with a sober red Sunday joint and a festoon of mottled sausages: Pike's Meat Purveyors, Main Street again. Funny, Jinnie hadn't noticed either of them on the way here. Spirella Corsets were at two o'clock. You could have fittings in the privacy of your own home, with Madame Irene, also Main Street. Then, would you believe it, an enormous naked lavatory pan squatted on

88

three o'clock: Tom Smith, Lanchester, and it should never have been allowed.

'Come on, Jin. We're going a bit farther back.'

The screen slipped out of the corner of her eye. Balconies, two of them, curved towards her, all twisting stems, stiff gold leaves, silver triangles of fruit and lily-of-the-valley bunches of lights.

'Pooh,' said Betsey, 'anybody'd think you'd never been inside the pictures in your life before.'

'Leave the lass alone,' said Ellen's soft voice. 'What if she hasn't? It is nice, isn't it, Jin?'

It was nice, right enough. And it grew better and better, hotter and hotter, smokier and smokier, fuller and fuller. More packed than a Sunday School Anniversary. Two men in Sunday-in-the-Park-bandsmen's uniforms started moving up and down the aisles, scanning the rows for empty seats.

A man in a butler's suit, the Manager, Nan said, came down the aisle. He unhooked the thick twisted rope of red and gold and silk separating the threepennies from the dearer seats. He replaced the rope, nearer the front still. The boys in the back of the threepennies cheered. They were fourpennies now. Which wasn't quite fair.

'Must be some queue,' said Nan. 'Full house already, I wouldn't be surprised.' She stood up and looked around. 'Good job we came nice and early.' Virtue rewarded was in Nan's voice and Jinnie thought pityingly of all the feckless last minuters still waiting anxiously outside.

Smoke was hanging in thick, hazy layers now. The layers were drifting higher and higher, dimming the lights and half-hiding the cherubs, pot-bellied and shameless, blowing trumpets at strange angles, that Jinnie had discovered among the rioting gilt round the screen and way up on the gorgeous ceiling. Three great empty-eyed, not-quite-faces that leered, scowled and just stared from the top of the great picture-frame were beginning to move and come alive behind the moving smoke.

Clapping and cheers broke out. At the front again. Jinnie stood up to have a look.

Below the picture-frame she saw a piano that she hadn't noticed before and a woman settling herself on a stool in front of it, all shameless bare arms and earphones of blonde hair; an enormous fiddle and medium fiddle over which two men, also dressed in butlers' suits, were bulging and fussing; and a beige woman dangling large beads who was putting an ordinary-sized fiddle under her chin and plucking sharp

89

sounds out of it. A band, a whole band, and nobody'd thought fit to mention it to Jinnie.

'Hi lass,' said a voice, 'you mek a better door than a window. Get yourself sat down, will you? I don't know what for you picked these seats, our Tom,' it went on; 'behind a lot of bloomin' jack-in-the boxes.'

Nan tugged Jinnie back into her seat and pulled a sideways face of disgust: about The Voice, of course, not Jinnie.

A bandsman's uniform went past yet again, this time squirting mist from a sort of bicycle pump. Spray settled on hands and face and legs: and smelt clean and nice.

'Not long now,' said Nan.

Nora took out a bag of toffee and started to pull the pieces apart.

At the front, fiddle strings squeaked and shuddered. Like a fork on a plate. The waiting became well nigh unbearable.

The lights began to dim, slowly: then the noise. The advertisements quivered. They whirred, hiccuped, and started to lurch upwards.

'Well, I'll be jiggered . . . would you credit it? . . . in the bloomin' boxes . . .'

Nan's indignant surprise and a great rich, woman's laugh that swept clean across the diminishing noise, came at almost the same moment. Jinnie looked towards the laugh and she knew that a lot of other folks were looking as well. The woman knew too. And knew she was worth looking at: tall, hair black as black, proud nose, gold hoops swinging at her ears, and glittering beads everywhere. The man with her matched her well: even taller and not at all diminished by the woman's glitter, nor by his own blue serge, not even by the woman's silver fox fur that he was carrying.

With his own hands the man like a butler was arranging elegant gilt chairs and fussing like a top-heavy pigeon.

'The cheek of it, the pair of them. In the boxes,' said Nan in a low voice, like Jinnie and everybody else ignoring the sparrow-like couple who were also in the box: 'for the whole of Consett to see. Where does she get nerve from? It's a good job our Will didn't come in with us.'

Nan was quite worked up. Betsey sniggered. Jinnie didn't understand. Of course it must cost a lot of money to sit up there and have the Manager himself arranging your chair, a wicked lot of money. But if there were no ordinary seats left, and if Aunt Polly was desperate to see Buster Keaton, which Jinnie could understand . . . . Of course, that Tot was with her again . . . .

90

The lights grew dimmer still. The advertisements creaked for the last time and disappeared. Safety Curtain said the next screen. Fire: folk trampling one another to death. It happened at Pictures and Theatres, Dad said: poor sinful souls, a judgement on them. Jinnie ignored the thought, her fingers were crossed, weren't they? The Safety Curtain followed the Advertisements. Where did they go to? This must be the real screen at last. In a sudden last swoosh the lights finished going out. Fresh whirrings and clickings came, and a thick beam of new light shot over their heads: blue, solid, firm-edged and revolving with smoke. It settled on the screen in a bright, white square. Jinnie had to know where it came from. She swivelled round.

'For Chris'sake sit down, will you? How many more times'll I have to tell you?' said the woman behind. She had a very piercing voice now that everybody else was quietening.

'For heaven's sake, Jinnie-man,' said Nan in a vexed whisper.

Jinnie subsided and tried to grow smaller.

The square of light had become bigger: thinner. It had spread over the whole screen, and slopped over the edges. Slowly it shrank and fitted the screen exactly. Something jumped into it: letters, words, lines, shapes. They didn't stay still. They jiggled and flickered. They were a drawing. They were a cat. A cat that walked upright like a human being. They were Felix the Cat. And Nan was so used to The Pictures she hadn't thought it worth the trouble to tell Jinnie she'd be seeing Felix, the Famous Cat.

Abruptly the fiddles and the piano abandoned 'Moonlight and Roses' and began to play Felix's own song. The front rows started singing 'Fee--lix kept on walking, kept on walking still.' Jinnie had no business to know the words, but she did. Everybody did. She joined in. Everybody joined in. 'With his hands behind him, You will always find him.' On and on went his adventures and at the end of every one he kept on walking still.

Suddenly the screen went blank and achingly white. The lights came on and the screen paled. Jinnie discovered that her seat was lumpy with springs; that her face was hot and her eyes were burning; that her ankles were itching; that she was at The Pictures and would never be quite the same again.

Nora's toffee was being passed along.

'Pooh,' said Betsey: 'who wants that kid's stuff?' She opened her bag, took out a packet of Woodbines. 'Anybody like a tab?'

91

Jinnie's mouth sagged open of its own accord and the others watched as Betsey struck a match, broke it, struck another and lit her cigarette. She puffed furiously. Jinnie's hot eyes began to water.

'All right. I will have one.' Nan held out her hand. Nan, of all folk! Betsey looked surprised as well, but she took a cigarette out of the packet and handed it to Nan.

'Anybody else fancy a go?' said Betsey.

'No thank you,' said Ellen politely. Nora didn't reply. Nor did Jinnie: she knew she wasn't included in Betsey's offer anyroad.

'Young madams,' said The Voice Behind. 'Not much more than bairns. What would their mothers say?'

What would Dad say? Smoking was one of the things he was against. Except for men of course. He smoked — a pipe and only one a day: after the shop was shut: and not in the house, in the lavatory. What if he found out Nan smoked? Coalgate might be a bad influence, he'd said. Jinnie didn't want Dad to be right about Coalgate.

The Voice hadn't finished. 'Fond brazzen,' it said. 'The lot of them.'

Jinnie stiffened. So did they all. Except Betsey. She turned, coolly surveyed the woman, then blew a long straight jet of smoke straight at her. The Voice was silent: for a moment. It came again, high, incredulous, outraged.

'The hussy. The impittent hussy.' It searched for words. 'Pit folk, I bet. Nowt but pit folk.'

'Oh you, you —' said Betsey. Another word Jinnie had never heard before. Another bad one. 'You know what you can do. Who d'you think you are, anyroad? Lady Muck from Todd Hall? You —'

This was a word Jinnie had heard: it was Swearing, all right. She half-sensed, half-saw out of the corner of her eye, the woman's anger.

'You, our Tom, sitting there sayin' nowt. You heard, didn't you? Why don't you stick up for your wife?'

The man moved uneasily. 'Oh, had your whisht, lass. Tak' no notice of a silly bairn showin' off.'

'All right,' said the woman; 'if you won't do owt, I will. One word more' and I'll fetch the Manager and have them thrown out. The lot of them. So watch yourself, you,' she said to Betsey.

Her voice had become louder and louder. Other folk were beginning to take notice. Jinnie felt ashamed. But mostly anxious. She couldn't bear it if she didn't see Buster Keaton

92

after all. And what a sinful waste of their fourpences. She sat rigid, looked fixedly at the head in front of her and hoped folk wouldn't know she was with Betsey.

'Go on, fetch him,' said Betsey. 'We've done nowt. Come to think, I wouldn't mind a word with the Manager myself.' She sniggered in the way Jinnie had already come to dislike. 'And mebbe the Manager wouldn't mind a word with me.'

'Well, of all . . . The impittent little bitch.' The Voice was positively spitting now and really loud. Folk were turning round to see what was happening, stopping their own talk so that they could hear. The hush was spreading, farther and farther out: and fast. It reached The Box.

Aunt Polly said something to Tot. Then she leant over the red plush.

'Why, it's our Nan: and Kate's lass,' she said. Aunt Polly had a Special voice, although it would be hard to say just what was Special about it: perhaps that it was warm and metallic at the same time. Certainly it was as penetrating as the woman's. Jinnie wanted to die of shame at being singled out in all this crowd. 'What's up, Nan lass? Somebody pesterin' you is there? D'you want me over there?' Oh dear: a Row. 'Leave the lasses alone, you, whoever you are. Or we'll come over there and make you.'

Aunt Polly stood up, Britannia's, no, Boadicea's, own self. She glared across the rows of heads, unerringly picking out the woman with The Voice. An attendant from the far side of the cinema who had been making his way across the front of the pit, hesitated a few rows away, changed his mind and turned back.

The woman was glaring back at Aunt Polly, right through the top of Jinnie's skull.

'I knew it,' she said. 'What'd I tell you, our Tom? Pit folk. I knew it.' How did she know? Jinnie wondered fleetingly. 'Pit yakkers and their fancy women.'

Whether she heard or not, Aunt Polly swelled for battle. Betsey sniggered again and swivelled right round to face the woman with The Voice.

'Men, anyroad,' she said loudly, staring at Our Tom. 'Women an' all,' to The Voice.

'Oh, hold your tongue, Betsey. Just shut yourself up, will you? There's no need for this carry on.' Surprisingly, it was Ellen who spoke. Nora remained isolated. Nan still said nothing, still looked in front of her. Still smoked the cigarette, though. Nobody seemed to know what to do next.

Please God, don't make trouble. Please. Jinnie forgot that

93

at The Pictures you hadn't the right to prayers. That **Betsey,** make her shut up. And Aunt Polly. Don't let them **get us** thrown out.

Miraculously, the direction of Aunt Polly's glare changed. It melted into a smile, at somebody somewhere near Nan's group. Not that Aunt Polly was withdrawing from the battle, mind you: that wasn't in her smile. In another miracle the lights began their slow dimming: the whirring began again. Two threepennies who had crawled under the rope and come down the aisle to see the fun hastily started back to their seats. And suddenly the Manager was there, stiff shirt bulging threateningly as he bent forward.

'I'll thank you ladies to be quiet,' he said. 'Can't have this sort of thing at The Royal, you know.'

He retreated in haste and dignity, and with a conciliatory glance at The Box, leaving The Voice still only half-way through its gasp of indignation. It started to say something. The lights blinked finally and went out. Aunt Polly, still smiling at the Manager, vanished from sight. The blue beam sped once more towards the screen. Somewhere not far away somebody hissed.

'Now enough's enough,' said Our Tom, firmly this time. 'Tak' no notice.'

High in the second balcony, a few voices, tantalized by the knowledge that they had missed something, took up the hissing with enthusiasm. Distant attendants shouted, 'Order, now. Order now.' The hissing drowned in the returning music. The Royal subsided into concentration once more. Nan stubbed out her cigarette, half-smoked. Jinnie's spine muscles relaxed.

'Go West,' said the screen at last and a whole new world appeared, and everything else was blotted out. And a strange new world it was, where the sun was always shining and even girls' plaits and old men's whiskers were different and grew at strange new angles. A silent world.

Through this strange, silent world moved a strange young man. He was like a real young man. And he wasn't. He had enormous eyes that never changed: a flat, fixed face that never changed. And a flat hat. He was a flat man altogether: a meccano man. Body leaning impossibly forward, or backward, feet flat on the ground, he loitered, he walked, he ran. He fell.

The strange new world was against the strange young man. It fell on him; bumped into him; ran into him; chased him; in curves, zigzags and circles. The young man took it all without

94

a flicker. But he fought back. He gave as good as he got. He was winning. He must. He must. He musn't. He mustn't. Not yet: not for long time yet.

But Jinnie couldn't hold back The End: or the lights: the 'Hurry along there, hurry along, please.'

'Did you like it, Jin? It was good, wasn't it, Jin?'

Jinnie didn't answer. She heard and didn't hear Nan's voice. She saw and didn't see Aunt Polly's parting wave.

'Hurry along, there. Hurry along. There's folk waiting to come in.'

Lucky folk, waiting to go into that strange new world.

'Hurry along, PLEASE.'

Out into her own strange old world where darkness had sneaked up while she'd been away and rain had polished the pavements. Shops were lit up now and still selling butter and bacon; cabbages and potatoes; carrots; legs of lamb. The jeweller's big clock was lit up. How could it be only a quarter past eight when she'd been at last to The Pictures? Without knowing, Jinnie set her chin defiantly. The Pictures was not Sinful. She didn't know yet just what it was. But not a Sin. Not Wicked.

So there. You. Whoever You Are Up There.

Twelve

'Well, well, well,' said Betsey. 'Look who's here.' But you could tell she wasn't surprised: she had expected to see the lads again. You could tell too that the lads had been looking out for them, hanging about on the edge of the market field where the stalls were thinly spread and not very interesting either, with their crockery and soap and remnants of cloth and home-made brooms.

Jinnie hadn't come back all the way into the real world yet and she couldn't be bothered with lads at any time, but everybody else was pleased. Nobody knew for a moment what to do, though.

'What're we just standing for, Nan? Aren't you going to do the introductions?' Betsey of course: and she was raising and lowering her wide blue eyes at the new lad who was now with Will and Stan. A proper show-off was Betsey: introductions indeed.

Nan was a little put out. 'This is Betsey, Kev. Betsey Smeaton. Betsey, this is Kevin Bourke. Sorry, I thought you would know each other already.' Fortunately, it never occurred to her that Jinnie didn't know Kevin either.

Kevin was looking awkward but Betsey was in her element.

'Pleased to meet you, I'm sure,' she said.

She stepped very close to Kevin and she looked very small beside him. Kevin Bourke. Of course. He must be Tot's brother. He was big enough to be, anyroad. Betsey stretched out her hand, daintily. Kevin blushed right up to his ears: then he held out his own large, rough, hand. Betsey took it, held it.

'My,' she said. She looked at Kev's hand, then up at him from under her fashionable hat and somehow round her shoulder. 'You're as big as your Tot. Bigger.'

Betsey wasn't a Flapper. She was a Vamp. Now, at last, Jinnie knew what a Vamp was: it was Betsey going on like this. And Vamps were Sinful: Scarlet Women. Dad was right.

But Kevin didn't mind Betsey being A Vamp. He went an even darker red, but he was smiling: in a silly sort of way. Betsey let his hand go at last.

96

'Where've you all been?' she said. 'The Green Man, I bet.'

'No, we haven't,' said Kevin, flattered. 'We've been to see "The Eagle." '

'Oh you never! Did you really? None of yuz eighteen. Are you? Of course, you all look eighteen. More than. Especially Kev.'

Betsey's voice could not have been more full of admiration if Kevin had been Rudolph Valentino, The Eagle, himself. She set herself in that posture of hers that was positively embarrassing, although Jinnie couldn't have said why.

'Nay, we're nigh on eighteen,' said Kevin. 'Anyroad, if we're old enough to go down the pit, I reckon we're old enough to see "The Eagle." '

'What's it like, Kev?' It was amazing how Betsey made it seem as if there was nobody there but her and Kevin. Yet Will had something to do with it as well. 'Tell uz, Kev.' She lowered her voice. 'Is it true that . . .'

'Oh be done, will you, Betsey? Come on. We'll never get to see Powsey at this rate,' said Nan. About time too. More and more folk were going past them now. 'Are you coming, Will?'

Betsey tossed her head. She actually did: like somebody in a story. 'Oh you, Nan Dunham,' she said and pulled a face. But she was only pretending to be vexed.

Round The Great Powsey's tower the crowd was dimayingly large. Of course you could see the tower, but the tank he was going to jump into was quite out of sight.

'We'll soon fettle that,' said Kevin and he took Jinnie's hand and started pushing a way through with unexpected assurance. They wanted to take the lass where she'd be able to see, he kept on explaining, to Jinnie's confusion. But nobody objected, although one woman at the ropes at the foot of the tower did say, 'Oh ay, cannie crack. All you lot?' She made way for them, though. Kevin put Jinnie in front of him, next to the rope barrier itself, and the others squeezed up behind and beside them.

'Just in time,' said Betsey, stretching her arm and displaying her new watch; 'nearly half past.'

The platform at the top of the wooden tower was high up in the night, hardly touched by the light rising from the smoky flares down below. The tank in front of the tower wasn't the swimming-bath Jinnie had expected. It was nothing but a wash-tub: an outsize one, but still a wash-tub. How could The Great Powsey be sure of landing in it? Her admiration and expectation grew.

'I hope we don't get splashed,' said Betsey. 'I don't want

97

my new coat spoiling with that mucky water: and oil mebbe. And sparks.' Even in the crowd Betsey managed to wiggle in peculiar way that made you notice her inside the new coat almost more than the coat itself.

'Suit yourself, Betsey,' said Nan. 'Move back if you want.'

Betsey stayed.

At one side of the tank were barrels: 'Inflammable'; 'Do Not Touch'; 'No Smoking'. That would be the oil, waiting to be poured on to the water and set ablaze when Powsey was ready to jump. That wooden tank . . . how did they get the water to burn without the tank catching fire? Maybe they *were* too close. What if the whole thing, tub, tower, barrels and all, caught fire? What a blaze it would be. Still, it wasn't as if they would be trapped in a building, and she did want a good look.

She concentrated on the tank. Round it were slotted grubby placards which read: 'The Great Powsey: 2.30: 8.30: 9.30: 10.30' and, 'Next Jump, 8.30'.

Somebody must come and light the tank before anything

98

else could happen. Sure enough, in a minute or two a little man in a greasy boiler-suit and greasier cap appeared from around the other side of the tank. The Great Powsey? Jinnie felt the beginning of disappointment. The little man stopped in front of 'Next Jump, 8.30'. She couldn't quite see . . . The little man moved. 'Next Jump' but it said '9.30' now. Jinnie could have cried.

Others started noticing, too.

'It's not good enough,' said the woman who had let them squeeze in beside her. A bit of a warrior she looked an' all. 'The' must think we've nowt to do but hang around here all night. Hi, you there. What's up?'

You could tell from the noises round about that other folk were vexed as well.

'Nay, I know it's an awful nuisance but it can't be helped,' said the little man in the dirty boiler-suit in a wheedling voice and Jinnie realized with surprise that he was in fact a woman.

'He went and had a sup too much. After the jump this afternoon. Can't really blame him, you know. That jump's no joke, you know. Anyroad, you'll just have to sleep it off, that's all, I sez to him. And made him have a lie down.'

The woman who had asked about the delay was full of sympathy now. She knew about men having a sup too much. So did most of the folk within earshot.

'The strain on him's something cruel, you know. On me, an' all.' The woman in the boiler-suit was accusing now. 'Riskin' his neck for a few bob a time. Bad enough when he's stone-cold sober. You wouldn't want him to jump when he's had a few. Now would you?' The wheedling note was back in her voice.

'Nay, lass, nay,' said the other woman; 'that I wouldn't. Poor soul.' Neighbouring clicks of sympathy agreed with her. 'You let the man have his sleep out. Never mind what anybody says.'

Nobody was saying anything: the crowd was already breaking up.

'That's fettled that then. We've missed it. We can't stop here until half past nine,' said Nan. 'What'll we do? Go straight home?'

'Why can't we stop?' said Betsey. 'We could get the quarter to ten bus, if we ran for it. That's not all that late.'

'Nay, lass, if you wait to see The Great Powsey the night, it'll more likely be the quarter to eleven you'll be gettin'. If that. Ben here said how it would be, didn't you, Ben?' A fresh voice, that had no business to be listening to other

99

folks' conversation, pushed its way in. It belonged to a middle-aged woman, one of a little group of older folk that Jinnie hadn't noticed before. You could see from his smug smile which was Ben.

'No jump at half past eight: nor at half past nine neither, Ben said. And it's turnin' out just the way he said.' The woman was positively pleased it was turnin' out the way Ben had said. 'You'll see, there'll be nowt but the one show the night: at half past ten. That's how it'll be, won't it, Ben?'

'Ay, will it,' said Ben with so much satisfaction that Jinnie could have hit him.

'How d'you know?' said Betsey resentfully. 'What makes you so sure?'

And why had they bothered to come, Jinnie wondered. Know-alls. Spoil-sports.

'Well,' said Ben, settling down pleasurably to his explanation, 'I'm from Stockton way, over here for the week-end, for a christening in the family the morrow. That's right isn't it, our Doris?' Doris nodded. 'Well, this here Powsey was at Stockton Market Easter Sat'day. Same tale there. Three jumps a night, they said. And now many times d'you think he actually did jump?' He looked at his audience triumphantly. 'That's right. Only the once. Nigh on eleven it was an' all.'

'Same excuse an' all, wasn't it, Ben?' said Doris, prompting him. 'He'd had a drop too much. Poor soul,' she said sarcastically.

'Ay, that's right,' said Ben. 'Mind you, it was summat worth watching when we did get to see him jump, him all on fire and everythin',' he added generously.

Which only made matters worse.

'But what's the point?' said Nan. She didn't want to believe Ben but you could see she did.

'Well,' said Ben, expanding, 'I've figured it out like this. Who d'you think pays him? Never thought about that, did you?' He was right: they hadn't. 'You don't think he'd risk his neck for the coppers folks'll toss into his wife's cap, do you? Half the folk that watch him, give nowt at all, anyroad. Slip off before the cap gets to them.' Jinnie felt herself go red. She could tell from their expressionless faces that Nan and the others felt guilty, too. They'd none of them even thought about paying. 'Hadn't thought about that, had you?' said Ben, pulling in his mouth in satisfaction. 'Well, the regular market folk club together and pay him. Bet the only ones that haven't put up some brass the night is the Salvation

100

Army and maybe the Miners' Strike wagon, which doesn't come often. Fetches the crowds, does Powsey. Look at all the folk here now. I'll back any money there's not many Sat'day nights as crowded at this; not at half-past eight. Am I right, our Doris?' He was. 'And what've the folk got to do now? Nowt but hang about. See?' Ben was clearly determined to hold his audience as long as possible. 'Well, it'll be a wonder if a good few of them don't spend a bob or two before half past ten. See?'

Jinnie saw.

'But look: it says "Next Jump half past *nine*",' said Betsey.

'Oh ay,' said Ben, pitying Betsey's simplicity, 'that's what it sez. Who's going to hang around for a couple of hours? But one hour now . . . that's not so bad. Then at half past nine, well . . . if they've waited that long, they might as well hang on a bit longer. So stay on's what most of them'll do. The ones with a bit of brass in their pockets. It'll be the bits of bairns with nowt anyroad that'll go home.' Ben looked at them half-accusingly, half-contemptuosly. Kev frowned: Will looked as if he might be going to Say Something. Ben went on hastily, 'So you see, it's all a question of trade. When he jumps, he's good for trade. And when he doesn't he's even better.' Ben laughed at his own cleverness. He had finished with them now, and moved away.

He was a Know-All, a Show-Off. But he was right. Because of The Shop, Jinnie knew about Good for Trade and Bad For Trade. Ben made sense and she was furious with Ben. Powsey had been Special. He leapt through darkness, a Falling Angel, trailing fire. Lucifer, all flames, hurled from a dark Heaven to a red and yellow Hell. Ben had diminished the glory, shrivelled The Great Powsey into Good For Trade. Jinnie concentrated her disappointment on the hateful Ben. But she couldn't blame him for everything, not honestly. Powsey's tower was rickety, his tank was nothing but a great wash-tub, his wife wore a dirty boiler-suit and told lies. It served Jinnie right. Dad and Mam were always warning her about Expecting Too Much. You be thankful for what you've got, Mam said. For what the Lord sends, Dad said. The Lord had sent Jinnie The Pictures. She was thankful. The Great Powsey couldn't be half as Special as Buster Keaton. Buster Keaton could jump off a tower twice as high, if he wanted to. Into a tank of gunpowder, if he wanted to. Jinnie began to feel better.

The others were disappointed as well. They were wrangling about what to do next. There was still plenty to see at the

101

Market; the Miners' Meeting, for a start, said Stan.

'Pooh, who wants to hear them harping on about The Subsidy, and the Owners and the Government?' said Betsey. 'I get enough of that at home. What about that fellow that gets chained up inside a big box? And the flame swallower?' Bet they're frauds like Powsey, thought Jinnie, wordly wise now, and determined not to Expect Too Much. 'They're always here; not like that old Powsey,' said Betsey. Nobody was very interested in them. 'The stalls then and we'll finish up at the Miners' wagon, if you like,' said Betsey.

But it didn't look as if Betsey was going to get her way, and she was beginning to sound bad-tempered.

'Oh, come on, Nan,' she said in the end, for Nan, more than anybody, wanted to go home by the next bus. 'What does it matter which bus you get?'

'I promised not to be late,' said Nan. 'But just me and Jinnie'll go,' she added reasonably. 'You lot don't have to come, any of you.'

Nora and Ellen said they didn't want to be late home either: they would go with Nan.

'Babbies,' said Betsey, which was much more insulting than babies. 'Well, I'm staying. Till half past nine: half past ten, if need be. How about you, Kev? Stan? You don't have to be in early, do you? For your mams to tuck you up?' She wiggled again and looked up from that hat of hers. 'Come on, Kev. You're a sport.' Kevin, embarrassed, shook his head and didn't look at Betsey. Nor did Stan. 'That leaves just you and me then, Will. Suits me fine,' said Betsey: and Goodness Only Knew what was in her voice and her look now.

'No,' said Will. He cleared his throat. Then, in a rush of courage, 'I'm taking Nora here home. If she'll let uz.'

Not a muscle moved in Nora's face: yet it was transformed by such happiness that Jinnie looked away. All because of Will. Ordinary Will. Of course, she knew from Edie that Taking Home meant something, but now Nan and Ellen and the lads were looking as if this time it was Extra Special. It was no use, Jinnie would never understand. But she didn't want to be a Grown-Up if Taking Home and ordinary lads were so important.

Betsey's face too had changed. She was looking at Will in a different way now.

'That's right,' she said. 'Save your money. Next Sat'day you'll be on strike. Of course, Nora'll likely pass you a bob or two out of the till . . . now.' She paused a second. Something even nastier was coming. 'I reckon you do right not to stay at

102

the market, Will. Then you'll not run into that mother of yours. She'll not be here yet. She'll be in the pub . . . with Tot Bourke . . . that fancy man of hers. A bloomin' Mick, at that. As for you, Kevin Bourke,' she added, 'I don't know how you have the cheek to show your face near Will Dunham. Or how Will Dunham can stick the sight of you, knowin' what he does about that brother of yours and his own Ma.' She paused again. 'Or are him and that runt of a Da of his the only ones that don't know?'

She had finished at last. She turned her back and left them, stepping over puddles, slipping in the mud but still wiggling, an insult in every wiggle.

Nora put a hand on Will's arm. The others were paralysed. I won't ask what she meant, thought Jinnie. Not ever. But she would, of course: one day. Soon. Fixed as a photograph, they all stared after Betsey. Then, without a word, Will flung off Nora's hand. He pulled himself out of the group and started to walk fast, with desolate, ugly steps, in the opposite direction from Betsey. Also without a word, Nora ran after him. It was after Nora and Will that the others stared now, not ready yet to look at one another.

'Good for trade, you see . . .'

Incredibly, Ben's voice drifted towards them. The prophet justified, he would enjoy his triumph all night.

103

Thirteen

'Nay, I hardly thought you'd be back so soon, or I'd've had the bath out,' said Gran. 'Good lasses. Come by the fire and get warmed.' She looked up from the long black stocking she was always knitting when she hadn't any other job to do, but her fingers worked busily on. The needles glinted rosily in the glow of the fire. 'And what's the matter? Faces like motherless foals the both of you. What's happened? Did you not get in at the pictures, or something?'

Trust Gran to guess immediately that there was something wrong. Yet the very last thing Nan had done before they went in was to tell Jinnie once again that she must not say a word, not one word, about Aunt Polly, or Tot, or Will.

'Oh ay; we got in all right,' said Nan. 'It was champion, wasn't it, Jin? It was Powsey we missed.' Hurriedly and wordily she started on an account of that part of the evening, missing bits out, of course.

Gran looked curiously from Nan to Jinnie. Jinnie braced herself for questions, but Gran only said, 'Well, that was a pity but never mind, mebbe he'll be back again some day. Good lasses for comin' home and not waitin': Nan'd've missed her bath for this week. Now you'll be wanting a bite of supper. I've done a bit of baking with your Mam and Dad comin' tomorrow.' The Market and Powsey had sobered Jinnie. On the way home she'd had plenty of time, while the others were talking, to think about Dad finding out about The Pictures. She wasn't looking forward to tomorrow. 'And I made a tatie cake for your supper. Light the gas, Nan, then fetch Jin a mug of milk from the pantry.'

Two places were already laid and in the middle of the table was a big basin of marrowfat peas with two round peasoakers sitting on top, waiting for Gran to pour boiling water over them before she went to bed. Another reminder that tomorrow was Sunday and Dad was coming.

She had supper by herself because it wouldn't do for Nan to fill her stomach just before a bath. By the time Jinnie was pressing the last crumbs of potato cake off her plate and into her mouth, Nan's bath was nearly ready. In front of the

104

fender, clean sacks were down to protect the mat. The big zinc bath had been fetched in from its nail outside the back door opposite the double-you, and wiped clean inside as well as out. The cold water was in and Nan, getting redder every minute, was adding the hot, jug after jugful, from the little brass tap beside the fire.

'Come on, Jin, hurry up,' said Gran. 'Get into your nightie, then let's do your hair. The rags are ready. Fetch them from the machine drawer.'

Jinnie hated having Saturday rags twisted into her hair, but on the whole she was glad Gran hadn't forgotten them. Curls were more fitting for Sunday than plaits. For the millionth time she wished Dad didn't think being bobbed was a Sin and a Shame.

'There you are: that's the last one,' said Gran and she'd hardly pulled Jinnie's hair at all. 'Now off to bed with you, Nan'll not be long after you. Here, Nan, I'll finish that,' for by now Nan was refilling the boiler with cold water from the pantry. 'Keep that door shut till Jinnie's into bed.' Jinnie gave Gran a good-night kiss and received a kiss and a hug and a slap on her bottom. 'You're quiet, lass. Must be tired. When our Nan comes to bed, don't spend half the night talkin' like last night. The pair of you'd best be asleep when I come up. And you can have a long lie in the mornin'. Get up just when you want.'

The high feather-bed sank alarmingly as Jinnie climbed into it, then curled comfortably round her, softer and warmer than her bed at home. She lay on her back, adjusted her rag curls on the pillow and put her hands under her head.

This was her favourite time for A Think: proper thinking, in words, not just the ordinary sort that you didn't notice. Lately The Scholarship had been particularly clamorous at bedtime. Funny, it wasn't bothering her now. Gran and Nan had put a stop to that, saying that Mam would see to it that Jinnie went to The Sec. Jinnie believed them: Gran never told lies. The Strike and Ruining the Country didn't seem so frightening now, either. Funny again, when she was at Coalgate, real pit country: pitmen everywhere.

Pale gaslight from the street lamp ruled a line across the bed, leaving her in darkness, strawberry-pitting its share of the patchwork quilt and turning the lace curtains into a kaleidoscope of shadows and shapes on the dim roses and trellises on the wall opposite her.

On the wall, half this side of darkness, a young woman, larger than she could ever have been in life, looked out of her

105

frame. Smooth-haired, mysterious, she gazed gently over her tight high bodice and sudden crinoline. Uncle Bob's mother, Nan said. Yet she was beautiful.

She was sad, too. Of course, she was Dead. Jinnie was feeling sad too. Uncle Bob was a queer man. She didn't know what to make of Uncle Bob. Was he at Consett, waiting for Powsey? Or was he getting drunk somewhere? Saturday night . . . and at Gran's folks didn't bother much about men having a sup. Dad did. Then Jinnie had a terrible thought. Gran must be Sinful. She'd go to Hell: and Nan and Jamesie. The thought couldn't be endured. Gran was Good. Jinnie didn't care what anybody said. Anybody. And she wasn't going to believe Gran was going to Hell. So there. You-Up-There.

Another worry was niggling. Tomorrow. Dad and The Pictures. Maybe Gran would make it All Right. Or maybe, more like, Dad would take Jinnie straight home when he found out, away from Bad Influences. He could. Dad wasn't afraid to Speak Out. All right, then. What if he did? Her holiday had been Special already, hadn't it? She didn't really mind all that much about The Dance. She was glad she'd been to The Pictures. So there. Again. You-Up-There.

She was tired. The quiet voices downstairs were soothing. Her thoughts drifted. They edged round Aunt Polly and Tot and Will. Back to The Pictures. To Gran. Everything was different at Gran's. It was muddling. The sounds below changed. She heard the round swish of water: the rattle of metal: the click of the back door. Nan had finished her bath. She'd be having her milk and potato cake. She'd be coming upstairs in a minute. Jinnie made herself more awake, started to phrase her thoughts, ready for the gossip with Nan.

The gentle murmur of voices began again. Nan didn't come. It wasn't Fair. What were they talking about all this time? Leaving Jinnie out. Grown-Ups. A few tears squeezed themselves out. That would show Nan. But not nearly as many as last night, not enough to moisten the pillow. Besides, she was very tired, after her latest night up ever. The voices grew dull, duller. The giant ratching of a coin wound into the gas meter scarcely touched her.

'Move over, Jin: you've got all the bed,' Nan whispered.

Jinnie rolled nearer the window, but she hadn't really heard.

106

Fourteen

Sunday dinner was much later at Gran's than at home and was still a pleasant memory in Jinnie's mouth as they waited on the quiet platform in a sober Sunday way. The train came into sight. She watched it grow bigger and bigger. Today Gran was stately in a long black coat and black hat. Nan and Jinnie were in their best too and gloved and hatted.

Unexpectedly Jinnie was feeling shy at the prospect of seeing Mam and Dad and Robbie again. At the moment they seemed like Company not Family at all. She was anxious, too, about how the visit would go, more so because she hadn't liked to tell Nan her worries. She had kept them to herself and they'd been bobbing up at odd moments all morning.

Dad was first off the train. His topcoat and grey Good Suit — older than you, our Jinnie — and especially his stiff trilby hat straightway marked him out as a stranger in blue-serge-cloth-cap-or-bowler-hat Coalgate. And he was carrying a brown paper parcel as no self-respecting pitman ever would. There's no disgrace in anything that's honourable, Dad said.

Mam climbed out next, beige cotton gloves, navy serge costume, the summer straw hat with blue forget-me-nots. Last of all Mam lifted Robbie down onto the platform. Jinnie felt a pang of love when he waved and came running towards them on his fat little legs. He was a Friday's child, loving and giving, right enough. And he had a mass of fair, bouncing curls so Jinnie felt a pang of envy as well, and for a moment begrudged sharing Coalgate and Gran and Nan and Vic with him.

When the greetings were over, Robbie wanted to cross over the railway track to the Way Out. Dad said no. Jinnie took Robbie's warm hand, feeling far more than three years older, and patronized him all the way up the stairs, over the bridge and down on the other side. Then she felt mean, so she let him take Vic's leash the rest of the way out of the station and even though it was Sunday, she ran with them down the ramp and right to the bridge under the train as they always did when they came to Coalgate. Then she let him set

107

Vic free to rush home ahead of them, to wait for them at the door, panting and pretending he was seeing them for the first time, and scarcely letting them in for his leaping and barking.

Uncle Bob was in his chair by the fire. He shuffled a little when they all arrived. 'Well there, Kate,' he said. 'And how's Josiah?' as if Josiah wasn't Dad but somebody somewhere else.

Jamesie stood up and smiled and would have looked shy, except that Grown-Ups were never shy. Were they?

'Hello, Kate lass,' he said. 'How's tha gannin on?' and sounded more Durham pitman than usual. Which was a pity with Dad there. He wouldn't hold his knife and fork properly at tea-time, either. Oh dear. 'And hello, there's wor lad: and a sight for sore eyes he is an' all.' Folk always liked Robbie a lot but Robbie was going home again this evening so Jinnie didn't mind this time.

Mam started to take Jinnie's hat off. She kissed her again. 'How've you been, hen?' she said. 'You're looking grand. Has she been a good lass?' she said to Gran.

'Of course she has, our Kate.' Gran smiled at Jinnie, shaking her head in a friendly way. 'And now where's me bonnie lad? Come and let's have a proper look at you,' she said. 'My, you grow more like your Mam every day.' She

108

smiled approvingly and gave Robbie another kiss. Nobody ever told Jinnie she was like her Mam. 'And how's Josiah?' Funny how it sounded different when Gran said it. 'Well, there's the kettle coming to the boil. Mash the tea, Nan. You'll be ready for a drink, Kate, Josh, awand?'

'Thank you kindly,' said Dad: which meant no. 'It'd just spoil our teas. And that reminds uz. I got Kate to boil a bit of ham: thought it'd help out for tea. It'd be just as well opened now.' He put the parcel near the teacups. 'Well, Jamesie,' he went straight on, 'what about this strike? Are you going to see sense? It'll ruin the country, as well as the industry. And you can't win, you know: the Government's got all its plans ready, you know. Against a General Strike as well.'

Dad wasn't afraid to Speak Out, right enough. Jinnie wished he wouldn't for once: not today, anyroad: at Coalgate, at Gran's. But he was settling down for a discussion you could see. And she *did* want Dad and Gran's folk to like each other today.

'Thank you, Kate lass,' said Gran, cutting the string of the parcel. 'It's a beautiful bit but there was no need, you know. We're not hungered yet. Put it on a plate in the pantry, Jinnie, will you?' Gran removed the outside wrappings and handed over the ham in its greaseproof paper. It did smell good. 'Jamesie's just off to Dottie's, Josh. He's fetchin' her for tea,' said Gran.

Jamesie was off like a shot. He grabbed a cap from the peg and was out of the back door so fast that he almost knocked the ham out of Jinnie's hands as she was making for the pantry. He didn't hear Gran call after him, 'Hi Jamesie, come back a minute. That's your old cap you've got.' Gran laughed. She turned to Mam. 'You'll have a cup, Kate?' as if Dad's refusal didn't include Mam as well. 'And the bairns'll never say no to a drink of pop, I back, before they go out to play.'

There was no hope. Things were starting to go wrong already.

Nay, his bairns had never broken the Sabbath yet, said Dad, and they weren't starting now.

He was right, of course. And when you were Right, you had to Speak Out. And if, when, somebody happened to mention The Pictures last night, he'd Speak Out then, to some tune. Jinnie wished again he wouldn't. Not today. Not to Gran. Then she remembered God. She hoped He wasn't listening to her thoughts. But He would be. It wasn't Fair:

109

you never had a single minute to yourself to think what you liked.

Mam looked into the fire. For a second nobody said anything. Then just as a preliminary grunt came from Uncle Bob, Gran said, 'Upstairs then. After the pop. Nan can show you her books again, Jinnie. And there's them postcards. Robbie'll like a look at them.' Gran's voice was the same as it always was. She added, 'And don't make too much noise the three of yuz. Your Mam and me want an hour or two's peace and a good crack.'

Jinnie didn't wait for pop: she escaped as fast as she could.

After a while she forgot to keep an ear open for sounds of Speaking Out below, or to worry about The Pictures. The books were wonderful. So were the cards. She left the books to join Robbie and the cards. Gran never threw out a card. There was a whole boot-foxful: Christmas cards going back to Before-The-War: every birthday card Nan had ever had, a glossy dozen of them, unbelievably beautiful with dewy red roses, angelic children and heavenward-looking young women with folded hands and masses of frizzy hair. And a holiday card of fat women bathing, from Aunt Polly from South Shields where the Miners' Outing went last summer.

The Family photographs were in the box, too. Some were familiar because Mam had them as well. Nan, aged four, fat-cheeked and solemn in muslin and ribbons; Jinnie and Robbie in sailor-suits holding hands; Aunt Nan, who had married a Catholic and died young, looking round-faced and still healthy. Uncle Davie was there, a young soldier in the Tyneside Scottish, neat moustache, high-buttoned tunic, criss-cross-bandaged soldier's legs. In another photograph, posh and pasted on stiff cardboard with the photographer's name in elegant gilt letters across the corner, Uncle Davie, a little older now, pop-eyed and half strangled by deep white collar, stood stiffly beside Aunt Polly, all black lace, black satin, black beads, black ear-rings, in a chair beside a potted palm, with a staring baby on her shiny knee. Boys of various sizes were ranged around them and Jinnie couldn't guess which was Will.

They came to a picture of a young woman, sweet and pretty in spite of piled-up hair, tight waist and bunchy skirt down to her feet. Aunt Kate, said Nan: and it was Mam, when you got used to her.

Then Nan took out of their special silk hankie wrapping the Uncle-Ted-who-was-killed-in-The-War's cards. She spread

110

them on the bed for them to see but not touch. Four Christmas cards, one for each year of The War. They were made of fine white card, covered with silk and embroidered: with white heather and a horseshoe; with roses; with forget-me-nots; and the last one, with gay crossed flags, the Union Jack and the Stars and Stripes most prominent.

Then they all stared at Uncle Ted himself: young, a soldier, legs like Uncle Dave's but his cap different. It was funny about people being alive in photographs but Dead really.

Last of all Nan showed them Uncle Ted's medals. They looked at them silently. Tears started to roll down Robbie's chubby little face while Jinnie felt sad and Sunday and it was a good thing The War had ended all War and she would try not be nasty to Robbie, not ever again. To comfort Robbie, Nan produced Snakes and Ladders from the cupboard, which brought Jinnie's worries back again, but she didn't care to say that Dad wouldn't like it and tried to rattle the dice quietly.

Mam came upstairs to tell them that Dottie had come and tea was ready. She didn't say anything when she saw the Snakes and Ladders, although she Looked. And as she tidied Jinnie's hair, she said Dad hadn't been at all suited when he heard about The Pictures: in fact he'd been bonnie and vexed and if it hadn't been for Gran ... And you needn't think you've heard the last of it, young woman. But there was no mention of packing Jinnie's things and taking her home; which was one load off Jinnie's mind for the time being.

When they went downstairs Dad was looking All Right. He was standing in the place of honour in front of the fire, warming his hands behind him and watching Gran pour tea out of a gigantic black teapot Jinnie'd never seen before into the best willow-pattern cups. A young woman who must be Dottie was putting the filled cups at the places round the table.

'Dottie, these is Kate's bairns,' said Jamesie, sounding shy.

'Well, hello there,' said Dottie, putting down a cup and turning towards them. Dottie wasn't shy. 'Hello, Jinnie. And there's our Robbie. Jamesie talks a lot about you.'

Instantly Jinnie disliked Dottie. She wasn't good enough for Jamesie, even if she was pretty. And she was: really pretty, with fair hair in earphones, and little curls at her neck and forehead.

She came forward and kissed Robbie, then Jinnie. Jinnie saw that her eyes were blue as blue, and she had a soft sweet bloom on her skin. She smelt nice. Of scent. Wasteful and full

111

of vanity, she was, as well as pretty. Chapel wouldn't approve of Dottie. Still, Dad didn't seem disapproving. In fact he looked as if he was enjoying himself: not actually smiling of course, but then he seldom did.

'Come on, pull up your chairs. Sit down will you, Josiah? Here.' She gave him the best place, Uncle Bob's. 'Kate . . . Dottie . . .' Gran showed them all where to sit.

It was more than a Sunday tea: it was a Company tea and better even than a Chapel Bazaar. The table was fairly carpeted with food. Three sides were neatly medallioned with cups of tea and plates of Mam's ham and Gran's home-made meat loaf. In the middle of the fourth, the window side, stood a large round cake-stand with a large round spice-cake. From it radiated more plates, dishes, jugs and bowls than you could take in with a single look: white pickled onions; dark beetroot; white snow-cake (Nan's speciality, baked this morning); red and yellow jam tarts (for Robbie); square chunks of pink, yellow and green ribbon-cake (Lizzie-Next-Door's); shaggy wedges of pink coconut-cake (Jinnie'd dipped them all by herself); prim slices of rice-cake. Not a nasty piece of seed-cake in sight, not even a slice of bread. And everything Home-Made. No wonder Dad was actually smiling now. Then — how could she have not seen it first? — right in front of her own place, a sun of cream horns and vanilla slices. Gran must've been hiding them, for a surprise. Shop cakes. A Sinful waste of good money. She'd have one of each: at the very end.

She looked up. From her place at the narrow side of the table, nearest the door, she could see straight along to the fire-place, where Gran was standing, a bowl of dough in her hands, to make girdle scones for after the ham and meat loaf. She and Uncle Bob would have their tea when everybody else had finished. Gran's eye was on her. She gave Jinnie an encouraging nod, and then a kind of wink. Gran-at-Barton'd never winked in her life, that was certain.

The fuss of getting into seats settled into subdued awkwardness. Then Dad began to Ask a Blessing. Jamesie dropped with a clatter the knife and fork he had just picked up. Nan made a squeaky noise and gave Jinnie a kick that must surely have been accidental. Dad finished the Blessing and began on the ham.

'Come on, then,' said Gran, for the rest of them were still suspended in the influence of The Blessing. 'Eat up. I'm starting the scones now, and you don't want them cold.' She began putting dollops of dough on the girdle.

112

'I'll have a bite of bread with my meat,' said Dad suddenly. Reprovingly he laid his knife and fork on his plate. No bread with cold meat was Wrong of course. But would've been Special . . . just this once, thought Jinnie. 'So'll the bairns, Kate.' He looked sternly round but nobody else asked for bread.

'I'll get it,' said Mam.

'That's a lot of meat Robbie's got there,' said Dad as he waited for the bread. 'Can you manage it all?'

'Yes,' said Robbie, his jaws working hard to prove it.

'Well . . . as long as you eat up your bread.' Mam brought it now: a good slice for Dad, thin halves for Jinnie and Robbie. 'And not too much sweet stuff, mind.'

'Nay,' said Uncle Bob, from his seat by the fire, 'the bairn can nobbut eat his fill,' and subsided again.

Everyone else was eating their fill, too busy to talk, and meat and pickles steadily diminished and disappeared. Gran gathered up meat plates as they became empty and moved them to the washing-up table. Then she gave everybody a small plate and a girdle scone. Except Robbie, still valiantly eating ham but obviously flagging.

'I knew all that meat was beyond him,' said Dad. 'If you can't finish it, give it here, Robbie. It'd be a Sin to let it go to waste.' Robbie surrendered his plate. 'Well, if nobody else wants it . . . ?' Nobody else did and Dad took a piece of the ham, drew it through the puddle of butter and scone crumbs on his own plate, and conveyed it carefully past his moustache into his mouth.

'Dottie,' said Gran, 'what about that tart? Folks is ready for it now. You dish it out, lass. Dottie's fetched us a rhubarb tart,' Gran explained. 'She's a rare light hand with pastry is Dot.' Jamesie looked pleased.

'How much fruit is there in it?' asked Dad while Dottie was taking the tart out of the oven. 'That's even more important. We like our tarts with plenty of fruit, don't we, Kate?'

Mam was busy wiping Robbie's fingers and didn't hear.

'I'll try a bit, though,' said Dad, finishing off his ham and scone. Dottie lifted a piece on to his plate. 'And I'll have the Carnation, Jamesie. Looks all right, Dorothy,' said Dad briskly, taking up his teaspoon. But Dottie didn't realize that All Right was high praise and didn't answer, just went on dishing out the tart.

When Jinnie's turn came, she said, 'No thank you.' Dottie's face didn't look over pleased but rhubarb was Jinnie's least

113

favourite tart and she must leave room for the cakes. Even as it was she omitted the rice-cake and the coconut-cake and went straight on to Nan's snow-cake. Then to Lizzie-Next-Door's and enjoyed pulling the ribbons apart.

The meal was slowing down now. Gran was refilling tea-cups with Nan helping. Dad was still busy, but Mam had started talking to Dottie and they seemed to be getting on all right. Mam asked about Auld Billy Reeves, the Church School master, because Dottie was the maid up at the School House. His missus was a bit of a tartar, Dottie said, but Billy was all right. 'His bark's worse than his bite. Soft as you know what, really, is Billy.' Dottie was Common, as well, thought Jinnie, listening.

'Ay, always was,' said Mam. 'Does he still slip out of school into the church for a funeral, if it's a bairn or some-body he's taught?' He did. Mam sighed. 'It's a bonnie lot he'll have been to,' she said.

'He remembers you, Kate,' said Dottie. 'He said to tell you he was askin' after you. I told him about me and Jamesie.' She smiled with that silly lad-lass look that Jinnie was begin-ning to recognize.

'Did he really?' Mam said, pleased.

Then everything stopped altogether when Mrs. Barker-Up-The-Street came in to borrow a cup of sugar: and to say hello to Kate, she said. To see what they were having for tea, Nan said, when Mrs. Barker had gone.

'Now, now,' said Gran: 'give over our Nan,' but half-heartedly. 'At least she didn't stop for a cup of tea when she was asked.' She looked around. 'Well, Josiah,' she said, 'are we ready for The Cake?'

Dad would have the first slice, of course, because fruit-cake to end the meal was as Special as meat to begin it. Liking spice-cake better than cream horns was one of the bits of being Grown-Up that put Jinnie off the whole business.

Judiciously Dad cut a morsel from his slice, tried it, tut-tutting over it with lips and tongue. 'It's All Right,' he said. 'A shade on the sad side, maybe. But better that than over-dry any day.' He helped himself to a substantial wedge of cheese to go with the cake. 'Nothing like a good home-made fruit-cake. Better than all your bought rubbish.' He looked in the direction of Jinnie and Robbie with a sort of mellowed severity. 'I'll just have another cup and that'll be about it.'

He was ready now for talk. Serious talk, of course. The only sort for Dad. An Idle Tongue was an offence to the

114

Lord: and only excusable in women. If then.

More than an hour till train time. A lot could happen in an hour. The last ring of cream horn was hard to swallow. Jinnie paused and looked at Nan eating a piece of fruit-cake. Jinnie loved Nan dearly but she was showing disappointing signs of Growing-Up.

'Well, as I was saying before you and Dorothy came in,' said Dad. Jinnie's stomach tightened threateningly, on the ham, the beetroot, the pickled onions, the cakes, the vanilla slice, the cream horn. A judgement. For not asking for more bread . . .

A whole hour. Still, things hadn't gone badly so far. Dad was in a good humour, although Uncle Bob was now champing his food something awful, and Jamesie hadn't held his knife and fork the proper way. But Dad was nothing if not Fair. He couldn't, he wouldn't, expect Coalgate Folk to know as much about Manners as he did. Or about anything . . . As long as nobody contradicted him it would be All Right. Even if they did, it would depend on how they did it. Dad liked a good discussion. And other folk had a right to their opinion, Dad said.

Jinnie finished swallowing the cream horn and crossed her fingers.

115

Fifteen

'As I was saying, Jamesie, before you and Dorothy came in,' said Dad, 'that Cook of yours is nothing but a Bolshie . . . a blooming Bolshie.' Blooming was strong, for Dad. 'Honest, I'll grant you.' Dad was always Fair. 'But misguided. He'll ruin the whole country with his ideas, not just the mines. Unless the rank and file see sense and refuse to come out next Saturday.' Dad shook his head, drew his breath through his moustache, and waited. The basket chair creaked uneasily but Jamesie said nothing. Uncle Bob was having his tea and couldn't be expected to talk just yet.

'Well, Jamesie? Will you come out?'

Jamesie had to reply now. 'Ay, we'll come out,' he said: 'if the Executive calls us out.'

Dad shook his head again regretfully. 'You'll be sorry,' he said. 'For a start, what're you going to live on when you're out? Your Union's got nothing.' Jamesie said something about war chests. 'War chests.' Dad actually snorted. 'Durham emptied theirs only in February. Reduced to appealing in the papers for donations, you were. For the men on strike at The Eden and the other Consett Iron pits round here.'

'Nay, there was nowt come in this house out of other folks's pockets,' said Jamesie, more audibly but still mildly.

'Well,' said Dad, 'you didn't win that strike and you'll not win this. Ay, it'll be the workhouse for some and the parish for the rest if it lasts long enough. And goodness knows what'll happen to the rates.'

'Nay,' said Jamesie. 'I'd starve sooner than go on the parish!'

'I dare say,' Dad said: 'but what for? If you go back on the Owners' terms in the end? And you will. You mark my words, you will. Because you can't win.'

Dad was Speaking Out with a vengeance now. He had to, of course. Jinnie looked at the clock again, but not very hopefully.

Jamesie muttered something about the General Strike.

'Ay, if it comes off,' said Dad. 'Like as not the T.U.C.'ll let

116

you down again. Another Black Friday.' Black Fridays, Red Fridays, Dad knew about them all. Jinnie's anxiety was mixed with pride. 'The Government's ready for you this time, as I said. They've got Emergency Powers. And they've got their plans: they've been organizing for this lot ever since last year. They weren't ready then. That's why you got The Subsidy. That's why you'll not get it now.'

Just what Gran had said to Jamesie. Not that she said anything now. Nobody did. They listened. Dad was a good talker. Mam'd said to Jinnie once that it was a pity Dad'd Never Had a Chance. He'd've done well at a job where he could use his talking. It was flowing now: in full spate: all about things Jinnie didn't know the meaning of then, but remembered for ever. Capital-letter things. Emergency Powers, The Subsidy, The Minimum, The Miners' Executive, The Federation, The Mining Association, The T.U.C., The O.M.S., and the Fridays. Names as well. She never forgot them either and they had a special sound for her for the rest of her life. A.J.Cook, Herbert Smith, J.H.Thomas, Baldwin of course, Ramsay MacDonald, Greenwood, Samuel, Straker, Robson, Ebby Edwards. On he went. Faster than the clock, though. And he was coming to a conclusion now. 'We'll just have to hope the Leaders'll come to their senses before they ruin the country,' he said. 'Not that they will, of course.' He gazed benevolently round, from his place on the hearth-rug.

Jinnie held her breath, hoping nobody would Argue. The clock ticked slowly on to train time. Still nobody spoke. Then:

'And what about the Government coming to *their* senses? Before they ruin workin' folk.'

It was Dottie who was speaking to Dad like that. A mere slip of a lass. Politics were for men, anyhow. Jinnie's heart sank. Now there was no knowing how The Visit would end.

Nobody looked at anybody. There was silence this time: that reached even Dottie.

'Nan,' said Gran, after an eternity, putting down her cup and speaking as if she hadn't noticed a silence was going on. 'You might as well get started on the pots. Your Uncle Bob and me's about finished.'

Everybody was anxious to help. Except Dad, of course. He was a Man as well as Company.

'Nay,' said Gran, a smile in her voice, 'there's no need for the lot of you to go at it like a cat at gut. Sit you down again, Kate. It's your day off for once. Leave it to the young uns. You an'all, Dorothy. You don't want to go splashing that

117

nice blouse.' A nice blouse it was, too — white, all embroidery, frills, and slotted blue ribbons. Too nice for that Dollie.

In the end Nan washed the dishes. Jinnie dried them and Gran and Robbie put first the food, then the dishes in the pantry. Nan was outside emptying the dishwater down the sink, Jinnie was wiping the last cup, when Vic started his silly carry-on that meant somebody was at the door. But worse than usual. He was leaping up as high as the door button in unmistakable rage.

'Ah,' said Gran, 'that'll be our Dave, Kate. I thought I knew them legs going past the window. Fetch that dog, Bob.'

Uncle Bob dragged Vic away from the door. The dog resisted all the way; you could hear his nails scratching the oilcloth as he tried to grip the floor.

Uncle Dave. Things were getting worse. Anything might happen now. Uncle Dave drank. Which was how he'd come to tread on Vic when he was still a puppy and had made the dog hate him for life. If he was drunk now ... Jinnie knew what Dad thought about Drink and Bad Examples and what Rotten Apples did to the rest of the barrel. Dad was vexed enough already, saying nothing and whistling thinly through his teeth. Before Jinnie knew it she'd be on that train with Dad and Mam and Robbie. You could hardly blame Dad, either: he did know more than anybody else there, especially that Dottie. Jinnie closed her eyes, crossed her fingers hard over the damp tea-towel and sent a hopeless prayer up to Heaven.

She opened her eyes again and caught Dorothy watching her. Dorothy winked, turned down her mouth conspiratorially. Cheek, when it was all her fault. Folk at Coalgate were always winking. Common, it was. Jinnie pretended not to notice.

'Have you got that —— dog out of the road?' called Uncle Dave's voice. Swearing. Of course.

Vic became even more enraged. Uncle Bob gave him a real clout. 'Now then, our Vic,' he said threateningly. Vic quietened, but Uncle Bob didn't let go of his collar.

'Ay, it's all right. Come on in,' said Gran. 'You're just in time for a bite to eat. Nan, get a plate and fetch that nice ham of your Uncle Josh's, for a start. Take your muffler off, lad.'

'I've just come by to see our Kate,' said Uncle Dave. 'What cheer, wor lass? How's tha gannin on?'

Uncle Dave was little and thin and his hair was grey where he wasn't bald. His skin was grey too: and his moustache and

118

his eyebrows. But his eyes were startingly brown, like Mam's, like all the Dunhams'.

'Well, what cheer, wor lass?' he said again. 'And how's Josh? And the bairns?' He came forward, shrugging his shoulders inside his jacket and rubbing his hands as if he was cold. For all that famous pound-a-week-for-his-pocket there was something sad about Uncle Dave. But he didn't look drunk.

'We're all champion,' said Mam: 'and how's Granpa?' She liked Uncle Dave, you could tell. And Uncle Dave liked her and he liked being called Granpa.

Then suddenly Dad was in a good humour again. Jinnie knew she'd never understand Grown-Ups, never, not if she lived to be a hundred. Dad and Uncle Dave were getting on like a house afire. Dad was saying that the country could do with more women like Aunt Polly who used their heads and weren't afraid to Speak Up. Uncle Dave had been in the pits all his life but between mouthfuls of ham and beetroot and pickles he didn't want This Strike either; although it wouldn't affect him because he was an Official and would still be going down, anyroad. Jamesie showed no inclination to join in, nor Dottie either this time. Jinnie's spirits rose fractionally again: maybe Dad wouldn't be so against Coalgate after all.

Quickly it was time for Mam and Dad and Robbie to leave. On the way to the station they were going to pop in at Cousin Joe's, Uncle Dave's eldest, and see the new baby, Uncle Dave's first grandbairn. Gran and Nan and Jinnie were going with them and to see them off on the train as well. Uncle Dave said he wouldn't mind having a look at his grandbairn either, so he would go as far as Young Joe's with them.

The new baby wasn't at all beautiful but Mam and Gran and even Nan went on as if he was. Cousin Evie was shy and nearly cried when Mam gave her the little smocked dress she'd brought him. It was so pretty, she said. Cousin Joe said she hadn't got her strength back and wasn't she a silly lass, and he looked as proud as if she'd done something clever although he was every bit as shy as Eva.

Fortunately they had only a few minutes left and Dad talked all the time to Uncle Dave and stayed in a good fettle.

On the station platform when the train was signalled, he felt in his back pocket and produced a sixpence. He gave it to Jinnie. 'For the Church Social tomorrow night,' he said. Church Social? Jinnie's eyes widened. Gran gave her a little look, so Jinnie just said thank you and gave Dad a special

119

hug, and felt quite sad when the train started to move. She ran alongside it to the very end of the platform, and waited and waved until the flutter of Dad's big white Sunday hankie in Robbie's hand disappeared into the darkening east side of evening.

Jinnie walked home to Grove Street in exhausted happiness. For once the fondness in their voices as Gran and Nan talked about the new baby and about Robbie — my but he was growing and wasn't he fair bonnie — roused no pang in her jealous heart.

The air was cool now and growing dim but the clouds over Consett way were edged with brightness against the pale sky. Church bells were ringing from St. Ives' on the hill. A group of Sunday summer straw hats, white gloves and prayer-books was crossing from Front Street to St. Ives' Road.

At the piece of open ground which was the terminus a bus was waiting. 'Why, look,' said Jinnie, 'there's Will and Nora,' then wondered if maybe she shouldn't have spoken since Nan had told her not to mention them to Gran.

'So it is, well,' said Gran. She gave them a wave.

Will waved back, handsome and happy, and Nora smiled in her quiet way and looked almost pretty.

'She's a nice sensible lass, is Nora,' said Gran. She didn't sound surprised, though. 'Just what that lad needs. Mebbe he'll get hisself put straight now.' She gave a little sigh. 'But mind, don't you go gettin' yourself tied up, our Nan. It's

120

College for you, and College and lads don't match. So 'just watch yourself. You an' all, our Jin.' She gave Jinnie's arm a squeeze.

But Jinnie didn't even like lads. The very idea of them scared her. Besides, she was going to be a Teacher. Miraculously all her worries had gone at last. She just knew she was going to get that Scholarship. All the other things, everything she wanted, would follow.

Sixteen

Monday began peacefully. For Nan and Jinnie, scarcely a quarter awake, a slice each of crisp, warm fried bread; for Gran a cup of tea and, 'Time to be up if you want that early start' — from Uncle Bob just off to the brickworks. It had hardly stopped being dark.

Later, Nan and Jinnie had breakfast with mats up off the floor and Gran in sack-apron: already half-way through the wash, she said — and Jamesie still fast asleep. Then Nan went off to school, Gran returned to the wash-tub and Jinnie to bed again, with a little stack of *Happy Mags* from behind the recess curtain. There'd be a William story in some of them, Nan'd said.

Upstairs it didn't feel like Wash Day. No shop bell ring ring ringing for blue-mottle soap and dolly blues. No coal-carts in the back lane and thumping on the yard door and, 'Hi, missus, Co-al,' and Mam dashing into the back lane to take down her clean washing out of the coalman's way. Only the sound of possing, and that was a comfortable distance away.

The sun got out: good for drying. Which was a blessing because a wet Washing Day was no joke for anybody. It had been a Holiday to lie in bed and read in peace. Now it would be a Holiday to help Gran. William could wait. Jinnie dressed and went downstairs. Jamesie was still asleep, Vic at the side of the bed. There was no sign of Gran, except that the biggest pan Jinnie'd ever seen was taking up the whole of the fire, slavering a little and puffing out steam and a smell of hot soap and boiling clothes.

She went outside. Gran was still busy in the roofed-over space between their lavatory and Lizzie-Next-Door's. She wasn't possing. She didn't, when Jamesie was on night-shift and still abed. Instead she was rubbing, slapping and pounding clothes on a sort of slithery board that was new to Jinnie. Nearly finished, she said: only the socks and dusters to do. If Jinnie would do the dusters on the board, Gran would get on with the socks, by hand.

Companionably they rubbed and slapped and pounded and splashed. The water grew so dirty it was a pleasure to see.

122

Then together they wheeled the tub to the big drain, emptied it and started again with clean, cold rinsing water from the pantry. Jinnie blued the water while Gran fetched the whites from inside.

The rest was easy: folding the whites, the sheets and towels; turning the mangle; pitching in the coloureds; folding and mangling again — and at last pegging out. Lizzie-Next-Door called from behind her own billowing sheets, 'See you've got a helper the day, Mrs. Dunham,' and Gran said Jinnie was a grand help, a body couldn't want a better, and Jinnie got a slap from a sheet that she wasn't expecting.

The cold blue water was warm and soapy in the end and Gran scrubbed the downstairs floor because it would be a shame to waste it. Jamesie woke up. Gran said he must've had some of his sleep out by now but he could just stop in bed till she'd finished and had got the mats down again. Nay, of course he'd still have time to be ready for Tot when he came for the pair of them to see to their pigeons.

Jamesie had his tea and bacon, Jinnie ate a sociable slice of tea-cake, and Gran got some socks, neatly rolled and ready, from her big work-basket. She put them into a brown-paper bag and said that when Jinnie was finished, mebbe she'd take them to Aunt Polly's, so that she could get on with Liza Daly's collars. And another bit was added to Aunt Polly's character: she didn't do her own mending.

'And here's a ha'penny for a cornet at Tommy's,' said Jamesie.

'Nay, you'll spoil the lass's dinner,' said Gran. However, she didn't say Jinnie wasn't to have it. Jinnie was glad because she'd never been to Aunt Polly's by herself, and not very often with Mam, and it would be an ordeal, so an ice-cream afterwards would be nice to look forward to. It wasn't until she was nearly to Aunt Polly's that it occurred to her to worry that maybe she shouldn't have taken the ha'penny, with The Strike coming up.

Aunt Polly's was the biggest house Jinnie knew. Of course, there were bigger houses, but Jinnie didn't expect ever to go inside them, so they didn't exist, not really. It belonged to the Pit and was, like the pound a week for his pocket, sure proof that Uncle Dave was clever and High Up at the Pit.

Aunt Polly's window was protected from the public gaze by great pot-bellied loops of lace curtain, a bamboo plant stand, an enormous brass plant pot and a forest of aspidistra leaves. Jinnie passed the window and paused at the front door. Go straight in, Gran had said, but had she meant the

123

front door? It didn't seem right somehow, not with such a grand house. Why didn't Aunt Polly mend her own socks like any respectable woman? And that brass door-knob hadn't been cleaned for Sunday, either.

The knob clumped a bit when Jinnie turned it but the door didn't open. She had no choice but to go round the back. Stepping uncomfortably on the nobbly cobbles, she made her way through Aunt Polly's archway, into her backyard. It was very big, Jinnie could see that, although she caught only glimpses of it through cracking sheets, somersaulting shirts and long-legged puffed-out linings which crisscrossed between the house, the clothes-posts and a big tree in the corner. It was some size, that backyard, and what was more, a garden seemed to be behind it.

The house looked still bigger from the back, perhaps because it had a full-length porch, if that was what you called it: it was more like a narrow, glass-roofed railway platform than anything. Jinnie dipped in and out of the clothes and towards the open back door and the sounds of washing. At the porch a dead creeper on a paint-peeling wooden pillar waved dispiritedly at her.

Dingy sunlight struggled through the glass roof onto the family litter near the back door: a bicycle upside down on its handlebars, inner tube hanging like a disease out of the front tyre and into a chipped enamel basin full of gritty water; a grubby push-chair; pit boots still waiting to be scraped clean; big zinc bath, of course. Aunt Polly's wasn't as impressive as it should be, somehow.

Jinnie hesitated in the doorway. A woman was working a noisy old-fashioned mangle. Bending and stretching, with one hand she turned the handle of the big metal wheel and with the other fed the fat wooden rollers with neat parcels of clothes that ballooned and fizzed then flattened as the water squeezed out. The woman wasn't Aunt Polly. Jinnie changed her mind again about Aunt Polly. She had a woman to do her washing. Like a Teacher. Aunt Polly was Posh.

The woman became aware of Jinnie. The mangle stopped. In the sudden quiet, Jinnie heard the clucking of clothes in a set-pot and, somewhere, voices. The woman straightened and with the back of a wet hand pushed a strand of hair off her damp forehead, knocking the untidy bun on the top of her head still further askew.

'If it's Polly you're wantin', she's in the kitchen. Go on through.' She looked at Jinnie with eyes bright and inquisitive as a duck's. She kicked a clothes-basket aside. Jinnie

124

squeezed past it and through the rest of the washing-day confusion. She hesitated again at the brown varnished door to the kitchen.

'You'll be Kate Dunham's lass?' said the woman.

Somebody else who knew Mam. 'Yes,' said Jinnie.

'You don't look much like her, though,' said the woman. 'Go on in. Fighting again, mind.' The voices, or one of them at any rate, did sound angry. 'Don't let it stop you, though. Polly doesn't care who knows. She doesn't care about owt.' The woman's voice couldn't decide whether to admire or blame Aunt Polly. In any case she had no business talking about Aunt Polly like that, not when she did Aunt Polly's washing.

'Make your mind up, lass,' said the woman. 'Here, if you like, give me your parcel: I'll take it in for you. But hurry up out of my road. I've got all this lot still to do before I get home to me own work.'

'It's all right, thank you,' said Jinnie with dignity. But she was uneasy, the sounds on the other side of the door were . . . well, she didn't want to walk into them. Her heart beat faster. She clutched the socks more tightly. She opened the door.

She saw Aunt Polly first: right in the middle of the room: right in the middle of everything. Jinnie never remembered her anywhere else. She was standing at a big battered oilcloth-covered table. Her hair, still in its night-time plait, hung down her back. Her large gold ear-rings were swinging thoughtfully as she tilted her head in critical admiration of the biggest, fanciest cake Jinnie'd ever seen outside a baker's window. A cake. On Washing Day. And what a cake: sides all gold and brown with toasted coconut, top all pink icing and spiralling peaks of cream and shiny red cherries.

Aunt Polly gave the sides a last smoothing stroke with an outsize knife. 'That's that,' she said. She put the knife down and started to lick her fingers. 'You know, I might take it to The Dance tonight myself — see how you're all getting on.' Her voice was tranquil, full of satisfaction with the cake. Jinnie hoped she'd get a slice of it tonight and that anger she'd heard must have been in her own imagination.

Opposite Aunt Polly, separated from her and the cake by a greasy plate, pint pot, seven-pound stone jar of jam, pint bottle of sauce sat, not Uncle Dave, as Jinnie'd expected, but Cousin Will. So it couldn't be a Fight. Could it?

Something was going on, all the same. Jinnie could see that from Will's face, his eyes which didn't move from Aunt

125

Polly's face. Whatever it was, it was between him and Aunt Polly. Everything else was outside it: the little girl on the po on the hearth-mat; the red jersey that must be Cousin George.

George was mounted on an ancient rocking-horse, with worn black spots, flaring red nostrils and depleted tail. He rose and sank, rose and sank and gazed into some pale blue distance of his own. The little girl saw nothing but Aunt Polly and Will. Jinnie stayed in the doorway, watching them too.

'Well, look who it is. Kate's lass. Come on in. Come on in.' Aunt Polly was warm and welcoming and not a bit upset at being caught with her hair still in a plait at nearly dinner-time. 'Take your coat off, Jinnie, and sit yourself down. Shift the cat off that chair. Would you like a cup of tea? No, of course you wouldn't; a drink of pop then. Will, fetch a bottle from the pantry, and the best biscuits.'

Will made no move: didn't even say hello.

'Where's your manners, our Will?' said Aunt Polly. 'First impittence, now sulks, is it? And all for what? Summat that's got nowt to do with you anyhow. None of it.'

'Has it not, though?' said Will, still as if Jinnie wasn't there. As if nobody was there but him and Aunt Polly. He was in A State again, the Will of Saturday-night-Consett-Market, not last night's Will-with-Nora. 'Has it not? Making a show of yourself for all Consett to see.' Well, certainly Aunt Polly'd got herself looked at on Saturday, in the box at The Pictures and calling out to Nan and that woman, but for Will to be still carrying on about it on Monday . . . well, it was out of all proportion as Mam would say. What could have set him off? He'd been all right last night.

'Oh, had away, man,' said Aunt Polly; 'you don't know what you're on about. You weren't even there. So we'll have no more of it.' Her tone was good-humoured but dismissing: as if she'd said all she was going to say. Then she changed her mind.

'Who's been doing all this talking you're on about, anyroad?' she said. 'Some daft bit of a lass, I'll awand, from the sound of it. A lot of fuss about nowt.' She sniffed scornfully.

Skilfully, with the big knife, she manoeuvred the cake onto a stand of paper lace and silver cardboard good enough for a wedding-cake. 'There, that's that,' she said. 'Come on right in, Jinnie, and sit yourself down. And if you're not

126

going to get that pop, our Will, it's time you took yourself off to bed. You're on night-shift, or had you forgotten?

Will would not be dismissed.

'Nowt you call it, a fuss about nowt?' he said. To Jinnie's dismay, he turned to her now. 'You were there. You saw her, didn't you? Stuck out front for all Consett to see her. With that . . .' Will was nerving himself to go on. His face was going all tight: a strange white edge came round his lips.

'Don't say it, Will,' interrupted Aunt Polly sharply. 'Don't.' Don't, Jinnie's mind echoed, not knowing why. 'There's things you don't understand. Not yet,' said Aunt Polly with a sort of warning defiance. 'Not yet. Some day, mebbe.'

'No, I don't understand,' said Will. 'I don't understand you. I'll never understand you. Never. And I don't understand . . . him . . . me . . .' He jerked his head in the direction of the room upstairs above them: and couldn't bring himself to say the name that should have come easily to his tongue: '. . . and why he didn't give you a good hiding . . .' A Good Hiding, for a Grown-Up? 'Years ago, if half the things folks say about you's true.'

Jinnie hadn't bothered much as a rule, about how Grown-Ups looked, not when they were real Grown-Ups, old Grown-Ups, They looked . . . Grown-Up. That was all. But Aunt Polly was a Grown-Up you did look at. And now with her large curving nose and big eyes, black and frightening, she was . . . she was . . . like, like Saturday again . . . No, not like Saturday . . .

'. . . I can understand that bugger, though . . . the . . .' A torrent of words came from Will's bleached mouth. Some of them Jinnie'd never heard before but she knew they were bad: and deep down she half, only half, knew what the words were about.

Will was shouting now. He was standing up, braces dangling stupidly, and glaring at his mother across the littered table.

'That's enough. You've said enough.' Aunt Polly was shouting now as well. 'It's got nowt to do with you, I tell you. It's between me and your father and . . .'

Will braced himself — unconsciously Jinnie did the same — and said the words that changed everything, even for Jinnie, especially for Jinnie. 'If he *is* my father.'

Dad had been right after all . . . about Coalgate folk, thought Jinnie calmly. They *were* Common. And what Nora could see in that Will . . . Jinnie looked past Will at a battered

127

dartboard hanging on a door opposite which must lead to the rest of the house. But she couldn't stop hearing the hate and the misery in Will's voice... And the names he was calling Aunt Polly. His voice rose in a last crescendo of accusation.

'I heard you come home Sat'day... and last night... only it wasn't last night, was it? It was this morning...'

'You... you...' Aunt Polly was screaming. 'Spied on. I'll not be spied on in my own house. Lying awake, were you? Waiting?' Aunt Polly took a deep breath, clutched her voice, brought it down to ordinary level, and Will to an ordinary naughty lad again. 'You oughtn't to talk to your ma like that.' Then unaccountably she flung her voice away again with a great wide movement of her arm. 'You... you little runt you... Nobody's asked what time you came in. Or where you'd been. Or what you'd been up to —' she paused, seeming to consider, then — 'with that stuffed face Nora of yours.'

Will closed his eyes.

'You mucky everything,' he said at last, not shouting now. Then he made a wild, wounded movement with his hand. His plate went skidding across the table, knocked the heavy mug on to its side. Tea dregs scattered and the mug rolled, crashed onto the bare floor and broke.

The rocking-horse creaked to a stop. George's big eyes, blue and round in all directions like glass alleys, looked at the floor where the broken pieces must be. Then he started sucking his thumb fiercely and his gaze moved back to its own faraway place. The rocking began again. The little girl gave a startled scream, then subsided into a whimper.

'Now look what you've done, frightening the life out of the bairns,' screeched Aunt Polly, like a ferocious parrot: except that parrots were funny.

The scullery door opened behind Jinnie. The washer-woman said soothingly, 'Now come on, the pair of yuz.'

Jinnie didn't move. She couldn't. Nobody took any notice of the woman.

'As if you cared about the bairns. You... you...' Will couldn't go on. He shut his lips tight, the white line around them again. For a second he looked as if he was going to cry, then in a kind of frenzy he looked at the table.

A great creaking of springs came from above, a thumping; then Uncle Dave's voice, angry and loud.

Aunt Polly looked up at the ceiling. 'Don't you start, you drunken sot you,' she screamed, not enjoying her screams any more: she had at first.

128

'Leave him alone. Don't start calling him names.' Will's voice had come back but it didn't belong to him somehow. 'You made him like he is. Oh ay, did you. You . . .' Another strange, ugly word. Will clenched a fist and his knuckles gleamed. It was going to be a Fight, a real one. It wasn't exciting; it wasn't funny; it wasn't the Donnellys, it was the Dunhams. It was worse, much worse, than Mum and Dad arguing. Jinnie was terrified now. She still didn't move. Will raised his fist. He looked around in a strange unseeing way. But he saw the cake.

'That's a fancy cake,' he said. 'You're good at fancy cakes. That's all you are good at . . . that and . . .' He brought his fist down with a great smashing movement right in the middle of the cake, the beautiful cake. Jinnie heard the washer-woman draw in her breath. Will laughed and held up his hand all splattered with cake and cream. 'Make that right again. If you can . . . fancy woman.' Calmly he shook cream onto the floor, then wiped his hand with a big khaki hankie. 'That's that,' he said. 'Well, I'll be off to bed now. Like you said . . . Ma.' His voice mocked but wobbled a little. He turned away.

Aunt Polly made a sound that drew Jinnie's eyes from the ruined cake and Will. She was staring at Will's back, moving towards the door. Her hand fumbled on the table, picked up the great knife, clumsily: threw it, hard. It caught Will on the arm, briefly, stuck a second in the door just below the dartboard, vibrated, then sagged and clattered on to the floor.

There was a sudden flash of silence. The rocking-horse stopped. The girl ceased her mewing. The cat dropped silently out of its chair, made its way across the hearth, along the edge of the room and out of the scullery door. Nothing, nobody else moved, until Will turned back and looked at his mother. It was a terrible look and Jinnie would never forget it. Then he looked down at his arm. Just below his rolled-up sleeve a red line was forming. It thickened, darkened, stopped being a line, became a great red patch. A dark trickle dropped onto the oilcloth. Unbelieving, Jinnie heard it splash, watched it spread, like spilt ink. If she shut her eyes the blood would go away. Everything would go away: she'd be back at home: where Sinful things like this didn't happen because the Friends were a Cut Above such Common Folk.

Nothing had gone away. She was still in Coalgate. Aunt Polly was still staring at Will and Will was still staring at his arm. Now he covered the blood with his hand. For a second

129

the blood was gone. It came back again, squeezing through the fingers, oozing fatly from the sides of his palm.

Aunt Polly came out of her trance with a high, loud laugh that set the child howling again. The laugh became a sob. Aunt Polly rushed at Will, flung her arms round him, sobbing, kissing, calling him her baby, shaking her ear-rings wildly and saying again and again that she'd never meant to, never, never, never.

Grown-Ups didn't go on like this. Not Jinnie's Grown-Ups. All she wanted was to get away. Yet she stood there, cold and sick and frightened and struggling with thoughts she couldn't give shape to, let alone find words for.

Suddenly the door opened, so violently that the dartboard swayed, tottered and almost came off its nail, the empty brass rings on the old curtain-rod on the top of the door shook like Aunt Polly's gold ones. The knife scraped across the lino and was pushed out of sight.

In the doorway stood Uncle Dave, little and tired and greyer than ever. Old. His feet were bare. His crumpled flannel trousers pulled on over his striped flannel night-shirt were sagging hopelessly. Faded braces, wrinkled with wear,

130

dangled down like Will's. That was Common as well. Decent Folk pulled their braces up, properly, over their shoulders before other folk saw them. Dad always did.

'What'n hell's goin' on down here?' said Uncle Dave. He glared at Will, still standing like stone; at Aunt Polly, still slobbering on Will's shoulder. 'Can't a man get . . .' He saw the blood. The grey in his face took on a yellow tinge. 'Christ,' he said: but it wasn't swearing. 'Is this what we've come to? One of these days somebody'll swing for you . . . you . . .'

He stood irresolutely, then he went on, 'For God's sake, woman, shut your gob, will you? Or d'you want me to shut't for you. A body'd think it was you'd been hurt. Shut up, will you? D'you want to fetch the whole town in here?'

Aunt Polly only cried the louder and clung the closer to Will, who in a peculiar mechanical way came to life at last and tried to push her away with his uninjured arm. Uncle Dave went to her. With a care that was almost funny, he pushed aside the long thick plait of dark hair and gave her a slap that could be heard above all the hullabaloo: right across her shoulders. Aunt Polly gave a loud yell and let go of Will. But she wasn't really hurt, you could tell: surprised mostly.

'Here, lad,' said Uncle Dave. 'Let's have a look. Let's see what she's done to you, the bad bitch.'

The washer-woman came to life. She rushed past Jinnie to Aunt Polly and put her arm round her.

'There, there,' she said, and made soothing baby noises. 'Sit you down, lass. Take no notice of him, Polly. Laying hands on a woman, the great ugly brute. I'll make a nice fresh cup of tea and you can drink it while I clean up this mess. Just look . . . that beautiful cake . . . and you takin' all that trouble just for poor Meggie Riddell's Social. Nobody'll lay hands on you again, not while Bella's here. I'll promise you that.'

'This is none of your business, Bella Telford. But you always were one for stickin' your shovel in,' said Uncle Dave. 'You can just take yourself out of this kitchen. To your washin': or back home if you want, to that man of yours that's never done a hand's turn for twenty years that I know of. I don't care which. You an' all,' he said to Jinnie, who wondered for a second if he didn't know she was Kate's lass. 'We want no big-eared, always-rights here,' and he might as well have struck her. Jinnie flinched.

Aunt Polly had calmed into quiet sobbing.

'That's right,' she said, 'do as he says, Bella.'

131

'Well,' said Bella, 'if that's all the thanks . . . Come on, lass. No good stoppin' where we're not wanted.'

Bella left the kitchen muttering whose washing was it and why didn't folks do their own and she'd a bonnie good mind to let them. But by the time Jinnie, trying desperately not to disgrace herself with public tears, was running clumsily through the archway, the poss stick was already thumping again, fit to batter the bottom out of the tub.

Seventeen

The sight of Gran's familiar street released Jinnie's tears and set her sobbing so painfully that she felt she must be sick at last. She managed to open Gran's door: indeed, she sent it clattering against the coat pegs on the wall at the bottom of the stairs. The inner door defeated her. She just could not pull out the big brass button to lift the sneck. She gave a thump with her knee that hurt and set Vic on the other side howling with vexation. She started kicking. The door opened and she fell against Gran's clean apron.

'Nay, nay, what a state you're in, lass. What's the matter then? Give up, Vic, will you?' Gran said so sharply that the dog retired to sulk under the window table. Not that Jinnie noticed. 'What ails you, bairnie?'

She drew Jinnie to the Windsor chair. She took from her, without comment, the parcel of socks that Jinnie hadn't known she was still clutching. Then she sat down, lifted Jinnie on to her knee and patted her and dried her cheeks with a clean white handkerchief, while Jamesie and Tot stood there looking awkward and as if they wanted to escape but didn't know how to. Jinnie was past caring who was there or who saw her crying.

'Now then. What've the' done to you, Jinnie? I'll settle them, the lot of them, for you. Who are they? Just tell uz, and your Gran'll be at them.'

Gran didn't know the awful things that'd been happening. She'd soon stop joking. Jinnie's sobs were threatening to turn to hiccups but she told Gran. About Will and the cake and Aunt Polly and the knife. And how Uncle Dave had hit Aunt Polly. And how he had called Jinnie a know-all and told her to get out. That set Jinnie sobbing again.

'It wasn't my fault I was there,' she said. Indignant, she drew in a long quavering breath and began to feel better. Then she looked at Gran's face and wanted to cry again but knew she mustn't.

'Well, so long then. I'd best be off. You don't want me here, Mrs. Dunham,' said Tot.

'Wait,' said Jamesie. 'I'm coming.'

133

'No, Tot Bourke. I don't,' said Gran, 'and I should've said it before this. But I couldn't bring meself, not even this morning when I was all set to. I've just kept hoping. . . The more's my blame. . .'

'You. . . Don't say it, Mrs. Dunham,' said Tot, half threatening, half defiant. 'I know what you're on about. But it's nowt to do with you . . . with anybody. . . It's between her and me.'

'That's just what it's not,' said Gran, 'not any more, if it ever was, and I can see by the look of you, you have the grace to know it for yourself, Tot Bourke, whatever you may say. So I don't know how you've had the face to keep on coming here — or why. Pretending . . . as if . . .'

'Nay, our Ma,' Jamesie started but he didn't go on. And Tot looked . . . well it would be hard to say just how Tot looked. And Jinnie wondered if something Awful was going to happen at Gran's now.

'The folks in this house, me most of all, ull always remember that if it hadn't been for you our Jamesie wouldn't be alive here now. Never think different, Tot Bourke. But that doesn't make right what's goin' on. Nay, I'm not goin' to tell you what you should do. I think you know anyroad. But I am tellin' you that you're not welcome in this house. Not any more.' Still Tot said nothing: nor Jamesie either. 'So get you off to your pigeons. You an' all, Jamesie Dunham. I'm not sayin' it's for you to fall out with Tot. Just take yourselves off and give uz a bit of peace, that's all,' she said and sounded very tired.

When Tot and Jamesie had gone, the room settled into quietness. On the mantelpiece, the clock fussed over the seconds as they passed as if all seconds were the same. Under the table, Vic, invisible, snuffled reproachfully. The fire rustled and shifted. Then the lid of the kettle rattled, water ran down and set fine ash flying. Mechanically and still holding Jinnie on her knee, Gran leant forward and eased the kettle half on to a cooler part of the coals, half on to the hob.

'No, Jin,' she said at last, 'it wasn't your fault you were there. But you were, the more's the pity. It was my blame: I shouldn't have sent you. That house's not a place for a lass like you. But . . . I don't know . . . Jamesie and me had some sort of notion to have it out with Tot. After what happened Sat'day night.' Would you believe it, Nan'd told Gran, after making Jinnie swear not to, but Jinnie hadn't time to be indignant. 'Then last night Will looked another lad al-

134

together . . . and I've never interfered in Polly's carrying-ons before. So . . . well . . . at the last minute I jibbed and still hadn't brought meself to say owt when. . .' Gran stopped. But she hadn't finished. 'Well, I've had me say now . . . and I'm still not sure if I've done right.' She sighed. 'Dear knows how it'll all end. I thought finding a good lass might make Will stop tewing himself to pieces over his ma. But it looks like it's made him take against Polly worse than ever.'

Jinnie thought Gran was talking to herself now, but she wasn't. 'Ay, it's a pity you got mixed up in such a sorry mess, Jinnie lass . . . . Still, you had to find out sooner or later that there's badness in the world. And bad folk.'

Jinnie didn't interrupt, but she had known about Badness already, long ago, from Dad and Chapel. As for bad folk, The Street at home was full of them. Gran was right, in a way, though. Some kinds of Wickedness she didn't rightly understand, not even now. 'And things don't go away because you shut your eyes. More like they will if you look at them fair and square, in a sort of way.'

Silence came again, during which Vic gave up his grievance, crept out, forgave them both with a yawn that showed all his teeth, nearly all his gums and most of his tongue, then stretched out on the mat again. After a long pause, Gran spoke again:

'She's a bad woman, your Aunt Polly, Jinnie lass. No better than she ought to be.'

That queer saying. Jinnie'd heard it before. It must mean some Sin too awful to name. The Sin Against The Holy Ghost, maybe. Now she could find out what that was. Gran would tell her. If she asked. Jinnie let the moment go. Time enough later. Some day. But Gran had already begun to explain. And all the bits were coming together to show what Aunt Polly really was.

'. . . she's a bad wife and a bad mother. She was a bad un from the start. Before Davie married her. But he wouldn't be told. Had to stand by her, he said. And nobody even sure the bairn was his: not Polly herself, if truth's to be told. A sorry day it was for him . . . and all of us. Ah well, that's water under the bridge, lass. He does go to the pub too much now, I dare say. She had no call to say what she did about him, all the same. And I'm glad the lad stuck up for him. Most men get drunk from time to time, Jin, and aren't worse men because of it.' Jinnie could hardly believe she'd heard aright. She'd take care she never repeated such a notion to Dad. 'He can afford it, when all's said. He's got a good paid job. And

135

never misses a shift. Not that that'd make any difference, he's got an upstanding wage, and will have all through the strike. Not many in Coalgate can say that, Jinnie: not pitmen, anyroad. And he always fetches it home. There's many a woman'd thank Heaven fasting for a man like your Uncle Davie. Don't you think different, never mind what he said to you. If only she'd made a good home, he could've been . . . he *is* . . . a good man. The bairns could've been summat an' all, instead of just dragged up anyhow: left to hing as they grow.'

Jinnie had scarcely dared to breathe in case Gran stopped talking. But that old kettle had to go and interrupt. Although it had been moved nearly off the fire, it suddenly became insistent, rattled its lid imperatively, splashed water right down to the clean hearth and sent Vic skittering out of range, protesting. This time Gran gently lifted Jinnie from her knee. She took the kettle off the fire altogether and stood it on the bright brass trivet. She hadn't quite finished yet but the stopping note was in her voice.

'You know, Jin: it's a funny thing. There's something about her . . . in spite of it all, there's times I can't help but like your Aunt Polly.' Which was what Nan'd said. 'Now how d'you account for that, Jin?' But she didn't expect an answer, and Aunt Polly was a puzzle again. 'There's nowt as queer as folk, lass.' Gran's everyday voice returned. 'My,' she said, 'just look at that clock.' Jinnie didn't like clocks, they were always bringing good things to an end. 'I haven't got those shirts done for Liza yet, and it'll soon be time for our dinners.'

Jinnie discovered she was hungry.

'But first I'll put the rags in your hair,' said Gran, 'so then you can go and have a lie down straight after your dinner. You haven't forgot the Social, have you? Lasts till quarter to eleven, you know. You need to get your rest forward a bit.'

Jinnie had forgotten the Social. Gran was going to let her stay till the very end. Coalgate was Special, right enough.

136

Eighteen

Gran finished tying Jinnie's hair-ribbon. 'Now don't you go pingering,' she said: 'it's fine. Pop upstairs and have a look at yourself. And tell our Nan to get herself away from that looking-glass and come on down and let us have a look at her instead.'

Nan turned right round from the glass when she heard Jinnie's step.

'Well?' she said, a little anxiously.

Nan was beautiful, thought Jinnie all over again. Last time at Coalgate, she had been just plump, nice Nan. Now she was Special. Even Jinnie's eleven-year-old eyes saw that. Even Jinnie's jealous heart, beginning to be aware of her own self in a new way, and afraid she would never be so beautiful, admired Nan.

'You look nice as well, Jinnie,' said Nan, pleased, as if Jinnie had spoken. 'And your hair's lovely.'

Until that moment Jinnie had liked the ringlets and ribbons too. Now they seemed . . . childish . . . babyish. So did her velvet Sunday dress.

'Come here a sec, Jinnie,' said Nan.

She picked up a tiny book from the dressing-table and tore out a page. Before Jinnie knew what she was doing, Nan had dabbed and rubbed the paper right, left, on Jinnie's cheeks.

'There,' she said. 'How's that? Come and have a good look at yourself.'

Face powder it was. Girls who powdered their faces were Fast, Chapel said. Daft as well, because Natural looked best, Dad said: and in the end their skin was ruined. Nan was Fast and Jinnie's skin was ruined for ever. It felt stiff already. It smelt nice, though.

It looked all right as well. Jinnie studied herself anxiously. Not long ago she'd had no doubt at all that it was more important than anything in the world to get eight out of ten for Composition on Tuesday, no mistakes in Dictation on Friday and all sums right every morning. But she was the only one in Ex-Seven who cared about such things. The others bothered most about what their faces were like, and their hair; and dresses;

137

and lads. They talked about little else, and Jinnie, well naturally, she'd begun to wonder . . . occasionally at any rate. At Coalgate she'd been wondering more still.

She leant close to the mirror. Her hair was fair, but pale-fair. It waved, but didn't curl: her ringlets came from rags. Her eyes were blue; no, be honest: grey. Her eyebrows were black: and her eyelashes. Which was silly, and didn't match her hair. Of course she hadn't any spots and the pink powder, when you got used to it, made her skin look quite nice. All the same, she was disappointing. She would never compare with Nan. It came from not being a Dunham like Nan. Jinnie was a Friend. She looked like Dad. You couldn't say Dad was exactly good-looking. As for the Friend Aunts, they were downright ugly.

Oh well, she was brainy. Gran said so. And she felt brainy sometimes. Teachers didn't have to be beautiful. Being a Teacher was a good way off, though. Being beautiful might matter long before then. Worst thought of all, even a Teacher might want to be beautiful: might enjoy things more: like going to Socials. Maybe tonight's Social would be better, if Jinnie was beautiful. Lucky Nan. It wasn't Fair.

The Social had started to nag Jinnie, in another way, as soon as she had woken up from her rest. Gran had been calling it a Social. It was to raise money for poor Meg Riddell whose husband'd been killed down the pit, Gran said. The Hall was costing nothing. The Refreshments were being given. Tom Elliot and Nin Bell were the band for nothing. So it couldn't be Sinful: it must be A Social. A Band was a bit suspicious, though. Chapel Socials never had a band. And Betsey and Nan called it A Dance, and on Friday night it was real dances they'd been practising, not the Grand Old Duke of York. Real dances were a Sin. Besides, she didn't know how to do them.

Now, as if she hadn't enough to worry about, there was something else: another worry was added. Did she look All Right? It was no use asking Nan. She'd say Jinnie looked marvellous and Jinnie would have no idea whether to believe her or not.

She was still worrying as they made their way up St. Ives' Road, mostly about dancing now. She didn't know how to dance. She didn't want to dance. You had to have a partner, anyway. She hated partner games: if lads had to be the partners. And they would be, at a Social. She didn't know any lads at Coalgate, and dancing was wicked: and did she look all right? Her thoughts went round and round until she

138

couldn't keep them to herself any longer, not all of them.

Nan was sympathetic at first. Jinnie needn't worry. Anybody could see she was only eleven. Nobody would expect her to dance. Nobody would ask her to.

But what if somebody did?

'They won't,' said Nan. 'I'll tell them not to, if you like.'

'Will you know everybody there?' asked Jinnie.

'No, of course not,' said Nan.

'Well then,' said Jinnie.

'I'll ask our Will to tell them. He'll know a good lot,' said Nan.

'But he mightn't even be there,' said Jinnie.

'Oh for heaven's sake,' said Nan, exasperated. 'Don't be such a misery: you're as bad as your dad. And don't be so bloomin' conceited. Who's going to want to dance with a kid anyway?'

Poor Jinnie wasn't feeling conceited at all and Nan relented immediately.

'Look,' she said. 'All you have to do is to say — nicely mind — you're sorry, you can't dance and you're only watching and thank you very much all the same.'

Nan was making it all seem much easier than it was going to be but Jinnie knew she'd better not say any more. She would concentrate on the Refreshments. They'd be Special, even if Aunt Polly's cake had been ruined. Refreshments Ladies always did their best when they were baking for A Good Cause.

Neary there now, near enough for 'Baby Face', Bay . . . bee . . . Face, to be coming bouncing like mad, out of the door. A Dancing tune, no question about that. Oh well . . . she just wouldn't tell Dad, ever; and anyroad, she'd have seen real dancing: one better than Edie-at-Home and *she* was twelve. Make the best of things, Mam said. That was just what Jinnie would do.

At a table near the door a man was taking sixpences. When it was Jinnie's turn he gave her threepence change from a big white pudding basin full of coins. Because she was still a bairn, he said. Inevitably he turned out to be another of Mam's old acquaintances.

'So she's Kate's lass, is she? Right bonnie she is an' all,' he said in a voice that came extra loud because he didn't know that piano, drum and 'Baby Face' would crash abruptly to a stop a second before he said it.

Two girls who had paid just before Nan and Jinnie, looked over their shoulders to see who the bonnie lass was: and *if*

139

she was. Their expressions were noncommittal. So maybe the man didn't mean what he said: you never knew with Grown-Ups. Jinnie felt better, all the same.

It was reassuring too, to find that the Church Hall was so like the Chapel Schoolroom at home: the same kind of entrance passage and stairs, the very same brown lino runners with light brown and beige patterned borders, the same brown and beige paint everywhere, the same shaped light-shades. Surely nothing Sinful would be allowed to happen here.

Upstairs had the familiar Chapel smell:. bare wooden floor and dust in the cracks; tea-urns heating, and the Chapel rattle of cups and spoons; and women's voices high with busyness. Jinnie's spirits rose. It was just like a Sunday School party.

You'd never guess, either, that the lads clustering not far from the door inside the big room were pit lads and going on strike on Saturday to ruin The Country. In shy best navy serge or dashing grey Oxford bags they could have been the Senior Boys inspecting the Senior Girls as they arrived, and nudging comments with their elbows.

But where were the girls? Hurrying in Nan's wake past the inspection, Jinnie had an impression that apart from the lads the big room was pretty well empty. They weren't the first, were they, the very thing Nan had wanted to avoid? Of course not, they couldn't be. There'd been two girls ahead of them at the table downstairs and whole clusters of them in front of them in St. Ives' Road.

They weren't the first and there were plenty of girls.

The girls were here, right enough. In the cloakroom, of course. Millions of them, well dozens, at any rate. All shapes and sizes of girls. At the clothes-pegs near the door, round the wall, at the mirrors, on the benches. Standing up, sitting down, changing shoes, straightening stockings, combing hair, powdering noses, tugging petticoats, smoothing dresses. Giggling, laughing, screeching, whispering, talking, shouting. Watching, being watched: approvingly, critically, enviously.

The air was warm and heavy with girls and lavender and Ashes of Roses and Californian Poppy.

And it shall come to pass that instead of sweet smell, there shall be stink, and instead of well-set hair baldness: and burning instead of beauty.

Jinnie shuddered. No doubt about it, Chapel wouldn't approve of this lot. Then suddenly, inexplicably, Jinnie didn't care what Chapel would think. Tonight was Special.

'Let's have your coat, our Jin,' said Nan, calm amidst the

140

tumult. Poking about she found a free peg and hung up Jinnie's coat and her own. 'Fourth from the far end; remember, Jin.'

The place settled down. Instead of just girls, Jinnie saw Lily Palmer from Fish and Chips, Elsie Nattrass from across the way at Gran's, Nora and her older sister Lizzie, Ellen. All looking better than usual. And wasn't that the other one of the girls that Nan had been standing talking to at the bus stop on Friday evening? 'Hello, Gwennie,' said Nan. Gwennie Bell. Jinnie heard all about her. You could see now at a glance as you couldn't on Friday when she was in Tech. uniform that she was one of Coalgate's Toffs; that her father owned a pub and was rich. Her dress was real crêpe de Chine and that was a solid lace hankie she was tucking into a little handbag that looked as if it was made of thousands of rings of purest silver. Jinnie'd never seen anything like it.

No wonder Nan didn't care much for Gwennie, all golden hair, blue eyes and pink and white skin. Not that Nan need worry. She was just as good-looking, only dark and warm like butter whereas Gwennie was cool and glittery like icing-sugar.

Nan pushed her way towards the other end of the cloakroom and the mirror over the fire-place. Jinnie followed. And saw Betsey. Immediately everybody else, even crêpe de Chine Gwennie, looked old-fashioned or ... something. A real flapper again, was Betsey. Fast. Face done up like a dinner; lips as well, hair slicked down. As for her dress ... It wasn't decent that dress: no sleeves at all: bare arms, bare all the way to her shoulders. And short ...

In the mirror Betsey saw Nan.

'Hi, everybody,' she called loudly. 'Watch this.' She turned and faced the room.

Somehow she contrived to make enough space in the throng to whirl round and start jigging — a real shimmy dance. Her dress jumped up and down. You could see the tops of her stockings. And fancy garters: wide, satin, ruched, black, and a red rosette on each.

Betsey stopped, holding up her dress to keep the garters on view: and wasn't she enjoying the shrieks of shock around her. Then she caught sight of Nora and Lizzie, who were working their way towards Nan. Betsey hitched her dress higher still.

'Like them, Nora?' she asked. 'How d'they look?' So Saturday's battle was still on. And once again Betsey seemed to be meaning more than she was saying.

Nora looked, judiciously. 'They look grand, Betsey,' she

141

said. 'Just right,' and added, '. . . for you.' Her voice was as pale and neutral as her face. Her sister Lizzie laughed. 'Good for you, our kid,' she said.

Nan said hastily, 'Hurry up, our Jin, are you not ready yet?' She abandoned the looking-glass. 'Come on. We didn't pay good money to stay clockin' in here all night.'

Of all the cheek. Jinnie'd been ready the moment she took her coat off. The music had started again and was sounding more and more alluringly every time the door opened. The cloakroom had been getting hotter and hotter, and Jinnie had started sweating a bit and she was beginning to think the powder would work into her pores and ruin her skin if she didn't get out of this crowd soon. Nan had a cheek, all right. Meekly Jinnie followed her into the big room.

People were dancing now: if you could call it that. Two lonely couples were shuffling sedately around, leaving tracks on the dusty floor. The piano was soft. 'Charmaine' . . . 'Charmaine'. . . . it almost said the words . . . and the drum was gentle. But only the dancers seemed to care.

The benches nearest the cloakroom were obviously for girls. Not that anybody was sitting down, but that was where girls were standing, in twos and threes and fours, mostly with their backs to the lads as if they didn't know the lads were there. They did, though.

The lads had grown bolder and had advanced farther into the hall, but were still within safe distance of the door. They stood in a big, untidy group, talking and laughing less than the girls. They still watched the girls: assessing them all over again. They approved of Nan. One whistled: then another, and then all of them. It was Common. Jinnie blushed, although she knew the whistles weren't for her. But Nan, calm as if she went to a Social every night of the week, was ignoring the whistles and accepting them at the same time. She started talking to a girl Jinnie didn't know. Jinnie concentrated on the dancers. One of the couples . . . my goodness, now she had a good look, they were every bit as old as Dad and Mam, she thought indignantly. What were they doing at a Dance? Nan said they were Lily and Lijah who'd been courting so long folk said they never would get wed now. And would Jinnie keep her voice down a bit?

The music slithered to a halt. So did the dancers. They clapped politely and waited. The drummer banged another full stop on a funny squashed-coolie-hat thing. A man in a nice grey suit climbed on to the platform and started talking to the man at the piano. The dancers moved away to a row of

142

benches at right angles to the Girls. They stayed hand in hand. Courting Couples; Keeping Company officially. Jinnie lost interest in them.

While the music was having a rest, Jinnie took the chance to find out about the man in the nice suit. He was the Em See, Mr. Gibbs, Nan said. 'You know, him and Uncle Davie have the same jobs at The Pit.' Jinnie could hardly believe it. She watched Mr. Gibbs go to a Special table just below the platform and join a woman there. She would be Mrs. Gibbs and she was as unlike Aunt Polly as could be and the boy with them, in grey flannels and blue Tech. blazer, belonged to a different world from poor Will. No wonder Gran was sad about Uncle Dave and Aunt Polly.

Meanwhile: what was an Em See? But Nan was very busy, what with talking to Nora and Ellen, and ignoring the lads, and deliberately not seeing Betsey whose entrance was now causing as much stir as Nan's had. So Jinnie didn't dare to interrupt. She gazed around at the hall itself but it was so like the Schoolroom at Chapel, it wasn't worth a second look.

The piano player looked hot. He had swivelled his stool round now and was bending forward and talking from the platform to the Gibbses, and all the while was running a loosening finger round the inside of his stiff white collar. The drummer was taking no notice of anything but his drum.

And now here was Dottie coming in. Jinnie wasn't expecting to see her. Jamesie wasn't coming, so Dottie had no business to come either. She had brought something for the Refreshments Ladies, and was carrying it as if it was Princess Mary's wedding-cake. She would. Show-off.

Jinnie flinched, caught unawares by a new crash on the metal hat. The Piano Man had swivelled back to his piano. His hands were poised above the keys. The drummer's sticks waited stiffly above the drum, while the brass hat still quivered. The Em See was back on the platform. He spread his hands and called out, and his voice was as nice as his suit: 'Take your partners, gentleman, for the . . . Boston Two-Step.' He looked towards the group near the door. 'And come on, lads, there's no need to be so shy.' The Piano Man's hands crashed down. The drummer whipped his drum, slashed the brass thing once more and away went the music, not gentle and moonie like 'Charmaine' this time, but rattling, bouncing stuff that fairly galloped away.

The lads looked self-conscious but they made no move. The dancing-floor looked big and empty: and the girls laughed and talked more than ever. Unabashed, the hands at

143

the piano leapt up and down and the drumsticks kept pace.

At last, at the Keeping Company benches, a solemn young man and a blank-faced young woman stood up, and set off across the floor, not slithering this time, but twisting, whirling together, marching, kicking, with sober abandon. The Boston Two-Step wouldn't do anybody's ankles any good, thought Jinnie.

The old couple who ought to know better were next and the rest of the Courting Couples, more numerous now, followed quickly, one after the other.

Still the lads made no move: still the girls avoided looking at them. Jinnie was glad she was only eleven and could look wherever she liked. Betsey didn't mind looking at the lads. She was fixing her gaze, or so Jinnie thought, on a smart young man with black patent leather shoes and black patent leather hair. And Nora was looking, although with eyes quite different from Betsey's, towards the group near the door. At Will, of course: scrubbed and shining and unexpectedly normal again, with no sign of a sling or anything. Will detached himself from the other lads and came over, crimson-faced but determined, to Nora. Calmly Nora took his hand and they joined the dancers, Will stumbling a bit and Nora not minding and not even seeing Betsey and the patent-leather lad go proficiently past them: not seeing anything but Will.

Then Stan from Saturday came and touched Nan on the shoulder and jerked his head towards the dance. Jinnie didn't think much of that, but Nan smiled and away they went. Lizzie was next. Then Gwennie was chosen. Kev Bourke came for Ellen. The lads grew bolder, the floor more crowded and the dancers less conspicuous.

The girls still waiting grew pinker and gayer. Then one or two went back to the cloakroom.

Jinnie had worried in case she was asked to dance: now she saw it might be worse for a girl not to be asked. It was like being left over when Leaders were choosing teams for games at school. Jinnie knew how that felt. And this was worse, somehow.

It was all very well for the lads. If they weren't dancing, it was because they didn't want to. If a girl wasn't dancing, it was because she hadn't been Chosen. It wasn't Fair at all, this choosing business. And it was why girls bothered about how they looked, and dresses. It was a good thing after all that Socials were Sinful. She wouldn't be going to one ever again. She would never have to worry about being Chosen, as she

144

didn't have to worry now, because as Nan said, she was only a kid and nobody expected a kid to dance.

In the meantime, there was that Betsey, wiggling something scandalous. And not only it wasn't Right for Dottie to be here and dancing, it wasn't Fair, either, when she had a lad all to herself already. Jinnie gave herself up to the pleasures of disapproval, and of watching.

The evening settled down. The pattern had been established and went on repeating itself. Being Chosen: dancing: stopping: pause. Being Chosen: dancing: stopping: pause. Again and again and again. Before long, Nan and Nora and Ellen, and Lizzie and Gwennie and Betsey, and all the other girls who could count on being Chosen every time, sat down during the pauses and didn't turn their backs on the lads any more. The big room grew hot. The dust on the floor disappeared and turned into slipperiness as Nan had said it would. The slow music grew moonier and the slow dances more slithery. The fast music grew gayer, and the fast dances faster. They were best: gayer and gayer. Even Will and Nora twirled a bit at corners and Jinnie's feet would have twitched if she'd let them. But she didn't in case somebody thought she wanted to be Chosen even though she was just eleven.

The Em See called for a foxtrot again. The Band began 'Sittin' on top of the World'. Will came straight for Nora. Kev Bourke made towards them as well. He seemed to like Ellen a lot, he chose her nearly every time. All the lads liked Nan. Who would come for her this time?

'May I have the pleasure of this dance?' said a polite voice from the side Jinnie wasn't watching. She nearly jumped out of her skin. It was the boy with the Tech. tie, the Gibbs's boy, and he was Choosing her. Dumbly she looked at him, then in appeal to Nan, and she felt her face going red. Nan smiled pleasantly and explained that Jinnie hadn't learnt to dance yet, otherwise she'd have been glad to dance with him.

'But how about asking me, Dick?' Nan added. 'You don't mind, do you?' she said to the patent-leather lad who appeared at that same moment and who clearly did mind.

Jinnie's eyes followed them. She was too embarrassed to look anywhere else. They were getting on well together, neither of them in the least put out that Nan was inches taller than Dick. Dick Gibbs was dancing properly, not just shuffling and hitching. 'I'm quittin' the blues of . . . the world . . .' sang the piano and really meant it. Jinnie began to feel disappointed. If only she'd had the sense to say she couldn't but she'd like to try. Still, she'd been Chosen. And

145

not by just anybody, but by Dick Gibbs who was a Cut Above everybody else. Several Cuts. Maybe she'd be Pretty yet. She must look All Right now.

Then Dottie's sister Annie and the young pitman she'd wed at Easter came and sat beside her. For a bit of a crack, they said. Matt said he wasn't much of a hand at the dancing but he liked the Band. Talking to them was easy.

They stayed on. A family group formed and Dottie came to it during the pauses. Nothing would get Jamesie to a dance, but he didn't want to stop her when she liked dancing, she said. 'And he knows I'm never short of a partner,' she added, smugly. It was true, though, and you could see she was a good dancer.

Then Uncle Davie's Joe arrived with Eva. 'Just for a little spell,' said Joe. Eva didn't like leaving the baby.

'The bairn's all right, you know. Fast asleep, most like. And her Ma sittin' in with him. But our Evie thinks he needs his own Ma. Includin' when his eyes is shut. We're not even stoppin' till Refreshments. Doesn't care if her man goes without grub as long as the bairn's all right. Women!' Joe pulled a face but you could see he was bursting with pride.

'Hark at him, will you?' said Evie. 'And him the one that's pleased when the bairn cries so's he can pick him up and nurse him. In the middle of the night, an' all. Did you ever hear of anybody so daft?'

They smiled at each other; not shy now, as they'd been with Mam and Dad yesterday. They didn't dance at all and did stay only a few minutes. It was a mystery why they'd bothered to get dressed up and come at all.

Anybody was sitting anywhere now. Nan's group had grown into the biggest at the dance and had spread from the Girls' benches round to what had originally been the Couples' side of the room. Now it included Grown-Ups, Dottie, Annie and Matt; Ellen's brother Richie, his girl Madge, and a bushy-haired man who seemed to be a friend of theirs. Will stayed with Nora all the time now, and Kev Bourke with Ellen. You couldn't have had a nicer group and in spite of all-dancing-and-no-games, Jinnie had forgotten all about Sin.

Then a parson came in. He'd be Church of England, of course, but he looked just like a Chapel minister. He had the same effect on folk as well. Lowered voices and awkwardness followed him like a ship's wake. Even the band felt obliged to come to a halt in the middle of their tune. Only the tea-urns took no notice of him. In the spreading quiet you could hear them gurgle and hiss, going full steam ahead for half-time and

146

Refreshments. The Vicar nodded and smiled at everybody, had a word with the band, then with the Refreshments Ladies, who were as shy and pleased as the Chapel Tea Committee would have been. He shook hands with the Em See and Mrs. Gibbs and Dick, who took the honour with conspicuous calmness, then he waved to the band and the dancers to carry on, sat down with the Gibbses and started talking not like a Somebody but just like an ordinary, real-life man.

Jinnie knew at last, once and for all, it really was All Right. She relaxed. It had been the truth that Dad'd been told. She ought to have known Gran didn't tell lies, not even to Dad. This *was* a Social: a Church Social. Maybe Dick Gibbs would Choose her again and show her how to dance. Tonight was Special without a doubt: as good as The Pictures. Touch wood. Cross your fingers. Don't think such thoughts or things'll go wrong.

And of course they did.

147

Nineteen

It was that Betsey's fault, as you might've expected. She hadn't said a word to any of them since the cloakroom. All the same, she'd never been far away at sitting-down times, near enough to hear what they were saying if she wanted to. And at Refreshments, it so happened that she settled next to them with Elsie Nattrass and the two lads who'd Chosen them. Would you believe it, you had to be Chosen even for Refreshments, or else go in disgrace to collect your own. Will and Kev and Matt had pulled benches round and made a big Family square, which was near the Em See's table and opposite the door. If, like Jinnie, you were facing the right way, you could survey pretty well the whole room.

They had finished their Refreshments and were laughing and funning a lot. Except Jinnie. She didn't believe in hurrying over food as good as this. The plate that Matt had brought for her couldn't have been better if she'd chosen it herself. The paste in the sandwiches had been meat, not fish. The scones had been thick with butter and full of neat, sweet little currants, not big, slippery sultanas to set her teeth on edge. The tart had been lemon-curd and perfect, sweet and sharp, soft and crusty crisp, all at the same time. Arranged on her plate in ascending order still remained a pink coconut snowball, a thick slice of chocolate roll and, best and last, a cream puff, which had been Annie's but by an unbelievable stroke of luck Annie couldn't eat another bite and had just put the puff on Jinnie's plate.

So Jinnie wasn't listening very hard. She was aware only that a lot of noise was going on and that it was Will who was in the middle of it, handsome and happy, and telling one joke after another in a very un-Will-like way. Maybe Will was going to be All Right, after all.

Hunching her shoulders in concentration Jinnie slowly sank her teeth into the prickly pink coconut, catching in her left hand the bits that fell. The coconut gritted noisily inside her head but she still heard Dorothy laugh extra loudly, then say, 'Oh go on, our Will.' Dottie wasn't in the Family yet: she had no business to call him Our Will. 'You pinched that un

148

from Jamesie.'

'Nay,' said Will promptly, 'Jamesie got it off me, more like.'

More screeches of laughter. It was funny the things Grown-Ups laughed at.

'Now who's for another cuppa? Come on, lads. Might as well do the job properly and get the seconds.'

They all laughed again. This time Jinnie did know why. Anything connected with eating and drinking, except beer, was women's work. Will and Kev and the other men went off to the Refreshments. Jinnie concentrated once more on the snowball. Not only the coconut but the creamy stuff inside was pink. Interesting: she'd only had white before. It tasted of raspberries. Pity she hadn't kept it until after the choco-late slice. Perhaps she could, still. No, that wouldn't be Manners now she'd had a bite out of it. Regretfully she took another mouthful.

Then a voice came through the coconut: and a laugh. Aunt Polly's. Funny how you always heard Aunt Polly. Over the top of the snowball she watched Aunt Polly going towards the Gibbses, or maybe the Refreshments. Tot was with her. Gran's word with Tot hadn't done any good. Jinnie's heart sank. Aunt-Polly-with-Tot was what upset Will and made Gran sad: and sent Uncle Davie to the pub. It made Aunt Polly a bad wife and a bad mother. Jinnie still didn't under-stand how, not exactly. Of course, if Aunt Polly stayed at home she could be mending socks, or keeping the house nice, or something.

Jinnie lowered the pink snowball and waited. She wasn't the only one who'd heard and was waiting, either.

'Well, ta, Daisy. Just a cup of tea, though. We're not stoppin',' said Aunt Polly to the Refreshments Ladies. 'Just dropped in for a minute to see how you're gettin' on without uz.' She laughed. Aunt Polly was always laughing. When she wasn't shouting in a rage.

'Thought I'd fetch a couple of spot prizes, Dick,' she said to Mr. Gibbs and Mrs. Gibbs, and to the whole room if they cared to listen. She handed over a big white paper bag. 'Seein' as you didn't get the cake I promised.'

Jinnie wished Aunt Polly hadn't mentioned the cake. She saw Nora's face. Nora knew. Nora's back was to Aunt Polly. She didn't turn to look at her: it was the Refreshments table Nora was watching, where Will would be.

'Thank you, Polly,' said Mr. Gibbs, 'they'll be very acceptable.' His voice was cool in spite of the 'Polly'.

149

A Refreshments Lady was going towards Aunt Polly, with two cups of tea. Aunt Polly moved to meet her.

'Why, there you are, our Will. I wondered where you'd got to. I saw our Nan and Dottie right away,' she said. 'And Nora,' she added meaningly. Was she making friends with Will, after this morning, or . . .? She must be. You should watch that imagination of yours, Our Jin, Mam said, or one of these days it'll run clean away with you. It was running away with Jinnie now, but in circles, getting her nowhere. Will's face was like a thundercloud. Aunt Polly took no notice. 'Off you go then, Will. Take your cups of tea to the lasses before it gets cold. Ta, Daisy.' Aunt Polly had finished with Will. She took a cup from the Refreshments Lady. 'And there's yours, Tot. You know, Dick, we might stay on a bit after all.' She seemed to be going to accept the chair young Dick Gibbs had politely vacated for her. 'Might even have a go: if you'll put on that Charleston. What'd'you say, Tot?' In spite of her teacup, she managed to do something very like a shimmy dance. Aunt Polly was really enjoying herself and her big gold ear-rings swung and bounced. Tot didn't reply. He was drinking his tea. He didn't look as if he was enjoying himself very much, though.

By now, the parson was raising his eyebrows and looking a question at the Em See and Aunt Polly. Aunt Polly, of course, knew who he was. Everybody in Coalgate knew, by sight at least, all the posh people: the four parsons, the three priests, the three doctors, the pit manager, the Co-op manager, the shopkeepers on Front Street, the pub owners and the school teachers.

'And mebbe the Reverend'll have a turn with uz.' Mrs. Gibbs looked shocked and Aunt Polly laughed again. The parson looked surprised: as if he didn't know what to say. He wouldn't meet anybody like Aunt Polly every day: or every year. Then he said something to Mr. Gibbs, and Mr. Gibbs said something back to him and then to Aunt Polly.

'Pleased to meet you, Mr. Chudleigh,' said Aunt Polly, holding out her free hand. 'I've heard a lot about you.' As if she was sharing a pleasant secret with the parson. It was a way she had. The parson shook Aunt Polly's hand. Then he held out his hand to Tot. Again Jinnie didn't catch what he said.

'Nay, this's not Mr. Dunham,' said Aunt Polly, cool as you please. 'This's Mr. Bourke. Just a friend of mine. Not one of yours, Reverend, one of theirs. You know — a holy Roman.'

The parson looked very uncomfortable now. His hand

150

wavered a little, but remained held out. Awkwardly Tot shook it. The Gibbses were embarrassed as well. Not Aunt Polly. Elegantly crooking her fingers, she sipped her tea, then put the cup down on the Gibbses' table. The parson sat back in his chair. Aunt Polly began to untie her extravagant fox-fur. Will started to move away from the Refreshments with his teacups. Then:

Somebody giggled. Jinnie didn't have to look to know who it was. A sly giggle. Snigger might be a better word for it. It was like that Maggie-Wilson-at-school's and nasty as a swear-word. It changed everybody, even Mr. Chudleigh. As for Will, he was like this morning again. Jinnie heard her teeth grit on a bit of coconut. There was going to be another Carry On. Like this morning's, but in front of dozens of folk this time. At a Church Social. The disgrace. What if Will threw those cups of tea at Aunt Polly? He looked savage enough. But it was Aunt Polly that went mad and threw things . . .

But Aunt Polly didn't bat an eyelid. At least, she did, but that was all. Her eyelids dropped for a second: only a second. And all she did was to run her fingers lovingly over her rich fur and then hand it to Tot.

'Put it down somewhere for uz, will you, Tot lad? And

151

you know, Daisy, I think I'll have another cup of tea after all. And then I'll have a word with some of the young uns. Don't they look lovely, bless them?'

Aunt Polly looked round the room. She let her eyes rest, for the first time, on Betsey. Who had giggled.

'Why, there's Betsey.' Aunt Polly waved across the room. Queen Mary herself couldn't have done it better. Aunt Polly raised her voice. Not that she needed to, the room wasn't all that big and everybody was listening. Folk always did, to Aunt Polly. 'And how's your ma, Betsey? She looked real poorly last time I saw her. Now when would that be? Let's see —' Aunt Polly paused, enjoying every moment — 'Friday, was it? Ay, it would be. Pay Day. That's right. Comin' out of Kidd's, she was. Had she been for that frock of yours, Betsey? Anyroad, it's real smart and you look champion, lass.'

Even Jinnie had heard of Kidd's. It was Coalgate's biggest pawn-shop. She knew about pawn-shops. A godsend to many a poor soul in hard times, Mam said. An encouragement to fecklessness, Dad said. But whatever you thought about them, if you knew somebody who went to them, you must never let on. Besides, pawning things might be all right, but pawning clothes was terrible. Even Poor Liza wouldn't pawn a dress of Betsey's.

Aunt Polly's insult was so enormous and so public Betsey was dumb and could only stare in fury. Maybe she regretted the giggle now. Serve her right.

'Mind you tell Liza I was askin' after her. Don't forget now, Betsey.' Aunt Polly took a sip from her fresh cup of tea and nodded agreeably over the rim at Betsey. It felt to Jinnie as if everybody was looking at Aunt Polly: they probably were, and Aunt Polly was loving it. She put her cup back in its saucer.

'You brew a real nice cup of tea, Daisy,' she said to the Refreshments Lady. Then she shook her sleeve away from her wrist so that she could look at her watch: gold, of course. 'My, my,' she said. 'Nine already. I don't think we can stay after all.'

'Not if you're going to the Colliery Engine.' Betsey found her voice, at last.

But the Colliery Engine wasn't much of a reply to Kidd's. Aunt Polly had won and Betsey knew it.

'Ta-ra well, Reverend,' said Aunt Polly, as if Betsey hadn't spoken, 'Dick, Emily.' Then she looked at Will, who was standing like a stone, smiled past him to Nan and Dottie and

152

the rest of them, and hypnotized, they smiled back. 'Enjoy yourselves, the lot of yuz,' she said. 'And if you can't be good, be careful.' For the last time her laugh came across the room, loud, warm and Common as always. Nothing Common, though, about the way she looked around and waved: Queen Mary all over again. She departed, followed by Tot, Aunt Polly's long fat fur still dangling foolishly over his arm.

For a second or two there was silence; then voices rushed into the vacuum Aunt Polly had left.

'Well,' said Dottie, first in the Family group to speak, 'isn't she the bloomin' limit?' Dottie was enjoying herself as much as Aunt Polly had been. 'Mind you, I don't know what poor Will gets hisself so upset for. He wants to take no notice. Nobody thinks the worse of him for Polly's goings-on. You want to tell him, Nora. As for that Betsey . . .' She raised her voice for Betsey to hear, but Betsey wasn't scared of Dottie, you could see. Then Dottie's gentle sister Annie, who had hardly said a word but had sat in quiet happiness hand in hand with Matt all evening, surprised them. 'Nay, Dottie,' she said, 'least said soonest mended. Leave the lad be: leave things be.' She looked startled at her own boldness and Matt patted her hand lovingly.

'Yes, you keep out of it, Dottie, will you?' said Nan. 'And say nothing when Will gets back,' for Will was taking a terribly long time to bring the tea.

'Well,' said Dottie. She retreated into a huff, but nobody took any notice.

'Come on, Nora,' said Nan. 'Let's go and help him and Kev with the tea.'

But by now Will was at the outside of the Family square, with the green-rimmed teacups that in some unreasonable way were becoming part of the trouble. The colour was back in his face. So was the sullenness that spoilt his good looks. He put the cups down carelessly. The tea that had already spilt into the saucers slopped on to the bench.

'What about a beer, Kev? Stan?' he said, not looking at Nora. Nobody was looking at Nora. Except Jinnie who just couldn't help it. 'Some of the lads's gone to the Fighting Cocks. I could do with a real drink meself. Not this woman's —' Jinnie drew her breath at the forbidden word spoken so defiantly, and in a Church Hall at that. Will was saying a lot more than a swear-word. He was saying that he hated his mother and that he hated Nora as well, maybe especially Nora at this moment. But what had Nora done? Jinnie was

153

getting fed-up with Will.

'Don't be daft, Will man,' said Kev in a light, coaxing voice. 'There's not time. The band'll be back any minute and the dancin'll be starting again.'

'Who cares?' said Will. 'I've had enough of — dancin'. I've had enough of this — Sunday School altogether.' The swear-words were fairly rolling out now. 'Well, how way, are you comin', Kev Bourke, or are you not? Make your mind up.'

'No,' said Kev. Then he tried to soften his refusal with a joke. 'I've paid me ticket, lad; might as well get me money's worth. Me and Ellen's goin' to win the spot prizes.' He couldn't have picked a worse subject to joke about and his face knew it.

'To hell with the spot prizes. And with you: the lot of yuz,' said Will savagely. 'I'll go by meself then.'

They watched Will's back push through the noisy group re-forming near the door. Betsey watched as well, pleased with herself once more.

'Pity about him,' said Dottie. 'Who does he think he is? What kind of folk did he think he was talking to? If Jamesie'd been here . . .'

Nan pushed aside Dottie's smug outrage.

'Nora . . .? D'you think . . .?'

'No,' said Nora in a flat, dead tone.

There's nowt as queer as folk, Mam said. It was true and Jinnie would never understand them. Never. Take Will and Nora. On Saturday when Will had rushed away, Nora had gone after him. Now she wouldn't. On Sunday and tonight, she'd been his girl and they'd both been happy. Now she didn't want to be and they were both miserable. That . . . that . . . Betsey with her sly triumphant face: she'd won, after all. But *what* had she won? She'd done something, to Will, but what, exactly? Come to that, what had she done to Aunt Polly? And what was Aunt-Polly-with-Tot all about? Really?

Jinnie had a lot to puzzle out. But not now. She bit again into the snowball. The coconut was very hard: it didn't go down easily. She heard herself swallow.

'You've got coconut on your nose, our Jin,' said Nan reproachfully. As if it was a crime.

And they all started talking again.

154

Twenty

Funnily enough, Will's departure made everybody more cheerful, not less. Even Nora laughed a lot. And for Jinnie the second half of the Social turned out to be even better than the first. She learnt to dance.

It began with Ellen not being Chosen. Not that this was shameful for Ellen. Kev had Chosen her so often it was beginning to look Serious. And now he wasn't dancing with another lass exactly, but with Nora.

'Like to have a go, Jin? Come on, I'll show you,' said Ellen. 'You'll soon get the hang of it. The foxtrot's easy.'

Jinnie herself had been thinking it might be. All you had to do was slither in time with the music and shuffle or hitch round the corners.

It wasn't as easy as she had expected, though. The floor had bumps in it. Walking backwards was nerve-wracking. Jinnie wanted to go her own way but Ellen said she must let herself be steered. Still, Ellen was patient. She only laughed when they had a collision or when Jinnie's feet got in the way. Jinnie's heart stopped thumping. When the music ceased she clapped like mad for an encore.

The next time a foxtrot was announced, without realizing, she glanced at the Em See's table. Dick Gibbs, young Dick, was looking at her. Hastily she looked away but not before she saw him stand up.

'Would you show me the foxtrot again, Ellen?' she said, very fast.

'Why yes, of course, Jin,' said Ellen, 'in a minute, when there's a few more on the floor.'

Dick Gibbs was coming towards them, but Jinnie couldn't say anything to Ellen: it would sound conceited. Anyway, he'd be coming for Nan. She tried not to see him. Calmly crossing the middle of the floor he was, not even going round the edge. Then that Keith Robson, the patent-leather lad, came and blocked the view. He made his smooth little bow. To Ellen. Thinks he's Rudolf Valentino, thought Jinnie spitefully, in the direction of his shining black hair. Without a word to Jinnie, Ellen stood up, and slid treacherously away.

155

And here, now, was Dick Gibbs, bowing politely: to her: Jinnie. 'You can do this one,' he said. 'I saw you,' and held out his hand. Jinnie felt terrible. She looked at Nan, just about to dance with Kev.

'That's right, Jin,' she said. 'Have a go. Dick won't eat you,' and she sailed away.

'Go on. Got to learn some time,' said Dottie, as she got up to dance. By now Dottie was firmly established in Jinnie's mind as someone who was always putting her shovel in where there was no muck, as Mam said. Even Annie smiled and nodded encouragingly. They were all against her. She durstn't say no. She stood up.

'I can't: honestly I can't,' she said and discovered her hands had turned hot and sweaty, which made matters worse.

'I bet you can,' he said and put an arm on her waist. She could feel its warmth. It'll leave a mark on the velvet, she thought miserably. What would Mam say? And what would she say to Mam? 'Anyway, I'll show you,' he said kindly. 'Now start off with your right foot.'

Jinnie found she had been balanced to start with her left. Dick trod on her toes. Jinnie apologized.

'Never, mind, you couldn't help it,' he said. It was Jinnie's toes that had been trodden on, mind you. 'Let's try again.'

This time they started without mishap. All she had to do now was to walk, backwards of course, to the far end of the room. She refused to think about getting round the corner. Suddenly her knees were all wrong. They kept on getting in the way. She couldn't bend them backwards. What on earth was she supposed to do with them? She couldn't get the right balance and slither into her feet either. It had been a lot easier with Ellen. She thought about the end of the room and turning the corner. Serve her right for coming to a Dance.

However, the corners were no problem after all because Dick took her round the room in an oval instead of a square. Then her feet caught the rhythm of the drum: at last. She still had to cling desperately to it, though, and Dick's polite conversation kept on threatening to shut it out. Mr. Dunham was her uncle, was he? Where did she live? What standard was she in at school? On and on, and Jinnie hardly knew what she answered and longed for the music to stop and the ordeal to end.

Yet when she was safely back in her seat beside Nan, she was sorry. She had hated it. She had loved it. It had been

156

Special. Just how Special she didn't want anyone to know.

'What did you make me dance for, our Nan,' she said, 'when you knew I didn't want to?' Jinnie tried to sound aggrieved.

'I couldn't let you refuse when you'd been on the floor already, with Ellen. Where's your manners, our Jin?'

'What's manners got to do with it?' said Jinnie. 'I'd've said no, politely.'

'It'd've been bad manners all the same,' said Nan.

'But how?' said Jinnie, becoming interested.

'Oh . . . I don't know,' said Nan, starting to lose patience. 'It'd make a lad look daft, I suppose. Anyroad, it would be: I've told you.'

'But that's not Fair,' said Jinnie indignantly. 'It's just not Fair. A girl can't ask, but . . .'

'Oh shut up, Jin,' said Nan. 'You don't know what you're on about.'

'But . . .'

'Go on,' said Dottie. 'I bet you enjoyed it really. Look: she's blushin'.'

Jinnie hadn't been. Now she was.

157

'Aa... haa,' said Dottie, wagging a finger. Jinnie could've bitten it.

Only just in time she remembered Mam's instructions. No Arguing, no Answering Back, our Jin: just you be a good lass. Jinnie said nothing. She gave Dottie a Look. Mind you, Jin's Look was worse than words sometimes, Mam said, so she oughtn't to have Looked either. She wasn't sorry, though.

The Parson was the first to leave, shaking hands, nodding, smiling. Then Matt and Annie thought it was time they were getting off home. Matt found a threepenny-bit in his pocket, gave it to Jinnie, said threateningly it was to spend, mind, not to put in her money-box. And they left. Quarter past ten.

The Dance was ebbing away fast now: like the tide at Tynemouth. You didn't notice at first then suddenly it was out. Jinnie hadn't seen many people go, but the hall was distinctly emptier.

Suddenly that Betsey was up on the platform, and a tall lad she'd been dancing with a lot. She was talking, goo-goo-eyed, to the Band. The Man at the Piano leant forward, saying something to the Em See. Betsey joined in, goo-goo-eyes all for the Em See now. At last, the Em See laughed, shook his head, shrugged all at the same time. Then he called out, 'Gentlemen... for the first-and-only-time-tonight, take your partners for the... Charleston.' He was saying some more but was drowned in a burst of applause.

Folks didn't take partners, though. Without anybody arranging it, they stood, and Jinnie found herself among them, in a circle and watched Betsey dance. If it was dancing. But if it wasn't — what else could it be? Strings of sound from piano and drum pulled, jolted, jarred, swivelled Betsey's head, arms, legs, knees, ankles and they all twisted and jerked independently. It was a miracle her joints held, but they did. Her shining shoes pounded, scraped, shuffled, slithered. Her flesh bounced. Her hair swung. Her beads jiggled. Her bangles clashed and rattled. Her dress swished and swayed and hid and showed, showed and hid those Sinful fancy garters.

Mam wouldn't like this lot, never mind Dad. Thank goodness he need never know. Betsey wasn't like a Church Social. Betsey was a Scarlet Woman. From the jungle. Well, at least Betsey would pay for it. Her ankles would thicken one and a half inches in a fortnight. That's what Chapel said. And the *North Mail*. She'd get water on the knees as well. Serve her right. There she was, eyes nearly shut, pretending to be concentrating, pretending not to know everybody was watching her. Because they were. Her partner was solemnly

158

shuffling, working his elbows, like running on the spot in drill at school. He'd go mad eventually, but nobody cared about him. It was all Betsey.

Betsey ran out of breath at last. She opened her eyes wide, stamped her feet to a stop, flung up her arms like a preacher and smiled an unpreacher smile. Who did she think she was? Everybody clapped, though. Like mad. The Em See, the piano man, the drummer, Nan, Dottie and to her own surprise, Jinnie.

'Come on lads,' cried the Em See. 'You've seen how it's done. Now's your chance.'

Quickly the floor filled up with folk, laughing and jerking and why they didn't kick one another was a mystery. Of course, when you looked properly, they weren't all going on like Betsey. Gwennie's garters were only pale pink, and Nan and Stan and Ellen and Kev, all the Family in fact, were quite respectable. Even Dottie's dress didn't bounce much. Maybe the Charleston was wicked only when folk like Betsey did it. Jinnie was beginning to realize that Sin wasn't as simple as she used to think. But she was relieved on the whole that Dick Gibbs didn't come for her and joggled sensibly round with his mother instead.

159

In a way the Charleston ended The Dance. After it, everything began to droop. Even the foxtrots were slower now. Not that clock, of course: it had been going faster, in the way clocks had.

'My,' said Dottie, 'twenty to eleven. Jamesie'll be here any minute. I'd best get my things before the rush starts. Don't want to keep him waiting and mebbe miss a shift. Not now.' Dottie was always letting you know one way or another that she and Jamesie were getting wed soon.

Other girls, also, began to emerge from the cloakroom, in coats and hats. And just as Dottie reappeared, the Em See called the last dance.

'Aa . . . haa,' said Dottie, back in the group. 'There's Dick Gibbs's lad looking your way, Jin. Shouldn't wonder but what he'll ask to take you home.'

'But what for?' said Jinnie, unthinkingly. 'I'm going home with our Nan, aren't I?' Then remembered. Taking Home meant Something Special.

'Oh, go on,' said Dottie. She screeched with laughter as loud as Aunt Polly's and not as nice.

Nan and Ellen and the rest smiled as well. Jinnie felt her face go red, and when Dick did come and Choose her, she felt stiff and awkward all over again: terrified he might be going to ask to Take her Home. And wondering, was this something else it wouldn't be Manners to say no to?

However, at the end, after they'd stood straight and silent for The King, all that happened was that Dick walked with her to her place for the last time and said, 'Thank you, Jinnie. I'm glad you came tonight. And I hope you win the Scholarship. I bet you will.'

Without doubt he was nice and a Cut Above everybody else. In a rush of gratitude and pride, Jinnie said, 'Thank you, Dick. For showing uz the foxtrot . . . and the waltz . . . and everything. And I hope you get to the . . . University . . . as well.' She hoped she'd managed the word properly: she'd heard it for the first time tonight.

'Thanks, Jinnie,' he said. 'Good-night.' He gave her a polite little bow, as well as a friendly smile, and returned to his parents leaving Jinnie feeling that this was perhaps the best moment of the whole wonderful evening.

Jamesie had arrived during the last dance. He was standing beside Dottie, all dressed up in Sunday clothes. Just to take Dottie home, half a street away, no more. And he'd have to change into his pit clothes in scarcely more than half an hour. He was red-faced and smelt of fresh air. He was twirling his

160

best cap as if he didn't know what to do with it, and looked shy. Goodness only knew why since he knew everybody in the group and probably most of the folk in the room.

Dottie wasn't shy. Nobody could get a word in edgeways for her chattering, and she was clinging to Jamesie as if she owned him. She was pretty, though, pinker and prettier than ever. That must be why Jamesie liked her and watched her all the time, and didn't mind the way she talked.

For all her clinging and chattering, she'd seen Dick's bow.

'Did you see that, then? Aren't we posh?' she said. 'Our Jinnie's clicked, Jamesie. Young Dick Gibbs, no less. Danced together all night they have.' She seemed to think Jinnie would be pleased. It wasn't even true.

'Nay,' said Jamesie, 'leave the lass be. She's nowt but a bairn. Dick an' all.'

Nan said, 'What's it like out, Jamesie? You look nethered.'

'I am,' he said. 'It's cold out. Bloody cold,' he added.

'Oh, Jamesie Dunham,' said Dottie, as if she'd never heard anybody swear before. 'Think on where you are. Time I took you off before you say worse.'

The others laughed. It hadn't taken much to make them laugh all evening, especially Nora. Jamesie became less shy.

'By the way,' he said, 'there's been a murder. So I heard tell.'

'Fancy not lettin' on about it till this minute, Jamesie Dunham,' said Dottie indignantly. And instantly everybody was asking questions.

A woman. On Robson's Field. Jinnie remembered it: they'd passed it on Saturday: a piece of waste ground between Consett and Coalgate, but nearer Coalgate. It must have been part of a farm once. Now it was pitted with subsidence, not safe for cattle to graze and fit only for gorse bushes, and coarse grass and weeds. From the road you could see a little row of deserted cottages, all ancient flaking whitewash, broken slates, sagging rafters, dead windows and doorways full of nettles.

The very place for a murder.

You'd have thought Jamesie'd shouted, the way other folk came crowding round. And it was funny how the murder relit the fag end of the evening. Who was it? Was she young? From Consett? Or Coalgate?

'Nay, what way would I know?' said Jamesie. 'I only heard about it from Arnie Foster off the last bus from Consett.' He couldn't say how Arnie knew, he hadn't had time to stop and talk. Nor how the woman'd been found: by a courting

161

couple, most like. Nor how she'd been killed. Nor if they'd got anybody for it: hardly likely yet, though.

'In fact, you know nowt about it,' said Dottie.

'That's what I've kept tellin' the lot of yuz all along,' said Jamesie; 'and isn't it about time we were all thinkin' about home?'

'All right,' said Dottie. She buttoned her coat, pulled her hat still further down so that you wondered how she could see. There was something Betsey-ish about that hat and about Dottie altogether. She took Jamesie's arm again. 'Now mind you two go straight home,' she said to Nan.

'Well, I was just wonderin',' said Jamesie, 'if the lasses might not come with uz, or mebbe stay here a few minutes and I'll come back and fetch them.'

'Don't be daft,' said Dottie sharply. 'You really might miss the shift then. Anyroad, there's a whole crowd of them'll be going home altogether.'

'Yes, but . . .' Jamesie was still a bit doubtful.

'Nay, Jamesie,' said Dottie, 'you want to stop readin' *The News of the World*, lad. Goin' on as if Jack the Ripper was back. In Coalgate. Who'd bother with bits of lasses, anyroad? It's the sort that's no better than the' should be that gets themselves murdered.'

'Why, Dottie, we don't know owt about the poor soul.'

'Anyroad, they all can go home together: the lads'll go with them,' said Dottie.

'All the same . . .' said Jamesie.

But the girls protested they weren't scared. The lads swore that they'd take them all to their very doors. Jamesie and Dottie departed.

The excitement died down. Nan and the rest were subdued or maybe just tired now. But Mr. Gibbs was standing at the door and making up groups, seeing that no one went home alone, so he was taking it seriously, like Jamesie.

The darkness outside was blinding for a moment. Then sky and earth moved apart and you wondered, as you always did, why it had been so black to begin with because now the sky was quite light, layered with soapsud clouds ranging from dark grey to patchy silver where the moon must be. Roofs made lines against the sky. Then it was another puzzle that although the sky was light, you couldn't see the houses, you just knew they were there, under the roofs. And you couldn't see the voices that were going down the hill. You couldn't see the street lamps either, only diagrams of yellow resting on the dark that were repeated and simplified at diminishing

162

intervals down the hill.

'Hang on to me, Jin,' said Nan through the dark. 'Ooh, it's cold. What say we all link home and keep warm?'

Because she was the smallest, they put Jinnie in the middle between Kev and Nan. Then somebody slipped off the pavement, so they made a chain across the road. And they'd be out of other folks' way as well.

'Let's run,' said Kev.

'Wait on a sec,' said Ellen.

'Right foot first,' said Nan.

Feet shuffled. Then, Ready, Steady, Off, they raced down the hill, so fast that in the end Kev and Nan swept Jinnie off her feet and carried her along.

At the bottom of the hill, somebody called a stop. They slowed down, bumped into one another and the chain broke. Everybody was breathless, and cheerful again. The Murder wasn't frightening any more. It was just the Special end to a Special evening.

The pubs were dark and silent. McElwain's hadn't been long shut, though, because the fanlight above his door was bright. In Gran's street, two or three blinds had lights behind them, but Gran's house was dark. Nan and Jinnie whispered good-night to Kev and Nora, who were the last of the group, and went in very quietly.

Vic greeted them with a half-bark then settled down again. Snores from the recess indicated that Uncle Bob was in bed. On the mantelpiece the clock panted and clicked ten times louder than during the day. The fire had been damped down for the night and was just an invisible smell of smoke. The only light came from the street lamp. It lay across part of the table beside the window and you could see Jamesie's water bottle and bait tin.

Gran was still up, in her chair at the top of the table, but at first you could see only her hands putting down her knitting.

Gran said she could tell without asking that they'd enjoyed themselves and that was champion. She wanted to hear all about it. But properly, so it'd have to wait till morning: it was very late. 'Later than you've ever been up before, Jin, I'll bet eh?' Now did they want a bite to eat? 'Sure, our Jin? Well then, bed.'

But they had to tell her about the murder. That couldn't wait till morning.

Gran didn't speak for a moment: then she said, 'Poor sinful soul. It'd be for none of her good deeds, a'll awand.

163

Not worth hangin' for, I doubt. And him that did it'll be thinkin' that by now. Poor devil.'

Her voice was soft as a sigh. She sounded sorry. For the woman who was dead? It must be. Murder was in the Ten Commandments. She wouldn't be sorry for a murderer. Would she?

Vic snuffled. Uncle Bob's snores measured out the time. Jinnie was floating in gentle melancholy, now.

'Our Jin's nearly asleep already,' said Gran. 'We'll not bother with a wash this once. Or your hair. Now take your nant, the pair of yuz. And no talking, our Nan.' She gave them their good-night kiss and hug. 'Off with you, then. I'll not be long out of bed meself, once I've got Jamesie off to the pit.'

In stocking feet, not to make a noise on Uncle Bob's head, Jinnie followed Nan up the steep stairs. It was very quiet. Nan's stockings hissed and crackled as she took them off. The click of a button hitting wood as Jinnie put her liberty bodice on her chair seemed loud enough to wake Uncle Bob.

She was first in bed, but she didn't go to sleep. In fact, she was becoming wider and wider awake. Music was still playing, feet were still slithering. Jinnie was still dancing: better and better every minute.

Downstairs the street door, then the inside door, opened. Voices murmured. Doors again. Jamesie's pit boots rang on the pavements. Other pit boots, stiff, steel-protected. No voices, not when wives and bairns were abed and just a wall away.

Nan was fast asleep now but Jinnie just couldn't stop thinking. Not about Dancing now: that would have been all right. It was Aunt Polly that kept pushing into her thoughts; and Will, and Uncle Davie this morning; and Tot, and Betsey.

And Dad. He'd have Something to Say if he ever found out that the Social had been A Dance: and Grown-Ups always found out. But the Parson — Nan said he was the Curate, not the Vicar — had been there. So it must've been All Right. Not Sinful. Sinful. Had it been Sinful?

Gran came quietly upstairs. Her clothes rustled. Her stays clicked. Her bed creaked. Jinnie lay still, pretending to be asleep. Gran's breathing settled down.

Still Jinnie was awake. She was Sinful. Without a doubt. No better than she should be ... Not for her good deeds, poor Sinful soul. Poor devil. That woman ... murdered. Dead. Jinnie didn't want to think about being dead. What was it like, being dead? She arranged herself, lay stiff and

164

straight. What happened after that?

'For heaven's sake lie still, our Jin,' said Nan, waking up, turning over and going straight to sleep again.

'You all right, Jin?' said Gran. 'Can't sleep for all this excitement, eh?' Her voice was smiling reassuringly. 'Want to come into my bed? Come on then, lass? That's right, then.'

And it was.

Twenty-One

Jamie struggled awake. Somebody was knocking on a door: with a heavy hand to be making all that noise. A dog was barking, leaping up, making a door rattle. Then she heard a voice. 'Whisht, will you?' it said softly, to the dog or the voice or both. Gran's voice and Jinnie was back inside herself again, and at Coalgate.

The knocking stopped and the barking dwindled to a low whine. The street door was opened.

'Is this Mrs. Dunham's?' A man's voice came straight up the stairs, after it Gran's, fierce this time but still soft. 'Whisht man, will you?' she said again and something about a bairn asleep upstairs.

Jinnie prepared to call down that it was all right, she was awake now, but the quiet voices had moved away from the bottom of the stairs and into the room. The inner door clicked shut and reduced the voices to a shapeless murmur, out of which she could make nothing. She stopped trying.

What time could it be? It was light, full daylight. She was still in Gran's bed. Nan's bed was empty, the sheet and blankets turned back to air. Nan's school hat and coat had gone from the peg on the cupboard door, and her schoolbag from beside the dressing-table. After eight o'clock then. But not nine yet. Jamesie wasn't back from the pit. His voice wasn't part of the sounds downstairs, she was sure. Unless he was already asleep in the bed under the stairs. Very late, then. But somehow it didn't feel very late. She was hungry, though: ready for her breakfast, but she'd have to wait until Whoever-it-was-who'd-knocked had left.

Whoever-it-was was a stranger. He'd asked if Gran was Mrs. Dunham. Funny how Gran and Mrs. Dunham and Annie didn't seem to be the same person at all. What could a stranger have come for? His wife was taken bad and he'd come to fetch Gran. Gran did look after poorly folk, especially wives. Sometimes she was fetched in the middle of the night, Nan said: in a hurry. She wasn't in a hurry at the moment, though: nor was Whoever-it-was. So that couldn't be it. Just as well. Jinnie didn't want to be left all by herself.

166

Especially not before she'd had any breakfast.

The voices stopped. The catch on the inside door clicked again. Gran came upstairs. And, oh dear, she was wearing her cap and shawl.

'Jin, hinnie,' she said, 'I've got to go out.' Her voice was different from usual somehow. 'But you'll be all right by yourself for a bit, won't you? You can get yourself a bite to eat; you know where things is, don't you? And I'll have a word with Lizzie-Next-Door so's you can go in to her, if you want.'

Jinnie was alarmed now. She *was* going to be left. She didn't say anything, of course: except, how long was Gran going to be?

'Well, I don't know, lass. I just don't know, but I'll be sharp as I can. You'll manage, I know. And don't forget there's Lizzie.' Gran hesitated. And she was avoiding Jinnie's eyes, no doubt about it. 'Now don't worry.' Why *should* she worry? 'I'll tell you about it when I get back.'

Gran was in a hurry and didn't want any questions. She gave Jinnie a quick little nod and a ghost of a smile and left her, wide awake now and wondering. Jinnie got out of bed and quickly and guiltily almost as if she was prying, tiptoed across to the window. She was just in time to see, not very far below her, Gran's shawl, side by side with dark blue shoulders, a glint of silver buttons and a blue domed hat spiked with silver.

A policeman.

Jinnie sat on the edge of Nan's bed. She was cold, especially her feet, chilled by the oilcloth floor. She ought to get her clothes on. But not just this minute. She had to think first. About Policemen.

Policemen came to Mickie Hind's at home. Often. Everytime there'd been a burglary, somewhere, anywhere, in the town, Dad said. Don't be daft, Jinnie Friend: Mickie was a burglar.

A Policeman had come to Peggy Allison's once, when her Dad was in The Infirmary. Mr. Allison had been taken a lot worse and Mrs. Allison had better go and see him straight away and not wait till Visiting Day, the Policeman said. Too late, though: Mr. Allison'd been dead when Mrs. Allison got there. That'd been about breakfast time as well. But Gran hadn't anybody bad in hospital. So that couldn't be it, either.

Now wait a minute. Old Daddy Brough that used to be Sunday School Superintendant. He was a boilermaker down at Swan's yard. Then one day last summer somebody

167

dropped a hammer from a height and he was killed. And him such a cannie fella, folks said. He was, too. At Sunday School they'd all liked him. Jinnie was coming home from school when she saw the ambulance at the Dead House, and the stretcher going inside. Then a bit later she'd heard that this time it was somebody she knew, and liked, and had vexed by giggling just last Sunday. She hadn't played outside that night, or the next, and Mam'd said she must be sickening for something. Anyway, after Chapel the next Sunday, folk were full of it, and Mrs. Brough and how she'd screeched and nearly gone out of the mind when the Policeman had come and told her about the accident. The Policeman.

An Accident. Jamesie. It was funny she hadn't thought of that first off. Or had she just not wanted to? Jamesie was a pitman. Jamesie had gone down the pit last night, all rosy and smelling of fresh air. Pitmen were always getting themselves killed. An accident down the pit. That was it. That must be it. It couldn't be anything else. But Gran had told her not to worry. Gran hadn't screeched either. But Gran wouldn't screech, ever, Jinnie was sure. She *had* looked queer, though, bonnie and queer.

She should've told Jinnie, all the same. It wasn't fair to

168

leave her, wondering and worrying and with nobody to talk to. From nowhere a picture came into her mind, of Jamesie, squashed, insides oozing out, like a black-clock's when you cracked it. She could see it: all of it. Jamesie. She couldn't bear it.

She put her hands over her ears, pressing the palms on and off: on and off. She shut her eyes, tight, making the lids squeeze her eyes; then opened them: shut them again. Again and again, until sound and no sound, light and no light, were all exploding together inside her head. As always it worked and her head was full of patterns, absorbing, and soothing, and after a little while she could think again.

Jamesie wasn't bound to be dead: or even hurt a lot. Maybe just a finger or two off, like Cousin Joe. That wouldn't be too bad and his compen, like Joe's, would come in handy for furnishing when he got wed. Or the victim mightn't be Jamesie, but Uncle Davie or Will, or one of Aunt Polly's other lads that she never seemed to see. She wouldn't mind them so much. Well, she'd just have to wait and see. She dressed and went downstairs.

Nearly half-past nine. Jamesie should've been home by now, without a doubt. She looked at Jamesie's clothes warming on the mantel rail, and the big rough towel beside them, the bath-tub on the hearth, the chipped enamel jug underneath the boiler tap. All waiting for Jamesie. She'd cry if she wasn't careful.

'It's not Fair,' she said to Vic. 'She had no business going off like that. Saying nothing. And no breakfast or anything.' But Vic was only a dog and didn't understand. He wasn't much comfort at all, breathing heavily like that down there on the mat where she could scarcely see him.

It was the very first time in her life Jinnie'd been all alone. At home there was always somebody about — Mam or Dad or Robbie — in the scullery or The Room; in the backyard, or The Shop. There'd always been somebody at Gran's, too. Now, empty, the house seemed different. Darker, for a start. There was daylight on the table next to the window and a bright glow on the fire, but everywhere else shadows and the dark had taken over, and were pushing forward threatening shapes, and threats without shape: and the room was full of rustlings and creakings.

As for going out the back to the pantry, where the cups and the bread and such like were, she simply durstn't. Perhaps with Vic, she might. But Vic was never allowed into the pantry. He probably wouldn't have obeyed her anyway.

169

She'd have to do without breakfast. But it wasn't Fair. She was very hungry.

She didn't feel right in herself either. She'd dressed without bothering about a wash: hadn't even thought about it, with no Grown-Up to tell her, or to get the water ready. Perhaps she should've: she'd had that powder on her face last night. Oh well, her skin was probably ruined already. Missing her wash couldn't have anything to do with the way her body and her clothes didn't seem to be getting on together. It must be her liberty bodice. When she'd fastened the last button, she'd found she had a buttonhole to spare. Maybe that was why her stockings were dragging now and making her feel lopsided. She wasn't going to take off her frock and petticoat and rebutton the bodice, though. Nor have a wash, neither. So there.

If only she knew what was happening: if Gran would come back soon: and Jamesie. Gabbing at McElwain's Corner he'd be, most like. He'd come clumping home any minute now. Of course he would. He must. Awful things happened to other folks. But Coalgate was different, it was no good hiding from that. Anything could happen at Coalgate. It was all Gran's fault, going off and leaving her by herself, wondering, and with no breakfast. Dad wouldn't like it, especially the no breakfast part.

Well, if she wasn't going to get anything to eat, she'd better find something to do. Nan's *Happy Magazines*. No, Nan's books. Maybe she hadn't taken all of them to school. Maybe her French book was still on the shelf in the cupboard upstairs.

Her hand was on the sneck of the inside door when behind her something creaked. Hot with fright, she stiffened, like Statues, every single bit of her motionless, except her heart which had stopped for a moment and now started leaping about all over, even into her ears. She durstn't look round, to see what had made the noise. Then she remembered the back door wouldn't be bolted: it never was in daytime. Somebody had crept in. With a knife, a big kitchen gully. Or a blunt instrument. A murderer. The Murderer. From last night. Any second now the knife would be in her back: between her shoulder-blades: exactly in the middle: quivering. Or the blunt instrument would descend and crack her skull wide open like an eggshell. Everybody would be sorry, of course. Especially Gran for leaving her. But that wouldn't be much use to Jinnie.

No more creaks. In the quietness she heard Vic's rhyth-

170

mical snuffle. He hadn't barked. And he would have, wouldn't he? Jinnie clutched around herself the tattered remnant of her courage. It was those *Thomson's Weeklies* and *News of the Worlds* at Betsey's on Friday night. Serve her right for reading such stuff, she'd known it was a Sin. She swallowed hard. Her heart went back to its proper place. Anyway, folk that got themselves killed weren't any better than they should be, everybody said. Jinnie was better than she should be. Wasn't she? Was she, though? What about The Pictures? What about The Dance? No, she couldn't expect any help to come down from the sky. She'd have to help herself, and for a start, she couldn't stop here all day. She made a determined movement and faced the room.

Nobody. Her pent-up breath came out with a rush. She wasn't going upstairs, though. French book or no French book. It was that back door that was the trouble. While she was upstairs somebody might slip quietly in. Nicely trapped she'd be, cut off up there. Just you go and bolt the door, Jinnie Friend, she ordered herself. Across the dark room past the dark pantry? It was no use. She couldn't do it. Just you try, Jinnie Friend. You know you'll not be happy till you're sure nobody can get in.

What if there was somebody in already? In that pantry, lurking. That settled it. Downstairs wasn't safe either. She wasn't staying here to be murdered. She'd have to go to Lizzie-Next-Door's: calmly, of course, and put her coat on first. Grown-Ups were fussy about coats. Luckily hers was on the nail on the inside door. She braced herself, turned her back on the room and put up her hand for the coat. Then startled out of her wits almost, she let out a yell. At least it would have been a yell but it choked as it came out.

It was only Vic, jumping up and barking like a loonie.

'Oh shut up, man,' she said. 'What'd'you want to do that for?' But she knew what usually set him barking. Somebody coming in. He skittered furiously towards the far door. He hurled himself at it, his bark worse than ever now; high and strangled. Her heart just about stopped this time. It was behaving very strangely this morning. Maybe she had A Heart, to add to her worries. Vic Knew. There was Somebody in the pantry. The dog kept on jumping up at the door, his nails scraping it in long streaks, and the door rattled. Then she realized another kind of rattle. Something dropped on the floor. Then Vic was back, crouching at her feet, slavering and whining through teeth clenched over his leash, which always hung on the far door.

171

Jinnie sagged with relief. The dog thought she was going for a walk and wanted her to take him. She knelt down, surprised to find she was trembling. She hugged the dog and for once didn't mind when he licked her face all over.

'Good dog, good dog,' she said. She got up again. 'All the same, we're not going for a walk, not now.' There wasn't any need. She'd stop being so silly and what would she have said to Lizzie-Next-Door. She shook her head and said sternly, 'Take it back. Go on.' Then, weakly, 'There's a good dog.'

Vic thumped his tail vigorously on the floor, dropped the slavery leash on to Jinnie's feet. He sat back on his haunches, head tilted up expectantly, tongue flapping, white teeth shining. Big teeth, bigger than she'd ever noticed before. Threatening. What if he turned nasty? Nasty things, dogs; wouldn't have one in the house, you never know when they'll turn on you, Dad said. Especially if they're spoilt, Dad said. Vic was spoilt, Dad said.

It wasn't Fair, Gran going off and leaving her. It was not. She'd better take Vic for that walk after all. She wished she knew more about dogs. But Vic wasn't A Dog: he was Vic. Frightened of Vic, indeed. Whatever was the matter with her this morning?

'No, not now,' she said firmly. 'Tell you what, though: we'll stand at the front door and watch out for Gran and Jamesie.' Which was a good idea really.

It wasn't as it turned out. The minute she opened the street door, Vic abandoned her for the lamp-post. He sniffed, left his visiting-card, as Mam would say, and trotted off to repeat the process at the other lamp-posts in the street and at sundry gratings and bootscrapers as well. She'd not be able to lure him back now, but he never got lost. She put him out of her mind and settled herself to wait for Gran, standing strategically sideways, her back to the hinges of the open door, so that she could keep an eye on the room as well as look down the street.

The Street was quiet: nobody out playing: nobody going to the shops: nobody going anywhere. Only Mattie was there, outside his open door, strange as ever under his shiny black chair cover. Somewhere in the distance a solitary poss-stick was thumping: on a Tuesday, mind you, which was Baking Day. More distant still a train whistled.

Dinner time was a long way off. She hadn't even had breakfast yet. It wasn't very warm out here, either, in spite of her coat. Some holiday this was. Now fair's fair, Jinnie Friend. What about the fish and chips, The Pictures, The

172

Market, The Dance? To keep herself company Jinnie started rehearsing conversations with Edie-at-Home

Then she heard Vic barking again. He came racing out of Ellen's archway at the bottom of the street — so that was where he'd got to — and just coming into sight from round the corner — how *did* that dog know when folk were coming home? — was Gran, and with her, not Jamesie but, of all people, Aunt Polly's George. He didn't wave. Nor did Gran. Jinnie didn't expect it from George, but Gran should've. Gran didn't take much notice of Vic either and he was making plenty of fuss of her. She gave him the merest pat and pushed him away. He stopped barking and jumping, stood surprised and undecided for a moment, then returned to his tour of inspection.

Gran was walking slowly. Did she always look so tired and old? And why was she bringing George with her? Cousin George with his pale blue stare and unblinking silence. Gran'd said nothing about going for George. And what about Jamesie? Why hadn't he come home yet?

Twenty-Two

Nay, said Gran, there'd been no accident down the pit. Jamesie was all right. He was at Uncle Davie's, that was all: staying with Davie for a bit. He'd be home before long, for a wash, and a bite to eat. And a lie-down. He needed his rest, no matter what happened. She'd brought George to stay with his Gran — her voice softened for George but George took no notice — while his Mam was in the hospital, she said. Aunt Polly in hospital: Jinnie was flabbergasted. Little Connie was with Eva, Gran said. Jinnie and George would have to be good bairns and look after theirselves a bit today: and after Jamesie when he came home. Gran might be out a lot today. She was going back to Uncle Davie's. She had things to attend to.

She went on explaining but not explaining: not like herself at all. So that Jinnie couldn't ask the questions she wanted to. What was the matter with Aunt Polly? She must've been taken bad pretty fast: she'd been all right last night. At least, the policeman was explained now: he'd fetched Gran to go to the hospital. But . . . Gran hadn't had time to go all the way to Consett to the hospital and back. And Uncle Davie wasn't at the hospital with Aunt Polly. He was in his own house with Jamesie.

'Now then,' said Gran, as if she'd explained everything, 'did you get yourself some breakfast, Jinnie?' and didn't wait for an answer. 'You'll can do with a bite more, anyroad, a'll awand. So can George. Give uz a hand, lass, will you? I'll fetch the bread and tea-cake and get on buttering. You fetch the pots and lay the table.' Which Jinnie did and it was funny how the pantry had lost its terrors now.

Gran didn't wait to have anything to eat herself. When the bread and tea-cake were buttered, she put her shawl on again.

'Be good bairns then,' she said. 'And mind, our George, you do as Jinnie says. And when you've had enough to eat, get into Jamesie's bed. You've got some sleep to catch up on. And I don't want him playing out, Jin. And if I'm not back, there's still a bite of ham on that bone and a morsel of meat roll — it'll have to do for your dinners — and some beetroot

174

and pickle. There's plenty of cake. And I'll tell you what.' She opened her purse: 'You can get some sweets, nice ones.' She put some pennies on the table near Jinnie's plate.

Something was wrong, right enough. Something Serious. Aunt Polly was going to die. Aunt Polly was dead already and Gran didn't want to Break the News to George yet.

Left sitting at the table with George, Jinnie felt excited, yet disappointed. And more than a bit resentful. Stuck here with George, even if Aunt Polly was dead. What on earth was she going to do all day? She knew her manners, though.

'Have a piece of bread, George,' she said politely, offering the plate.

'Na,' said George, and took some tea-cake.

'You should always have bread to start with,' said Jinnie. She always had to, at home. George stared at her. 'Come on. Just that little bit.'

'Na,' said George, starting on the tea-cake. 'She didn't say I had to. And she said I could have some sweets.' He looked at the pennies.

Jinnie ignored that. Gran hadn't meant sweets for breakfast. 'All right,' she said. 'For this once. Gran did say for you to do as I tell you, didn't she, though?'

George didn't answer. He was too busy demolishing the tea-cake.

'Don't gobble so, George. You'll make yourself sick,' she said. That was what Mam and Dad always told her and Robbie. And Robbie had been, once. A thought struck her: if George *was* sick, who would clean it up? 'You will, George, really you will,' she said anxiously.

Teeth buried in tea-cake, nose almost touching the butter, George stopped a second. His pale eyes looked briefly at Jinnie. She stared back, urgently. George just lowered his gaze again, finished the bite, went on eating. He had long black lashes: longer than Robbie's even. What a waste, on George. And she could see that George was going to be a handful, for all his quietness.

He wasn't, as it turned out. Not as long as Jinnie let him have his own way. He showed no signs of being sick either, for all his gobbling.

The pile of tea-cake soon vanished.

'How about bed now?' said Jinnie. 'Gran said you didn't get much sleep last night;' hoping George might tell her about last night.

'Na,' said George. He climbed down from his place at the table and went to the sewing-machine, to a pile of ancient

175

comics that Gran had brought with him. He selected one, then settled himself in the Windsor chair by the fire. There he sat, legs, too short to reach the floor, dangling, body bent forward to let the firelight rest on his *Film Fun*. He looked like a little old man.

She was tempted to sit opposite him and look at a *Film Fun* herself. She didn't often get to read a comic. But that would be encouraging George's disobedience.

'Well, I suppose we'd better tidy the table and wash the pots,' she said instead. She should have known that hints would be wasted on George. Righteously she started the jobs. She'd have a good read when she'd finished. But she hadn't even sat down after safely bestowing the last mug in the pantry, when George said, 'She said I could have some sweets.'

'She's the cat's mother,' said Jinnie. 'You shouldn't say she.'

'She said I could.' George's eyes fixed accusingly on the four pennies still on the table.

Jinnie didn't care for going messages and didn't often have to, because of The Shop.

'Oh, all right,' she said. 'What sort?'

'Paradise Fruits,' said George. Not what Jinnie would've chosen herself, but all right.

'What if they haven't any?'

'Mintoes,' said George.

'And if they haven't . . .?' Jinnie liked to be prepared for all eventualities.

'Gob-stoppers,' said George. Jinnie was sorry she'd asked. She didn't care for gob-stoppers.

Whitehead's smelt of yeast and warm dough. Sticks were crackling and sparking like mad under the oven. Loaf tins were warming on the hearth. Mrs. Whitehead was at the table, hands and arms busy with a great mound of dough. So busy she didn't notice Jinnie.

Jinnie waited. She was timid about tapping on the counter. Dad didn't like it. If a Grown-Up tapped, never mind a bairn, he was annoyed. As if he had nothing to do but come running, he said. So she waited, trying not to look at Mr. Whitehead beside the fire-place as usual, in case she seemed to be blaming him. However, at last, Mr. Whitehead thumped his stick on the metal hearth cover and Mrs. Whitehead looked round. She started to shake flour and bits of dough off her hands, then changed her mind.

'Nora. Our Nora. Sho-op,' she shouted. 'She'll be here in a

176

minute. She's putting the bairn down for his bit sleep. Nora! You're Mrs. Dunham's grand-bairn, aren't you?' she said, pummelling the dough. 'Kate's lass.'

'Yes,' said Jinnie, resigned. Some day she might be herself, but the time seemed a long way off.

'And how's . . . how's . . . your Mam?'

Jinnie had a feeling that wasn't what Mrs. Whitehead had intended to say.

'She's all right, thank you,' she said. 'She was here on Sunday.'

'Ay, I heard tell. Well, when you go home, say I was askin' after her.'

Mrs. Whitehead concentrated on her dough, punching and kneading and turning it round. She started cutting it into pieces.

'Is that Nora not down yet? What is't you want, lass, and I'll get it.'

But at that moment Nora came down the stairs. She stopped at the bottom beside Jinnie.

'Oh,' she said, 'it's you;' not at all friendly. 'What'd'you want?'

Her face was paler than usual, if that was possible, and her eyes looked sore. She didn't say a word as she weighed out the Fruits and took Jinnie's fourpence. A quiet lot the Whiteheads, kept themselves to themselves, Gran said, except Lizzie, of course. All the same Jinnie was a customer, and not exactly a stranger, either. Still, Mrs. Whitehead herself was making an effort. 'Now don't forget,' she said as she moulded a piece of dough and put it into a tin, 'tell your Mam I was asking after her.' Then she added, 'And your Grandma.' Which was a bit unexpected since they lived in the same street.

About half-way between Whitehead's and Gran's a door was open wide. Mabel Barker's it would be. Mabel was like Mrs. Parks at home, all day watching folk go by. Ears always half-way down the street, Gran said. Only bit of her that ever does owt, them and her tongue, the lazy faggot, Jamesie said. Impittent with it, an' all, Uncle Bob said.

There she was now, sure enough, eyes bright and bulging.

'Hey lass,' she said. 'Stop a minute. I want you.' Reluctantly Jinnie slowed down. 'How's your Aunt Polly?' So she'd heard about Aunt Polly, had she? 'Is she dead yet?' What a way to ask. 'Poor soul,' Mabel added, but you could tell she'd be disappointed if Aunt Polly wasn't dead. Jinnie shook her head. Mabel hadn't finished, though. 'Who've they got for it?

177

I saw the poliss at your Gran's. Was it her man? Or was it that Tot?'

'Sorry, Mrs. Parks,' said Jinnie scarcely knowing what she said and surprised that she could say anything, and so calmly at that, 'I'm in a hurry.' She waved her bags of sweets and started to run, stupid with shock and new thoughts and old thoughts: and she'd been far too polite to that impittent old faggot, even if she was a Grown-Up.

She heard Mabel call after her, 'Stuck up little madam. Who d'you think you are, Lady Muck from Todd Hall? Like that Nan, her and her fancy school. This'll take you down a peg or two: the lot of yuz, you . . .' Mabel finished with a volley of swear-words and Jinnie felt that the whole street had become full of ears.

George accepted his pleasures as stoically as his sorrows. Or maybe he never felt either pleasure or sorrow. Jinnie had never met anybody quite like George. He took the Fruits without a thank-you and frustrated Jinnie's generous intention of taking only one for herself by assuming that they were all for him and not offering her any at all. Greedy little pig, she thought.

178

Indignation was warm and pleasant, an escape from all those other thoughts about Aunt Polly and Uncle Davie and Gran and what would Dad say if it all got into the papers? As it would. She couldn't bear to have Dad say anything about Coalgate and how he'd been right after all.

George was making a lot of noise with those sweets. His sucking and cracking got on her nerves. Common, George was: but what could you expect? She couldn't tell him to stop the noise, though. She'd have to be careful what she said to George from now on. He was Special, now, set apart from ordinary folk by all kinds of awful things that Jinnie could still only guess at.

'George,' she said. 'What about bed, when you've finished them sweets? You must be tired . . . if you've missed a lot of your sleep . . .?' still hoping George might Say Something.

But all George said was, 'Na, she said when Jamesie come home.'

Had Gran said that? Jinnie wasn't going to argue with George, though. Especially not now. Pity she couldn't tell what went on behind those pale blank eyes of his. No, fair's fair, she wouldn't like anybody to be able to see what was going on in *her* head. It was bad enough God always knowing. She took her eyes away from George. He returned to his sucking and his *Film Fun*. Jamesie would be home any minute. Maybe he'd tell her what had happened. When George was asleep, of course. You didn't talk about Awful Things in front of children.

It wasn't long, Thank Goodness, before she heard heavy hobnailed steps at the back door and the flat ordinary sound of a jacket banged against the wall to shake off loose coal-dust. Gran had said for her to look after Jamesie. And she'd thought for a while that he was dead. She went and opened the door for him. He was taking off his boots now, and putting them on to the upside-down wash-tub to dry out. His pit bottle and bait tin were on the ground. Jinnie picked them up.

'Hello, Jamesie,' she said. 'You've come.'

'Ay, lass, I've come home.'

Jinnie hadn't expected Jamesie to be as he'd been yesterday when he returned from the pit: funning all the time, pretending to rumple her hair with his black hands, to give her a coaly kiss on the end of her nose, and teeth smiling all the time white as white in his streaky black face. But she hadn't expected him to be quite so different either. Somewhere in this tired, faceless man must be the Jamesie she

179

knew but at this moment she couldn't find him.

'Come on, George,' she said. 'That's Jamesie's chair. You sit over there.'

'Nay lass, leave the bairn be,' said Jamesie. His voice had had all the stuffing knocked out of it as well. George clambered out of the Windsor chair and settled himself on the patchwork cushion in the basket chair and even his light weight set it creaking.

Jamesie sat down. He bent forward and loosened the knee-band of his britches. Jinnie saw briefly the black skin of his neck and the top of his back. Then he sat up again, stretched his feet to warm at the fire: his purple pit stockings were mostly black now. He said nothing. He shifted his position, clasped hands round his knees, as if he was holding himself together, so tightly that his knuckles showed little white patches on his black skin. He rocked back and forwards, just the merest little bit. He looked into the fire, and George looked at him. Somebody would have to say something soon.

'What about a bite and a sup then?' To her surprise Jinnie's voice and words came out just like Gran's.

'Nay,' said Jamesie, 'I don't want nowt just now. Thanks all the same.'

'Will I get the hot water out then?'

'Nay, leave uz alone, lass. I just want to sit for a bit. I'm dead felled. Stop clockin' like a broody hen.' Then he realized Jinnie was hurt and he made an effort to lighten his voice. 'Tha's as bad as thee Gran. All right, lass. A pot of tea, then. And after that we'll see about me bath. Can't sit here idle all day.'

He became aware of George's gaze, clinging to him relentlessly.

'Well, George lad,' he said awkwardly and looked away.

'You and me Da,' said George, '... what were you bubbling for?'

Grown men crying. The neat firm tube of water Jinnie was pouring from the kettle wobbled and almost missed the opening of the teapot.

'Look out, lass,' said Jamesie, 'you'll scald yourself. Me and George an' all.' Jamesie sounded almost pleased at the prospect. 'Can't have that, can we, George?'

George was not to be put off.

'Is me Ma dead?' he said. 'Is she? Is she down the bury-hole?' George's voice was not much different from usual. 'And where's our Will?'

180

At last. Something would come out now: everything maybe. Jamesie would have to answer George. Carefully Jinnie put the teapot on the hob, to brew the tea, and the kettle back on the edge of the fire: and waited.

Jamesie said nothing. His rocking stopped. The skin on his hands stretched tighter still. Then slow tears came into his eyes. They grew, spilt over and ran down his grimy cheeks. He did nothing to stop the tears. Perhaps he didn't know they were there.

Until this moment, Jinnie'd been outside it all, whatever it was. Watching, guessing, resenting, enjoying. Not feeling it at all. Now for a second she shared the pain, the whole Grown-Up world of pain in Jamesie's eyes. Only for a second: it was more than she could endure. The moment passed leaving a great ache in her throat and a tightness somewhere in her ribs that hurt like a bruise.

'No,' said Jamesie at last: or maybe it was straight away. 'She's not dead. But she's very bad and it's no good me tellin' you no different.'

George's expression didn't change. Then he asked, 'What did the poliss come to me Da for? And what for does nobody know where our Will is? Where is he?'

'Nay,' said Jamesie, 'if I could tell you that, somebody *would* know where he is. Now isn't that right?' he said reasonably. 'And the poliss come about your Ma being in the hospital. And that's about all I can tell you, Geordie lad.' Or was that all Jamesie wanted to tell? It seemed to satisfy George, though. At least he didn't ask any more questions.

'Now, our Jin, let's be havin' that tea you've made before it's brewed to death. And Geordie, them bullets you're eatin', what about one for Jinnie?' Obediently George started fishing about in the bag. 'Nay, that's not the way, lad. Offer her the bag, to take one herself. Nay, I'll never get you learnt your manners, our George.'

Jamesie sounded more like himself again: looked more like. But with Grown-Ups you never knew: not even with Jamesie who had never Grown-Up.

181

Twenty-Three

After George and Jamesie lay down for their rest, there was a lot for Jinnie to do: tidy up the hearth; put Jamesie's pit clothes on the rail to dry; fill up the boiler; empty the teapot; wash Jamesie's mug and plate. She hadn't finished but was outside emptying out the dish-water when Gran came home. Gran wasn't alone.

'Jinnie,' she said, 'here's somebody wants to talk to you.'

To her? She'd never seen the man before. She guessed, though, what he was. But why did he want to talk to her? Maybe she could guess that as well, after what that Mabel had said. He didn't waste any time.

'Now, Jinnie,' he said, 'you look like a clever lass. Don't be nervous. I only want you to tell uz about yesterday. Yesterday morning at your Aunt Polly's.'

She was right: he was another policeman. A Special Plain Clothes Man. And it *was* the fight at Aunt Polly's he wanted to know about.

She looked at Gran.

'Go on, Jin, just tell him what you told me and we'll get it over with.'

'It's all right,' said Jamesie from the bed under the stairs, 'you lot can stop whisperin'. I haven't been to sleep yet. Couldn't get off.' Jinnie had gone tiptoeing round her jobs. What a waste of effort. 'And a brass band couldn't wake George up now,' said Jamesie. He lay on his back, hands under head, elbows jutting, and listened. They all listened. To Jinnie. So much listening made her embarrassed at first, but she soon got into her stride and told the Plain Clothes Man about the row at Aunt Polly's: the cake and the knife and Will and Uncle Dave.

The man didn't interrupt her much, just once asked a question and then a few more when she'd finished, particularly about what Uncle Dave had said — exactly. And Will.

'Well, I hope you're satisfied now,' said Gran. 'Botherin' a bairn: to tell you what that Bella Telford's come runnin' to you with already. And nobody's denied, anyrod.'

'It's the truth we're after, Mrs. Dunham,' said the man

182

mildly. 'That's all. Now then, I'm not saying any lies've been told. Different folks remember different things, that's all, and a bairn often remembers what other folks don't. She's got a good pair of eyes in her head, has the lass. And a good memory. No reason, either, to remember ought but what she actually saw and heard. Ay, she'd make a good witness. They'd believe her in any court.'

A witness. In a murder trial. Witnesses were important. They got their pictures in real papers, as well as in Thomson's. Edie would be green with envy.

But Gran was upset. 'You'll never put the lass in court, will you? A bit of a bairn? And I don't know what her Dad'll have to say.' Jinnie didn't either. But she didn't care. She'd never had such a chance to be Special in her life before.

'It'll not be for her Dad to say. Nor me,' said the man. 'But maybe it'll not come to that, Mrs. Dunham. Maybe what happened yesterday morning has nothing to do with this . . . business.' All the same, you could tell he thought it had.

'It hasn't. It hasn't. I'm sure on't, sure as I've ever been of anything. There's some other explanation. There has to be,' said Gran. 'I know Dave . . . it's her that's the bad un. He wouldn't harm a fly . . . Too soft for his own good, that's what his trouble's always been, not . . .'

'That's what the mothers always say, Mrs. Dunham,' said the man. He sounded sorry, not a bit like a Plain Clothes Man. 'And that's the very sort that sometimes turns.'

'There's . . . others . . . you know,' said Gran.

'Yes,' said the man. 'I know. There usually is. I'll be going into them an' all. Now I know it's no good me telling you, Mrs. Dunham,' said the man, 'but try not to worry too much. It may not be as bad as it looks. And we'll find your grandson for you an' all. He can't be far, you know.'

'He's a cannie fella, yon,' said Gran in a dull surprised way, when the Plain Clothes Man had gone.

'Ay, he is,' said Jamesie, who had got up the minute the door had shut again. 'You know,' he said awkwardly taking Gran's hand, 'we're all going on as if this was bound to be a hanging matter; as if she was dead. She's not, you know: not yet. And she's a tough un, is Polly.'

Aunt Polly was a tough un, right enough. All that laughing and shouting and being scared of nobody. Jamesie was right. You couldn't imagine Aunt Polly dead. Of course, if she wasn't, it'd mean Jinnie wouldn't be a Witness and in the papers: but for Gran's sake she'd give that up, willingly.

Nobody seemed to hear the gentle tap on the door except

183

Jinnie. Then 'Can I come in, Mrs. Dunham?' and Lizzie-Next-Door was standing just inside the room, tall and clean and starched and carrying something covered by a fresh red-and-white cloth.

'Seems like you're in, Lizzie,' said Gran trying to make a joke. 'Sit you down. I was just trying to stir meself to make a cup of tea. You'll have one with uz, won't you, lass?'

'That's what I've come for, Mrs. Dunham, to make you a cup. It's not long off dinner-time and I thought mebbe you could eat something and I've been bakin'. Anyroad, Jamesie and the bairns . . . you'll not've had any time.'

'Nay, but you're a grand neighbour, Lizzie. Times like this you find where your friends is. But you shouldn't've, you know. You've got enough on your own plate.'

'Now, Mrs. Dunham, none of that,' said Lizzie, pretending to be offended, 'or I'll start on about the shirt collars you've turned, the nights you've sat up with Anty, the . . . Oh well.'

The something Lizzie had brought was pasties. Jinnie saw and smelt them as Lizzie put them into the oven to keep warm. Then Lizzie set about making the tea. The job took Lizzie half the time it would've taken Jinnie. Grown-Ups were depressing that way.

'Well, I'll be off,' she said, 'the lads'll be in from school any minute. Don't bother about the dish. Jinnie can fetch it, or I'll bob in for it meself.'

The tea put new heart into her, Gran said. She wasn't hungry, though. Jamesie and Jinnie must have her pasty between them. George's could go in the pantry, until he woke up. 'Now get on with your meat, you two,' she said. 'I want a bit of peace. To think.'

The pasties tasted every bit as good as they looked. Jamesie was as hungry as Jinnie now, and ready for cake when the pasties were finished. Fruit-cake for him, and a big wedge of Nan's snow-cake for Jinnie.

After a while Gran stopped thinking. 'That's it; Billy Reeves,' she said; 'no point fetchin' Bob from the Brickworks. I'll go and see Billy. He's been to College. He'll know what we can do for the best. Can't do any harm, anyroad.' Jamesie thought it was a grand idea. 'Can't sit clockin' here all day.' Gran stood up. 'I'll go now. School'll be out, and by the time I get meself changed and up to the Hills', he'll've had his dinner.'

Through the snow-cake, Jinnie heard Gran moving about upstairs. She wasn't there long but when she came down again she was in her Sunday clothes, right to gleaming steel

184

hat-pins and black gloves.

'I'll away now,' she said. 'Be a good lass and look after things a bit longer for uz, will you, Jinnie?' More dishwashing, thought Jinnie. 'You've been a grand help. I just don't know what I'd've done without you.' And Jinnie knew it was time she learnt to think of other folks beside herself: Mam had told her often enough. 'And our Jamesie, clockin' by the fire all day's no good to anybody. All right, you can't sleep, but you can get yourself properly stretched out on that bed: it'll rest your limbs if it does nowt else.'

Jinnie washed up again, full of thoughts about being a Witness and glad she was going to be a Teacher, because this washing-up business came round far too often. George slept on. Jamesie lay resting silently.

He came to life again and got up when Gran returned.

'Well,' he said, 'what'd he have to say?'

Gran put her handbag down, removed her hat-pins, then her hat. 'That's better,' she said.

'Come on, our Ma,' said Jamesie. 'Had he owt to say?'

'Ay, had he,' said Gran, ' . . . and I don't know if I've done right . . . but Billy says, if it was his Family, there's only one thing he could think of: go to see a lawyer. Right away. And see what *he* had to say. It was up to uz, Billy said, but that's what *he'd* do.'

Jamesie was flabbergasted, and indignant. 'Nay, that's a good un. That's as much as sayin' you . . . he . . . thinks Davie did do it. Or mebbe Will.'

'That's not what Billy says, and he's been to College, he should know. He says there's all sorts a lawyer can do that you can't; would never even think of, he says. Well, that's what he'd do. If it was his son. Right away, before he was a day older.' Gran sat down, in a chair near the door and made no move to take off her coat, not even her gloves.

'That's not all, is it our Ma?' You could just about hear Jamesie thinking.

'No. He's fixed for uz to see a good man in Consett the day, two o'clock. Billy went to see the Vicar, and the' fixed it between them. The Vicar's got one of them telephones.'

The Vicar knew about Aunt Polly. Betsey would know. She was a maid at the Vicarage. Betsey would be pleased. She'd won.

'But what about paying? Did Billy say owt about that? It's all very fine for him and the Vicar: they've got plenty of money. Where do the' think pit folk can get that kind of money from, to pay a lawyer? Costs a fortune every time one

185

of them opens his mouth, so I've heard tell.'

'This un's a poor man's lawyer, Billy says. Does it a lot cheaper.'

'Nay,' said Jamesie, suddenly accepting the idea of a lawyer, 'we want a good un, while we're on. Paddy Hastings.' Paddy Hastings was Famous. A Witness, Paddy Hastings asking her questions. Jinnie'd be in all papers: picture, headlines, everything. Even Dad might not object. Paddy Hastings was a top man. He was Labour, of course.

'Don't be daft, man,' said Gran. 'Now who's goin' on as if Davie'd done it? And yon's a rich man's lawyer, our Jamesie, even I know that. And Billy says the Vicar says this man in Consett's a good un.' Oh, well, thought Jinnie. She did let her imagination go running away with her. 'It'll take uz all our time to pay a poor man's lawyer, never mind Paddy Hastings,' said Gran. 'Sir Patrick.'

'And how *are* we goin' to pay him,' said Jamesie, down to earth again, like Jinnie. 'You haven't answered that 'un. Our Davie'll have nowt. That's a certainty.'

'I'll manage. Somehow,' said Gran. 'I've got a bit put by. In the Store. And if that's not enough, Bob'll lend uz his bit, I know he will.'

'Nay,' said Jamesie, shocked. 'Bob's is for when he has to give up the Brickyard. He can't hardly live on ten bob a week pension, our Mam.' Jamesie didn't seem to doubt, though, that Uncle Bob would give his savings. 'And Nan . . . That's our Nan's College money. You'd never get it made up again, not by the time it'll be needed. It was going to take the next three years to get enough scraped together as it was. You can't use that money. You can't. It wouldn't be fair to Nan either.'

This more than anything brought home to Jinnie how serious it all was. So serious that Nan was threatened now. Nan was going to College: Nan was going to be a Teacher. Jinnie could hardly remember a time when it had not been so. Jinnie couldn't even begin to *un*think Nan-at-College.

'Nan'll understand,' said Gran. 'But I'm not sure there's any call for her to know.' Then she realized Jinnie was there. 'Jin'll not tell, if we ask her not to. She can keep a secret. Can't you, lass?' Jinnie knew that wild horses wouldn't drag out of her a secret of Gran's: not even Edie would. She nodded solemnly. 'Anyroad, Nan'll understand. I know she will. But the money'll get put back. I don't know how, not yet, but it will: if I have to beg, borrow or steal it.' Gran looked as if she meant it, but she couldn't, could she? Not

186

the steal bit. 'I can still scrub floors,' she said: 'and take in washin'.'

'Dottie and me's got a bit put by an' all,' said Jamesie. 'Davie can have a lend of that. It'd have to be a lend,' he went apologetically. 'It was for Dottie and me to set up with.'

'Nay, but you're a good lad, Jamesie Dunham,' said Gran. 'We'll try if we can manage without that. Josh'll lend us a bit, if we ask them, I know.' Jinnie hoped Gran was right but she didn't think Dad had any spare money: and he didn't hold with family fights: or the Coalgate folk, either. And what he would say when he found out about all this . . . But maybe he knew already. Maybe it'd been in the paper, this morning. 'And Dottie'll need to have her say, you know. She might not be so anxious to. You couldn't blame her: you'd have to put off gettin' wed.'

'Dottie'll see it the same way as me,' said Jamesie. 'I'll bet on that.'

'Well, there's time yet to think about it,' said Gran, 'and I'd best be getting meself off if I'm goin' to be in Consett by two. I'll just go upstairs for me Store bank book, though, to show the man. He'll do none the worse for knowin' we've got a bit of money behind uz.' Gran picked up her handbag — it had been Aunt Polly's once, but after she bought it she decided she didn't like it: funny how you kept on coming back to Aunt Polly — and went upstairs. They heard her steps crossing the room, then the rattle of the dressing-table drawer.

Then came another sound, another step and who should burst in but Dottie, out of breath and pretty as ever in spite of everyday coat, black woollen stockings and flat heavy shoes.

'Nay lass, what's tha doin' here? Why isn't tha at work?' said Jamesie.

'My, Jamesie Dunham,' said Dottie, pulling a face that would have been downright silly if she hadn't been so pretty. 'Here was me thinkin' you'd be glad to see uz. That's a fine welcome for a body, isn't it, Jin?' She didn't expect Jinnie to answer, though. 'As a matter of fact, I've got all the rest of the day off. Your Ma might could do with a bit of help, the Missus said. Billy slipped over to tell her your Ma'd been to see him. Where is she, by the way? It'd be Billy told the Missus to let uz off. Catch the old faggot turning out the parlour on her own, if she could help it.

'D'you know, that was the first we'd heard about Polly

187

being the woman found on Robson's Field.' Dottie shivered with excitement. 'Who'd've thought it, when you told uz last night? Mind, she's just the sort really, when you come to think about it. Fair asked for it she did: the talk of the place: her and her fancy men. Can't say I blame your Davie.'

'Now, Dottie . . .' said Jamesie.

'Wonder is he didn't do for her years ago, if half they say's true. Of course, it might've been Will. The Missus said he'd taken his nant. But why should he, really?'

'Now, Dottie,' said Jamesie again.

'Oh there you are, Mrs. Dunham. I was askin' where you'd got to.' She looked questioningly at Gran's Sunday clothes. 'The Missus sent uz to see if there's any jobs you want doin'. Oh isn't it awful, Mrs. Dunham?' Dottie's voice didn't sound as if anything was awful at all.

'Thank you kindly, Dottie, and tell Mrs. Reeves thanks when you see her the morrow. It's very good of the woman. But the Reeveses is cannie folk.' Dottie sniffed. Gran didn't notice. 'I wouldn't've thought of askin', Dottie, but since you're here . . . Today's bakin' day, and I haven't got a thing done. And there's the dinner for Bob and Nan, and all of us, come to that. Look, lass. I'll just leave it to you, anythin' you can manage. There's money in the machine drawer and Jinnie'll run any messages you want. And I really must get meself off to Consett, now.'

She picked up her hat, and set about skewering it to her hair again, with the first and fiercest of her hat-pins.

'To Consett?' said Dottie.

Jamesie explained. 'And I said they could have the lend of our money,' he finished.

'You said what?' said Dottie, shrilly.

'I said . . .'

Dottie didn't let him finish. 'I heard very well what you said, Jamesie Dunham. And you can just un-say it. That's our money for settin' up. That we were never goin' to touch for owt else. Not for the last strike, not for this strike, not even if it goes on for months. When would we ever get it together again? Nay, just you listen.' But Jamesie was listening all right. 'If you .think I'm goin' to wait for you for ever, till we're another Lily and Lijah, still courtin' when we're thirty, you've got another think comin', Jamesie Dunham.'

Dottie's voice was going higher and higher. Fancy anybody wanting to get wed as much as Dottie seemed to.

'You're not the only pebble on the beach you know.'

'But, Dottie,' Jamesie was so bewildered by the storm it

188

was almost laughable, 'I know what we said. But this is somethin' we never even thought of . . . This is . . . Family, Dottie. He's me brother, Dottie. You can't . . .'

Gran was standing motionless, final hat-pin still in her hand. She didn't say a word. George was making sounds of waking up and no wonder. As for Jinnie, it was all so interesting she forgot she was Jinnie, for once.

'Ay: and I'm your lass. Or was,' said Dottie. 'What about me? What about us? It's not fair. All the money they've had through their hands. More than you and me'll ever have. Spent it like water they did, the both of them. And now he wants ours. Mine,' she said. She was quiet now, and calm. 'Well he's not gettin' his hands on a brass farthin'. Don't you go thinkin' owt else. It's him or me. Make your mind up to that, Jamesie. Or will I make it up for you?'

'But Dottie, you've got it all wrong,' said Jamesie. 'He's never asked for it. He knows nowt about this: or the lawyer or anythin', yet. It was Billy Reeves that . . .'

'Billy Reeves,' said Dottie bitterly. 'What's it got to do with Billy Reeves? Who does he think he is, sticking his shovel where's there's no muck?' Only she didn't say muck, as Mam did. 'I bet he didn't offer to put his hand in his own pocket.'

Now Gran did speak. 'Nay, Dottie lass, it was me went to Mr. Reeves,' she said gently. 'And he knew I'd never take a penny, not as long as there was somebody in the Family to borrow from: not unless things was a lot worse than they is as yet.'

'Well, Mrs. Dunham,' said Dot, sharply, 'I'm not Family: not yet. Mebbe I never will be.'

'Dottie,' said Jamesie.

'So don't count on owt I've got. And the Post Office book's in my name. Remember?'

'Nay, Dottie, you'd never . . . you're not sayin' . . .?'

'Wouldn't I, though?' said Dottie. 'It'd make up for the time I've wasted on you.'

'Whisht, Dottie, whisht. Before we any of uz say somethin' we'll be sorry for. Sit down. Make yourself a cup of tea.'

'All right, Mrs. Dunham. I'll shut up now,' said Dottie. 'But I meant every word I've said and I'll stick by it. And I'm not stoppin' here now. I'm not goin' back to work neither. The old bitch can get her own hands mucky for once.'

She went away, without another word and not bothering to shut even the street door behind her.

'Come you in, you bad dog, you,' said Gran. Jinnie'd never

189

given Vic another thought since he'd vanished this morning. There he stood looking doubtfully into the room, uncertain what his reception would be. 'Where've you been, you bad dog, you? Just look at your feet. And your back. What've you been up to?' Gran was really angry. Vic looked guiltier than ever. Gran went and closed the street door. 'Come in, will you? Have we not enough to do, without you comin' back filthy mucky, needin' a bath?' At the word bath, Vic slunk past them all, and disappeared from sight under the bed.

'I'll have to leave him to you, Jamesie,' said Gran. 'And d'you think you could get George upstairs into my bed where it's quieter. Don't let him sleep much after three, though. Don't want him awake half the night again.'

'Ay,' said Jamesie, 'and for goodness' sake get yourself off, will you? You'll only just catch that bus. We can look after ourselves, you know. And might even manage a dog.'

'Don't worry, Jamesie,' said Gran. 'She didn't mean it. She was upset. She'll be back, any minute. You'll see. She will.'

But Gran was wrong, for once. Dottie didn't come back.

Not ever.

190

Twenty-Four

Already this was without doubt the queerest day Jinnie'd ever had. One of the queerest things about it was that in spite of the strange things happening it was so dull a lot of the time. All this making tea and washing dishes or just waiting. It was so shapeless as well. Everybody (except Jinnie) coming and going, and eating at the wrong times. Then, so much being by herself (George asleep didn't count) or with Grown-Ups was a strain. Especially as the Grown-Ups had changed so you hardly recognized them. Nobody told her anything either, and she knew she mustn't Pester.

Not having anybody she could talk to was worst of all. She longed for Nan to come home, although Nan wasn't the same as she used to be. And if she found out she might not be going to College, she'd be as changed as Jamesie.

Still, she was glad Tuesday was Games Day when Nan finished early, and hadn't so far to come home either.

She couldn't expect Nan yet, though, and she'd have to fill in the time somehow. Talking to Jamesie was out of the question now. Jinnie hardly durst look at him, never mind talk. She didn't like to read either. A comic or a weekly, or even a book, seemed unfeeling, as if she didn't care about Jamesie's troubles. Now if there'd been a newspaper, reading wouldn't have seemed so bad somehow, but Gran didn't take a morning paper regularly. No, there was nothing else for it: she'd just have to sit here. And Think, of course. But there were so many things, old and new, jostling around in her mind that thinking was no pleasure; it wasn't even easy. In fact, she didn't seem able to think properly at all in front of Jamesie. It was talking she needed. She'd burst if she sat here much longer in all this silence. It would be ages and ages before Nan came home.

The quiet after Gran had gone must have seemed like forgiveness to Vic. He crept out, tentatively, found himself ignored and settled cautiously in his usual place. He was dirty and no mistake: he must have been rolling in horse muck, or worse: he smelt of it, as well as of dog. When was Jamesie going to bath him? She durstn't remind him, though.

191

Jamesie roused himself. 'I think I'll away and feed the pigeons,' he said. 'It's past their time. Mebbe you'd better stay here, to be in the house if George wakes up. D'you mind, Jinnie?

Pigeons were fine, from a distance, on roof-tops and walls, cooing and rainbow-necked, but close up, in Jamesie's cree, they were all sharp eyes and sharp beaks and sharp claws. Of course Jinnie didn't mind staying with George and missing the pigeons. She wished Jamesie would wash Vic first, though.

'There's a few other jobs need doin' on the allotment as well,' said Jamesie. 'So I'll get meself off. Nan won't be long now, and if owt happens give uz a shout, or fetch uz, will you?'

Jamesie's pigeon-cree was on his allotment, one of a number on the other side of the wall of Gran's backyard easily reached through a gate next to the old disused midden. Jinnie said yes she would call him.

'Well, get yourself reading or something. It'll do you no good clockin' by the fire all afternoon.' Clocking was a new sin to Jinnie, a special Coalgate one.

It was a relief to be free to read. She still hadn't worked her way through all the William stories, so she got the magazines from their shelf. But for the first time William failed her. Her eyes kept on closing, her head kept on falling forward. As bad as Uncle Bob, she thought. Jinnie hoped Gran wouldn't be disappointed about Uncle Bob's savings. He had a name for being careful had Uncle Bob. And he was always full of disapproval or silence. He'd be worse than ever now. Thank Goodness Nan would be home before him for sure. Time was passing. Nan would be here any minute now. She wouldn't sit silent leaving Jinnie to guess what had happened. Nan would tell her all about last night and Aunt Polly.

But maybe Nan didn't know anything about it. She'd gone to school before the policeman came. She'd been at school all day. Well then, Jinnie would have the pleasure of telling Nan about it. Come to think of it, there was quite a bit she did have to tell.

Nan didn't know: anything. Jinnie could tell that from the ordinary way Nan opened the door: the everyday voice in which she called out, 'It's me-ee. I'm ho-me.'

'Whisht,' said Jinnie importantly, going to meet her. 'Not so loud. You'll wake George.'

'George . . .?' said Nan.

192

'Ay,' said Jinnie, he's upstairs asleep.' Coalgate folks were used to being quiet because somebody was asleep. Nan said no more until she was in the room with the inside door safely shut.

'What on earth's George doing here? And where's everybody?' she said.

'Aunt Polly's in hospital,' said Jinnie.

'In hospital . . . What's the matter with her?' said Nan.

'I'll tell you in a minute . . . I don't really know . . . She's had an accident,' said Jinnie.

'An accident . . . What sort of an accident?'

'I don't exactly know,' said Jinnie.

'You don't know . . . Well, where's our Mam?' said Nan.

'She's gone to Consett.'

'To Consett . . . To the hospital? Is Aunt Polly dying?' asked Nan.

'No. I don't know. She hasn't gone to the hospital, she's gone to see a lawyer.'

'A lawyer?'

Nan didn't seem able to do anything except echo Jinnie in a most satisfactory way. But she'd be asking all sorts of questions in a minute and the mention of a lawyer was getting close to the business of Nan maybe not being able to go to College.

She'd better share the job of telling Nan about today after all.

'Jamesie's on the allotment,' she said. 'He said to give him a shout when you came. And Dottie's been here.' Nan had to be warned. 'She's fallen out with Jamesie. For good, she says.' Too late Jinnie realized this also might lead to awkward questions. 'Don't mention Dottie to Jamesie,' she said hurriedly. 'He's all upset.'

'Dottie . . .?'

Things had happened a bit at a time throughout the day. Nan was hearing about everything at once: no wonder she was stupefied.

Between them Jamesie and Jinnie told Nan all there was to know, except that neither of them mentioned Dottie, and Nan didn't either. Nan couldn't take it in, for a while.

'It wasn't Will. I know it wasn't. It wouldn't make sense,' Nan said after a time. She sounded just like Gran. 'It was never Uncle Davie either. He wouldn't. He couldn't.' Just like Gran, again. 'It was Tot . . . I bet it was.' You could hear her welcoming this solution.

'Tot? Nay,' but Jinnie saw that Jamesie wasn't sure: that

193

he'd thought of Tot as well. Jinnie hadn't. Why should Tot...?

'It was. It must've been. Did he go down the pit last night? Did he?'

Jamesie shook his head.

'There you are then. Why should he miss the shift else?'

'Had on, lass. What does that prove? Like as not he was going to miss it all along.'

'Was he going to? Did he tell you?'

'No, he didn't,' said Jamesie, 'but Tot doesn't tell uz everything, you know; not these days.'

'He'd've told you that,' said Nan.

'That's as maybe,' said Jamesie. 'Like as not, he did intend to miss the shift. He would be goin' to Durham the day, to the meetin' of the County Association. He's the Eden Lodge man there in case you've forgotten. He'd know he'd be at Durham all the day. The Durham men are decidin' the day how to vote at the Federation Meeting in London on Thursday. Tot's a Durham delegate to the Federation, as well, our Nan. He's a busy man these days. There's still a strike set for Saturday, you know. Or have you forgot?' It wasn't like Jamesie to be sarcastic, but Jamesie was changed. 'He's got more important things on his mind than our Polly.' Here Jamesie sounded doubtful, though. 'Anyroad, what would he want to go doing that for?'

'Well,' said Nan, 'they could've fallen out. She always does fall out with them in the end.'

Jamesie looked frowningly at Nan, then tilted his head in Jinnie's direction. It's all right, you needn't bother. I know; Jinnie wanted to say.

'And she's had plenty to say against The Strike. She went to that meeting in London, got herself in the papers.'

'Nay, lass,' said Jamesie, roused to indignation. 'I never heard tell yet of a woman gettin' herself nigh on murdered because she didn't like a strike. Yon's a bonnie queer notion to be gettin'. Nay, we'll just have to leave it to the police. They're not a bad lot, really.' He relapsed into his gloom for a minute, then made an effort to be more cheerful. 'Suppose we just shut up. We're not gettin' any wiser. And it's time that dog had the stink washed off him. And that bairn'd better be woke up, if he's goin' to get any sleep the night. He'll want summat to eat, our Nan, if you don't. So will Bob when he comes.'

Food again. Everything always came back to eating, and washing-up after, of course.

194

Uncle Bob came home as usual. Jamesie told him about Aunt Polly and everything. He didn't say much, just that Annie'd done right to go to Consett like Billie'd said. But his silence was All Right somehow and he didn't retreat to the Windsor chair.

They were all still sitting at the table when a car stopped just outside. You didn't see a motor in Grove Street very often, or in Coalgate come to that. Jinnie and George and even nearly-Grown-Up Nan rushed to the front door to have a good look. There, of all folk, closing the car door and saying something to the driver, was Gran: calm as you please, as if this wasn't the very first time in her life she'd had a ride in a motor.

Ay, she'd got on all right, she said taking her hat-pins out once again. This Mr. Harcourt was a cannie sort of a fellow. No side. Brought her back home from the police-station hisself. She felt a bit better knowing he was in charge. She looked a lot better as well, Jinnie saw. Billy'd been right; there was things a lawyer could do that an ordinary body couldn't. She didn't tell them what, which wasn't Fair at all. You could tell she was more hopeful, though.

'Now, what about a cup of that tea you've made, our Nan?' she said. 'My throat's like a kiln.'

Would you believe it was Uncle Bob that poured the tea. Wonders would never cease, thought Jinnie.

Gran actually had some bread and jam, as well. Which was a good sign. Half the trouble in the world came from not eating properly. And at the proper time, Dad said. And chewing properly, of course. Not bolting.

Jinnie wished Gran would bolt, though: just this once. She could hardly wait to hear what had been happening. Surely Gran would tell them in a minute.

But Gran chewed every mouthful slowly and drank her tea in sips. Nobody asked a question, not even Uncle Bob who was nearly as old as Gran herself.

Of course. Jinnie remembered. It would be because of George. George was Too Young. You had to be Grown-Up, or nearly, to hear about Aunt Polly.

Besides, Aunt Polly was his mother. It would be sickening all the same, if the rest of them had to wait till George was back in bed and asleep again before they heard about the Lawyer and the Police and everything.

After an age, Gran put her cup and saucer on her plate, then balanced her knife on the saucer.

'Now, our George, if you're going to get any sleep the

195

night, a breath of fresh air and a bit of a walk's what you need. You an' all Jinnie. You've been clockin' in here all the day.' Well, if that wasn't unfair, and Jinnie hadn't come to Coalgate to have a new Sin, Clocking, added to her list. 'And George'll be wantin' to see Connie,' said Gran. For once George showed a flicker of surprise but he didn't argue with that note in Gran's voice. 'So, Jin, go down to Evie's with George, will you? You've been such a grand help all day, I don't know how we'd've managed without you.' Jinnie wasn't taken in by that. It was true, of course. 'And Evie'll be glad of a hand with Connie and the baby.'

Gran needn't think Jinnie didn't know she was being got shot of so that the rest of them could Talk. Well, she couldn't stop Jinnie being a witness and that was more than Nan would be.

'And our Jamesie, you're not goin' down the pit the night. Oh no you're not: not without sleep you're not. So you can get a breath of air an' all and take the bairns to Evie's.' So Jinnie was a bairn again, lumped together with George, now they had no more use for her.

But Gran was going on. 'You an' all, our Nan.' Jinnie cheered up. They were all being got shot of. Gran was going to talk to Uncle Bob alone. Jinnie would never know now what he thought, or about his Savings, but Nan wouldn't either.

'Heck,' said Nan, 'it's been games all afternoon. I'm tired.'

'Can't help that,' said Gran. 'You can come straight back from Evie's. That's all.'

As they turned into Evie's street, they saw Evie coming towards her house from the opposite direction, the baby in her arm, Aunt Polly's Connie clutching her free hand. They'd been to Evie's mother's, she said. She went most afternoons. If Joe wasn't home, of course.

She was glad to see them. 'Aren't we, Connie?' she said, but Connie, overcome, buried her head in Evie's coat. And it would be grand to have Jinnie's help with the bairns.

'Go on in, Jinnie, the door's open,' she said. 'Take your coat off. You an' all, George. What about you, Jamesie? And Nan? I'll be makin' a cup of tea soon as the kettle boils.'

Jamesie said he'd be getting straight back, thanks all the same; Nan as well. They stayed with Evie at the door a little while, talking, though.

Jinnie kept her ears on them, but the only thing she found out was that Joe was at Pa Dunham's, which didn't amount to much even when she had worked out that Pa Dunham was Uncle Davie.

196

Soon Jinnie forgot to be shy, or to wonder what she was missing at Gran's, Evie was so nice and a baby such a novelty. And once Connie got used to Jinnie she took a flattering liking to her.

When it was Jackie's bath-time, Evie let Jinnie hold him, while she climbed the ladder to the upstairs room and brought down his night things to warm on the big fireguard and then got the bath ready. The baby was warm and happy, but a bit of a responsibility because he waved his arms and legs a lot and wouldn't stay still, so Jinnie was not sorry to surrender him to Evie and, with Connie and George, watch his antics in the bath. Jackie had tired himself out by now. He fell asleep while he was having his bottle and didn't even open his eyes when Evie settled him down for the night, in a big old-fashioned clothes-basket, which she put on top of the chest of drawers in the corner. Till her own bedtime, she said.

'Your turn now,' Evie said to Connie. 'Start on her buttons, will you, Jin? While I put a drop more warm in the bath.'

Connie started to winge: it wasn't bedtime yet, and she didn't have to get washed to go to bed.

'In this house you do,' said Evie. 'Now come on and be a good bairn, and I'll mebbe let you stay up a bit, after. Just this once mind, because George's here and your Cousin Jinnie.'

Evie topped up the baby's bath with jugfuls of hot water from the boiler. Connie made no further protest but submitted quietly to a bedtime wash: hand, face, neck and knees. Then, clean and shiny, and wrapped in the baby's everyday shawl, she sat as good as gold in the rocking-chair near the fire while Evie and Jinnie restored the hearth to normal.

Then they all sat round the fire eating cake, and Evie let them put their feet on the bright steel fender while she showed Connie and George how to look for pictures in the crags and craters of the hot coal. They all found different pictures and nobody could see anybody else's, except Evie, but Jinnie suspected her of pretending. The game could have gone on all night because the fire kept on settling and changing.

'Well, that's enough of that,' said Evie after a while: 'or we'll be hurting our eyes.' And sure enough, Jinnie discovered hers were beginning to water.

Evie never once mentioned the clock, or Connie going to

197

bed, although in the end it was very late with the gas lit inside and darkness outside.

They were all so happy that nobody noticed Joe coming in until a gust of cold air swirled round their feet.

'Our Will's home, anyroad,' he said. 'Run off to Newcastle: to join the Army, last train last night, the great daft gowk,' he said affectionately. 'Didn't even know about our Ma.' Then as if somebody had asked a question, 'Na, nowt else,' he said, soberly now.

'Well, there you are, our George, and Jinnie. Granma Dunham says it's bedtime for the pair of yuz.' So Joe had been at Gran's. What else had been happening while Jinnie was at Evie's? 'I'll take you,' he said. Then to Evie, 'I'll not stop,' he said.

'Nay, if there's owt you can do,' said Evie.

'There's nowt nobody can do the night,' said Joe: 'except the hospital. Holdin' her own, they say which is summat. Come on you two, coats on,' and when they were ready, 'I'll be straight back,' he said to Evie.

He didn't go into Gran's with Jinnie and George, just tapped on the lighted window and waved, then turned and went home.

Gran's house was warm right to the door, cheerful with the smell of new baked bread and as crowded as on Sunday. Gran was normal again, in weekday skirt and grey-striped flannel blouse. Uncle Bob was in the basket chair, solemn but for once not nodding off to sleep. Jamesie was looking pale and tired. Nan had changed out of school uniform into her everyday serge frock as usual. But Jinnie was only half aware of them, because in the place of honour in the Windsor chair sat Will. Handsome again: and happy, undoubtedly, unbelievably happy.

Jinnie had half expected Will to be at Gran's. But not Nora. Yet there she was, sitting on a little stool beside him, positively rosy for once, and shamelessly holding his hand. Jinnie gave up. Nora was Beyond her. Everything that had happened this week was Beyond her. And today had been her queerest day ever.

She'd expected a Real Holiday at Coalgate to be Special, but this had been more Special than she'd ever dreamt of. She didn't believe anybody, not Anybody, could ever have had a holiday like this.

And it wasn't over yet. She still had the whole of tomorrow, all Thursday and a bit of Friday. No, the holiday wasn't over yet, not by a long way.

198

Twenty-Five

But the holiday *was* over. Breakfast things hadn't been cleared away next morning when in walked Mam, surprising them all and come to fetch Jinnie home.

But they'd said she could stay till Friday: hadn't they? They'd promised. Hadn't they, Gran?

'Now don't Argue, our Jin,' said Mam. 'We always said we'd see how things went, you know that. We never promised anything.'

'You did, our Mam, you did. You said you'd told Miss Middleton I'd be back at school Friday afternoon. You know you did.' Only George's pale stare kept Jinnie from bursting into tears.

'Now, Jinnie, all I ever said was Miss Middleton said Friday afternoon would be all right for you to get your last-minute instructions for The Scholarship on Saturday. That's all I ever said. Now be a good lass and don't Argue.'

Don't Argue. That was what They always said when You were in the right and They didn't want to admit it. All the

199

same you could tell from her voice that Ma was a bit upset herself. Feeling guilty, most like.

'I don't know what your Dad'd say if he heard you carrying on like this, our Jin. He said as soon as he saw last night's *Chronicle* that you'd have to come home. He'd've set out for you straight away if it hadn't been for the Class Meeting at Chapel. You know what he is,' she said to Gran apologetically. 'He's a worrier.'

'Ay,' said Gran, 'I know what he is.'

'You'll just be in everybody's road an' all, Jin. So be a good lass.' Why should she be a good lass when Mam was spoiling everything?

'Nay our Kate,' said Gran, 'no bairn's ever in the road, not in this house. So don't you go sayin' it. And Jinnie's been a grand help. We couldn't've managed without her yesterday.' Nothing about today. Of course: Nan was staying at home: they didn't need Jinnie any more. 'Could we, George?'

'Na,' said George surprisingly. Now Jinnie's tears did begin to splash over.

'The lass's welcome to stay till Friday, no matter what. A promise is a promise, specially to a bairn. And the lass thought you'd promised right enough, our Kate.'

'That's all very well,' said Mam, daunted, 'but she's a big lass now, and there's times when with the best will in the world you can't keep a promise.' Mam was as good as admitting They had promised. 'It'll do her no harm to find that out. Nobody could've foreseen this lot. And who's to say how it's all going to end? Like her Dad says, she'll be best out of it, at home.'

But she couldn't be out of it. She was a Witness. Wait till Mam found that out. Serve her right.

'And for another thing,' Mam said, surer of herself now, 'you can do with her bed. I can see that. You know you can. You could go in with Nan, then George could have your bed, and Jamesie and Bob can have their bed to themselves again.'

'Nay,' said Jamesie, 'we're not grumblin', Kate.'

Gran said nothing.

Without warning, Mam gave way.

'Oh, all right,' she said. 'Jinnie can be the one to decide: although I don't know what Josh's going to say if I go back without her.'

They all looked at Jinnie. It wasn't Fair: it was not.

'All right,' said Jinnie, 'I'll go home. I'll not stay where I'm not wanted. I hate you, our Mam. I hate the whole lot of you. You just want to get rid of uz.'

200

This wasn't Fair either. Gran hadn't asked Mam to come, she'd been as surprised to see her as Jinnie had. But Jinnie couldn't stop herself. She pushed past Gran's arms, almost knocked George off his chair and rushed upstairs. At least They wouldn't have the pleasure of seeing her cry.

But her tears had dried up. She aimed a vicious kick at Nan's schoolbag. It hurt her toes: but she didn't care. Then she sat down with a thump on the window-sill and looked without seeing, beyond the lamp-post, at the house across the street.

There was a brief silence below, then quiet voices and then, of course — what else could you expect of Grown-Ups? — the rattle of teacups. She was fed up with Them and their everlasting tea. There they were, drinking the stuff by the warm fire, and leaving her to freeze up here. Well, they needn't expect her to wash-up after them. That was something else she was fed up with: washing-up.

Saying nasty things, they'd be: about her. She didn't care. She'd show them. She would... she would... Jinnie couldn't think of a single thing to do to Show Them. Except to go on staying still and quiet, which didn't amount to much. Still, it'd make them wonder what she was up to. If she didn't stir for a long time, a long, long time, maybe they'd think she was dead... struck down in the flower of her youth... of grief. The Cruelty Man would have something to say to them then. She would lie still and pale, on her lips a faint smile of forgiveness. Like Ludovic in Dad's old Sunday School prize. They'd cry over her and say what a beautiful corpse she made, like Mary Brown in The Street last year. And wish they hadn't been so cruel. *She* hadn't done a single thing to deserve to die, after all.

Aunt Polly had: and look at the stew everybody was in about her. And her not even dead yet. And No-Better-Than-She-Should-Be. At long last Jinnie had found out what that meant. It meant going to The Pictures, or The Pub, or a Dance with a fancy man. She knew what that was as well: somebody better-looking than your husband. Like Tot. Not that Tot seemed very fancy to Jinnie. Of course he was tall and had fair hair that curled, but his face wasn't up to much, all ugly blue marks. Shot marks from blasting down the pit, Nan said. Altogether Jinnie had learnt a lot at Coalgate. She'd been to The Pictures as well: and a Dance.

She was going to have to be careful what she said about Coalgate, though, when she got home. Dad wouldn't like her knowing about Tot, she felt sure. But it wouldn't be hard to

201

avoid mentioning *him*. The Dance would be much harder. It might slip out. She'd better stop calling it a Dance right away and start remembering it had been a Church Social For a Good Cause. A Dance, said her conscience. She was going to have trouble with her conscience, she could see. There was no need to, though, it was a Grown-Up who had let her go. Gran. And Gran had spoken up for her just now. She wasn't going to cause any more bother for Gran by owning up about The Dance. She often found herself Owning Up when she hadn't intended to. She'd just have to be extra careful and not even talk about Coalgate in front of Dad.

Not that she expected another Real Holiday at Coalgate ever again, but Dad might stop their day trips to Gran's. Then she'd have to wait until she was a Grown-Up and could do as she liked before she saw some of them again: Evie and the baby and Joe and Will and ... it was a long list and included George. None of them ever came to Wallsend, only Gran and Nan. Of course Mam would still want to come and she might Speak Up to Dad. Jinnie sighed. Things were more complicated than she used to think, when she was young.

Mrs. Nattrass opposite, opening her window to air the beds, gave Jinnie a friendly wave and Jinnie realized she'd been guilty of Staring again and only half waved back.

The stairs creaked. I won't look round, Jinnie thought: not even to see who it is. And if they expected *her* to say sorry, well, she wasn't going to.

'Give's a hand with the beds, there's a good lass. These feather ticks is more than one body can manage. Fetch the beater out of that cupboard, will you?'

Jinnie couldn't pretend she hadn't heard. And it wasn't Gran's fault Mam'd come to take her away. She fetched the beater. They started with the big bed and Jinnie walloped it until she was breathless. Then they turned the little mattress of Gran's bed and she had a go at that. Gran said it would be a shame to spoil it by sleeping on it.

'I hear your Uncle Reg and Aunt Nell've sent a card that they'll be at your house this afternoon,' said Gran sociably. 'D'you know I've never seen them since the day your Mam and Dad got wed? I've only seen them that once, come to think. Cannie souls, they seemed.'

Would you believe it, Wallsend had gone so far away that Jinnie had clean forgotten that Wednesday often meant Uncle Reg and Aunt Nell to tea, because their shop on the other side of Newcastle was a lock-up, a Cut Above Dad's, and

202

had half-day closing. Jinnie liked Uncle Reg and Aunt Nell, for themselves as well as for Christmas presents and the tuppenny bars of Fry's cream or Cadbury's Milk they always brought for Jinnie and Robbie — a whole one each. Jinnie began to feel better.

'And our Nan's going to Byers's for a paper. Would you like to go with her? You haven't bought any presents yet, have you?' No more she hadn't.

'All right, Nan,' Gran called out. 'Hang on ... We'll be down in a minute and Jinnie's goin' with you.'

Presents for Mam and Dad had selected themselves all that time ago when she'd run away from meeting Nan: for Dad a cigar (threepence); for Mam a fancy box with two tiny pieces of pink soap, and a miniature tube of golden scent (sixpence). Jinnie thought Robbie might be harder. Byers's had a whole windowful of things she coveted. But when she reached the shop she found that without knowing it, she had narrowed her choice to two things: the beautiful pencil-box and a clown she'd hardly been aware of noticing. It was almost impossible to choose. The pencil-box was achingly beautiful while Joey the Clown, on a renewed acquaintance, was just like Buster Keaton, flat and straight-faced. She moved his arms and legs at all four joints and stood him up and made him lean forward at an impossible angle: more like Buster Keaton than ever.

'Hi, come on, Jin,' said Nan, 'get a move on. We haven't got all day, you know.'

'Any lad'd like Joey,' said Mrs. Byers. 'How old did you say your brother was? Eight? Joey's just the job, then. Don't let me make your mind up for you, though.'

The shop bell jangled and Mrs. Byers went to the other counter to serve the new customer. A tuppenny packet of tabs. Jinnie recognized the voice. Betsey, and why wasn't she at work? Jinnie looked round, then was vexed with herself for doing so. Betsey saw her at once but pretended not to.

'I see Coalgate's in all the papers, Mrs. Byers,' said Betsey. 'The place'll be getting a bad name after this lot. Still, I don't suppose folks'll go thinking we're all as bad as the Dunhams ...'

'Well, if there's nowt else, Betsey,' said Mrs. Byers loudly and firmly, 'would you mind shuttin' the door properly after you? It's cold this morning.' Mrs. Byers returned to Nan and Jinnie. The door slammed and the bell jangled again and that was the last Jinnie saw of Betsey.

Joey was sixpence more than the pencil-box. That decided

203

it. Robbie hadn't had a Real Holiday, Jinnie could afford to be generous.

'I'll take him,' she said resolutely and stopped looking at the pencil-box. 'Could you put him in a separate paper please?'

Miraculously Mam admired Joey so much the minute she set eyes on him that she didn't notice Nan smuggle the box of soap and the cigar to Gran who said she'd just pop upstairs and finish parcelling Jinnie's clothes. George pushed Joey into more and more ridiculous postures and Mam laughed; Vic barked jealously and Jinnie felt a bit like Christmas for a moment. Then Jamesie came in from the back and tried to admire Joey too and Jinnie felt guilty.

When Gran came downstairs with the parcel, she thought Jinnie's choice was capital. 'But that's enough, our George. You'll wear him out before Robbie ever lays hands on him. Pop him into your bag, Kate. And just look at that clock, will you, the lot of yuz.' The enemy clock again: forever ending good things. ' . . . if you want to get that train, our Kate . . . If you get off now, I'll see you onto the train, before I go back to our Davie's.'

Jinnie· hadn't known Gran had been to Watling Street already this morning: it must've been before breakfast. She hadn't said anything, but at least Aunt Polly wasn't dead yet, or Uncle Davie in jail. She'd have had to tell them that and of course she wouldn't have been coming to the station with them either. But somehow Aunt-Polly-and-Uncle-Davie were less important now.

Coalgate was changing too. The houses, the shops, the pubs, the people, had grown familiar during the last few days. Now as she was going home, Mattie-in-His-Chair and Lizzie-Next-Door out washing her front step, McElwain's Billiard Saloon and the pitmen sitting on their hunkers, The Colliery Engine, Byers's even, were all strange again. Yet not strangers either. At least not in the way they had been when she came on Friday. They didn't make her feel excited now, or shy: but sober instead, sad almost.

Sent on ahead of Mam and Gran — so that the Grown-Ups could talk, of course, but Jinnie didn't care now — the three of them, George and Nan and Jinnie with nothing to say all of a sudden, walked to the Station. Sedately their steps echoed under the bridge, changed tune on the corrugations of the ramp, then changed again on the wooden platform.

Tommy Wilson punched Jinnie's ticket and they waited just inside the gate for Mam and Gran.

204

'Sorry to hear about all the trouble you're havin', Mrs. Dunham,' Tommy said as he punched Mam's ticket. 'Everybody is. Me Mam nearly came round yesterday to see if there was owt she could do. You've only to ask, you know, Mrs. Dunham.'

'I know, Tommy,' said Gran. 'Thank you kindly, but there's nowt anybody can do but wait. And hope. She's still unconscious, but a bit better they said this morning. The signal's still up, I see.'

'Ay,' said Tommy, 'the train'll be minute or two yet. There's a fire lit in the Waiting-Room, Mrs. Dunham; Kate.

The fire in the Waiting-Room — Ladies Only, but George didn't count — was scarcely worth talking about, all smell and fuss, still crackling and spitting wood splinters, the merest flickers of flame coming and going among black lumps of coal and torrents of yellow grey smoke. All the same, Mam and Gran sat down on one of the long brown benches.

'You can go and watch for the signal, if you like,' said Gran. 'But not too near the edge, our Nan. Did you hear that, George?'

The signal showed no sign of moving and watching it soon palled. Jinnie wanted to investigate the red slot-machine again. It would be a long time before she had another chance.

'All right. If you really want,' said Nan, in a Grown-Up humouring voice. 'You can have first go. Then you, George. I'll lift you up. Only for a pull mind. No wasting pennies.'

It now seemed rather pointless, and Jinnie's melancholy was deepening, but she felt committed to the machine. After all, You Never Knew. And Special things had happened already at Coalgate. She pulled the drawer, extra hard, with both hands. As if by magic and would you believe it? the drawer came out: so unexpectedly that Jinnie almost overbalanced. Not only did it come out, but it held a neat red-and-gold-wrapped oblong of Nestle's Milk.

'Well I never,' said Nan. 'How did that happen?'

Somebody must've put a penny in and the machine hadn't worked. More important, what should they do about it?

'It's yours, of course,' said Nan. 'It was your idea.'

Jinnie hesitated. She coveted the rich red and gold wrapping almost as much as the chocolate itself. But she hadn't paid for it. Taking it would be Sinful. People who took things they hadn't paid for ended up in Trouble Street. Is this where the girl lives who took that chocolate at Coalgate Station? the Plain Clothes Man would say. To Dad.

'Go on, take it,' said Nan.

205

'It's not mine, not really,' said Jinnie.

'Don't be so daft. You take it,' said Nan. 'We're not leaving it for the next one that comes along, nor for Tommy Wilson, neither. We'll all have a share if you're not going to take it.'

They hadn't heard the signal rattle down. Now, in the near-by office, the last-minute bell started buzzing furiously, making Jinnie jump and setting the pigeon baskets fluttering. They'd have to make up their minds about the chocolate pretty quickly.

'Keep it for me Mam,' said George suddenly.

It was the perfect solution. Jinnie extracted the chocolate, pushed the drawer shut again.

'You look after it,' she said, and handed it to Nan with scarcely a pang of renunciation.

Mam and Gran emerged, talking earnestly, from the Waiting-Room Ladies Only. Tommy Wilson was taking up his stand beside the pigeon baskets. With a smell and a billow of dark smoke and huffing steam and cheerfully chuntering pistons and wheels, the train came curving neatly over the bridge, which from up here you'd never guess was a bridge at all, and on to the platform.

Mam kissed Gran. 'Now don't forget what I said . . . and if there's owt me or Josh can do, anything at all . . .' Gran gave Jinnie a hug, then grabbed her hand and pushed into it two threepenny bits. 'One for you and one for Robbie.' Imagine Gran remembering, at a time like this. Mam opened a carriage door. 'Say thanks to your Gran, our Jin, and ta-ta to Nan and George. Hurry up now. The train'll not be standing long.'

Mam got in first, put down the parcel of Jinnie's clothes. Then she turned again to the door and hoisted Jinnie in. 'Mind now. Stand well back, Jinnie.' She slammed the heavy door. She struggled with the thick leather strap at the window. Why did they always have such stiff ones? Jinnie was in despair. The strap yielded. The window fell with a crash.

Not a moment too soon. The guard was blowing his whistle. Behind Gran's head the green flag was waving. Then came the familiar hiss and rush of steam from underneath the train and blotted out George, Nan and Gran. As they always did, buffers clashed, infectiously bang bang bang along the train. The steam cleared. Gran and Nan and George were already turning from sideways-facing-the-train to frontways-looking-down-the-platform. Receding. Dwindling. Smaller and smaller. Gran-and-Nan-and-George were a single dot. Then it was no use waving any more.

'Come away from that window now, our Jin. You'll get

206

your death of cold. Oh my goodness, look at the muck you've got on yourself. Your good coat an' all. You look better than you did, though.'

The Holiday was over.

From *The Newcastle Mail* – 1926

Friday, 29 April

Coalgate Victim Gives Valuable Lead.

.... Mrs. Polly Dunham .... regained consciousness late last night in Consett General Hospital. She was able to give the police a full description of her assailant, who appears to have been a foreigner, aged about thirty...........

Readers will remember Mrs. Dunham as the miner's wife who took part in the march in London on 17th April, of the Women's Guild of Empire and who later addressed the meeting of 20,000 women in the Albert Hall ....

Thursday, 15 July

Northumberland Scholarship Winners:

....

Wallsend: Girls: Mary M. Little, Jane A. Friend, Doris S. Wilson, Dorothy Simpson, Doris L. Duncan, Catherine Robson, Alice I. Higgins, Margaret M. Cope, Constance S. Baker, Millicent N. Banks.

Boys: ....

Glossary

A good seam	A seam is a line of separation between two strata—a layer of coal between layers of other materials.
A'll awand	I warrant; I'm sure.
Anyroad	Used in the sense of "anyway," "anyhow."
Apollyon	The devil, from Greek, "destroyer."
Bairn	Child.
Black clock	Black beetle.
Brazzen	Brazen; bold as brass; impudent.
Cannie	Nice.
Chauntering pistons	The author is describing the noise made by the pistons of the train. "Chauntering" is a North Country expression meaning to grumble or to complain.
Clocking	Brooding.
Compen	Compensation for injury at work.
Crack	Talk. Cannie crack: fine talk (always sarcastic).
Cree	Shed; hut.
Creels	Large wicker baskets for fish—often worn on the back.
Cullercoats	A fishing village in Northumberland.
Dick	Head louse.
Durstn't	Dare not.
Felled	Very tired.
Fettle	Arrange; put right. What fettle the day?: How are you today?
Gawp at	Gape at; stare at (with excessive curiosity or amazement).
Gob-stoppers	Form of candy, sometimes on a stick. "Gob" is slang for "mouth."
Gully	A butcher's knife; a carving knife.
Had a pash	Had a crush on ("pash" is slang for "passion").

209

Had away	Go away; go on with you.
Had your whisht	Be quiet.
Hunkers	Calves of the legs. To sit on your hunkers: to squat as a miner does, i.e. to sit on the toes with thighs resting on the calves of the legs.
I'll be jiggered	An exclamation of surprise or astonishment.
Impittent	Impertinent; very impudent.
Jemmies	Crowbar used by burglars.
Knuckle-dusters	Metal instrument protecting knuckles from injury in striking. The main purpose of these is to inflict extra damage during a fight rather than to protect the user.
Linings	Tightly fitting ankle-length underpants worn by men.
Make on	Pretend.
Marra	Mate who works on the same seam of coal.
Midden	Heap of dung or rubbish.
Montoes	Mint-flavored confectionery.
Nant	Leave. To take your nant: be off; go away.
Nowt	Nothing.
On a ticket	On the installment plan.
On tick	On credit; the debt to be settled at the end of the week.
Owt	Anything.
Panel	Doctor's list of patients entitled to free treatment by virtue of weekly contributions deducted by employers and paid to the doctor. Hence, on the panel, panel patients.
Pigeon-cree	Pigeon roost.
Pingering	Spoiling by fingering too much.
Pinnie	Pinafore.
Poss stick	A wooden stick used to beat clothes as part of the washing process.
Progger	Hook used in mat-making.
Put your shovel in where there's no muck	Interfere in things that do not concern you.
Queue	Line; to wait in line.
Quoit	Heavy, flattish, sharp-edged iron ring thrown to encircle iron peg or to stick in ground near it in game of quoits.

210

Ruched	Made with irregular pleats.
Sannie	Sanatorium for patients suffering from tuberculosis.
Scones	Soft cake of barley meal or wheat flour of size for a single portion cooked on griddle or in the oven.
She's wantin' summat	She wants something.
Shop was very tying	Jinnie's parents felt tied to the shop.
Skem	An imprecise term of abuse.
Snib	Bolt, fastening catch of door, window, etc.
The Store	The Co-operative Society.
Tabs	Slang for "cigarettes."
Taties	Potatoes.
Tew	Exhaust; wear to shreds.
Trilby hat	A soft felt hat, something like an American Homburg.
Tuppenny	An article worth two pennies (old sterling currency).
Winge	Whine; complain.
Yakker	A pitman (a term of contempt).

211

About the Author

Winifred Cawley was born and raised in Northumberland, England. It is this area and its people that have inspired all of her books. Though Mr. and Mrs. Cawley consider England their home, they have lived in Romania, Yugoslavia, Egypt, Iceland, and Australia. When not traveling about the world, the Cawleys make their home in Yorkshire, England.

Winifred Cawley won the 1974 *Guardian* book award for this book.

c.1

F
CAW
Cawley, Winifred

Gran at Coalgate

DATE			